The
Things

of

Man

THE THINGS OF MAN

A Novel

Vince Wheeler

BELLE LUTTE PRESS

Published by Belle Lutte Press. www.BelleLutte.com

ISBN 978-0-9973260-0-0

Library of Congress Control Number available upon request.

Printed in the United States of America

Cover Illustration by Roy Scott. www.RoyScott.com
Cover Design by Vanessa Maynard. www.VanessaNoHeart.net
The circle within a circle design that precedes this page, and is used later in the work, uses material from www.texturefabrik.com

——————————————

BELLE LUTTE PRESS

While today's media maximizes profits by force-feeding the populace cheap and unoriginal thought, Belle Lutte Press is fighting the good fight—hell-bent on publishing original, high-quality novels.

For Pam.

Contents

"Hast thou eyes of flesh?
or seest thou as man seeth?
Are thy days as the days of man?"
—The Book of Job

BEFORE

Days of Summers Past

On a hot August night he sat in the darkest part of a dead-end alley amid the stench of rotting garbage and the waste of men and animals. His face lay hidden, draped by a mask of filthy hair, his body naked and coated thick with something red and sticky.

Out along the street, hookers prowled.

"Cuanto para usted?" a man shouted from a passing car.

A woman told him to come find out.

Another man called her an ugly bitch.

There was more shouting. A commingling of voices.

A short drunken man, his shirttail out, one tennis shoe untied, weaved along the sidewalk and turned down the alley. He staggered past the one sitting there, taking no notice, and clomped on to the terminus of the backstreet, where he unzipped his pants, urinating on the wall and, to a lesser extent, his shoes and pant cuffs. Finished, he turned to go back as he had come and, oblivious, nearly walked into the taller figure now standing directly ahead, an unbending shadow blocking his way.

With a start, the man stepped in retreat, rocking and almost falling over.

"What do you want?" he asked.

The shaded form came closer. "Do you know who I am?"

"No," the man said, backpedalling.

"I think you do."

Seconds later, the man struck the end wall upon which he had relieved himself. Boxed in, panic took hold. His drunken face withered.

The other, trailing the odor of death, drew within inches. "You know who I am."

The man shook his head, not wanting to believe.

And yet he did. He knew.

"You're *him*. The one who . . ." He trembled, struggling to breathe. ". . . does things."

"Yes."

The man put his hands to his head, begging, weeping.

"Why are you doing that?"

"Because I don't want to die!" the man wailed. "Not here."

"You have to die somewhere."

"But not like this. I have a wife."

"Many men have wives."

"And children. Three children."

"Men have children, too. Such are the things of men."

Hands reached out and closed around the man's throat, the horrible, squalid thing that held him looking almost human, and at the same time, more something else.

Then, in what seemed a reprieve, the grip loosened, and the voice, before cold and mechanized, spoke in a desperate tenor.

"What is it like," it said, "to be a man?"

In another August, on a sun-filled morning, he entered the wide, high atrium of an office building in a suit and tie. Hair cut short and styled. Briefcase in hand. Shiny black dress shoes sounding echoes on the marble floor.

He punched for an elevator and the car arrived with a ding. It was empty. He boarded and the doors closed. As he went skyward, he felt less and less himself. And when the car stopped and the doors opened, he was gone.

PART ONE

DAYS
OF
AUTUMN

Chapter 1

Home

Brad and Sally Manford had an apartment near the beach in Santa Monica. Once or twice, a few years ago, he had said something about moving to Kansas. She had ignored it. Thought he was joking.

Now they were moving to Kansas.

It was verging on midnight. He had just made it official. Just walked in from the airport—from a twelve-hundred-mile trip, on the other end of which he had spent a full day interviewing with a dozen-plus lawyers at the firm he would call his new employer—and dropped it on her.

Standing in an oversized sleeveless tee that passed for a nightshirt, she huffed and sat down hard on the couch, crossing her thin bare arms and legs, top foot bobbing at a hostile clip.

He sat beside her and opened his laptop.

"I think you've lost your damn mind," she said.

He had been hearing that for two weeks. He had answered an online job listing. His prospects had looked good. He had tried to prepare her.

Great opportunity, he had said. *Senior associate. Prominent firm.*

Wichita? She had almost laughed, but, seeing him serious, had not.

Sal, I think it's the right place. I do. I really want to go there.

Wich-i-ta? She had sounded disbelieving. And a little scared. As if talking to a man unbalanced. *Brad, honey, nobody really wants to go to Wichita.*

As he moved his laptop cursor, her foot, still bobbing, came to a sudden stop.

"What are you doing?" she said.

"Looking for a house."

5

"Good God."

That was when he saw it: Two-story colonial. White siding. Black shutters. Wood floors. Walkout basement.

. . . *And all,* the ad said, *at the end of a quiet suburban cul-de-sac.*

There was a virtual tour. The images grabbed him. Held him.

But there was something else. Something not in the pictures.

"Right here," he said, tapping the screen. "This is it."

Grudgingly, she glanced over. "For who? George Washington?"

"You don't like it?"

She rolled her eyes. Green eyes. The greenest he would ever know.

"I think it's a bit much," she said.

"Too pretentious?"

"No, it's lovely."

"Too big?"

"Not necessarily." She rose and walked away.

"What, then?"

Stopping, she turned back.

"A bit *much*," she said, rubbing thumb on index finger.

Indeed, the place would not come cheaply. The down payment would drain their savings. But Brad would keep that from her, just as he kept from her so many things.

———————

They flew in over a sunlit Labor Day weekend. Brad had arranged for a realtor to meet them at the property. The owners, a couple who had built the house two years previous, were long gone, the rooms devoid of furnishings. The realtor led them through a sweep of the interior, then, from the kitchen, out a French door onto a deck above the basement patio, where, almost at once, his cell phone rang and he excused himself to return inside.

From the deck, they looked out over an enormous back yard enclosed by a five-foot wrought-iron fence, the deep cul-de-sac lot growing ever wider as it stretched to its rear boundary.

"My lord," she said, "this would be a bitch to mow."

"We'll hire someone."

"That would cost plenty."

"Then we'll get a rider."

"That would also cost plenty. Look," she said, "if we're going to have a yard, I'll mow it myself, and with a regular old lawnmower. I need the exercise, anyway."

"Okay, so what's the problem?"

Her expression implied nausea. "I don't even know where to start." She turned to go in. "Let's see something else."

"Sal . . ."

"Brad . . ."

Catching her with his arm around her small waist, he drew her in, sliding his hand down to the curve of her hip.

"Brad, the guy's just inside."

"He's busy."

"And probably watching."

"I don't care." Gazing into the yard, he pulled her close. "I like this place. I think we belong here."

"And I think you've lost your damn mind."

"I wish you'd quit saying that."

"But Brad, this house is *expensive*. And you're not going to make what you did in L.A."

"Yeah, but the cost of living here is so much less."

"I know, but still . . ."

"It'll work out. Trust me."

"Oh, Brad." She shook her head, eyes closed. "A house is a big step. Maybe we should just get an apartment."

"No, no more apartments."

"Then a different house."

"No, this is the place for me." He corrected himself: "For *us*, I mean."

"But we don't have even half enough furniture to fill it, and what we have looks like crap."

"We'll buy furniture. Anything you like."

For a moment, she fell quiet. "God, I hope you know what you're doing."

He didn't. He knew he didn't. He knew only that this was where he had to be. There was no doubting it. And it was not so much the house, the property, but the space it occupied, the ground beneath.

Somehow, strangely, he felt part of it. Like he had been here before and never really left.

And he had known—known even before he had seen those pictures online—that it would be this way.

He pulled her closer. "There must be something you like about this place."

"Not really."

"Oh, I'll bet there is. I'll bet if you go back and take another look, you'll find plenty of things. And on the way, try to imagine stuff on the walls. And furniture. And the smell of fresh bread in the kitchen."

"Brad, give me a break."

"Just try."

With a long, unhappy sigh, she did. And alone, he descended to the yard.

———

Some distance from the deck stairs and to his left—the yard's west side—was a small, simple, octagonal gazebo, painted white. To his right, more or less centered on the eastern half of the lot and laid in a square roughly 10' x 10', were what appeared to be four sections of sawed-off wooden utility poles, constituting, he assumed, a flower box. A vernal cottonwood tree, itself at most ten feet, grew from the middle of the weed-infested rectangle. Nearer the gazebo were three young pear trees, and along the back of the yard, abutting the fence, was an evergreen hedge trimmed flat on its top and sides, its boxy shape interrupted only enough to accommodate access to a gate, presently padlocked.

There was a solitude about the place. The lots on either side were vacant, awaiting development. Residences down the street were largely out of sight. And just past the rear fence line, bordering a narrow strip of open commons, stood a wooded area where a lofty wall of cedars obscured the view of everything beyond.

A path of smooth stones led to the gazebo, and Brad started on the paved way, but within a few steps, for no discernible reason, veered off into lush, ankle-deep grass and turned in the direction of the little cottonwood.

The grass became even taller and thicker as he neared the tree, and as he reached the grouping of poles surrounding it, he saw he had been mistaken. This was no flower box. Its confines held a thin layer of hard-packed sand, and under the covering weeds lay a rusted toy truck and a miniature plastic shovel.

It was a bit odd, he thought, placing a child's sandbox around a tree. And the tree itself was not necessarily desirable. He had heard of seedless cottonwoods, but if this was not of that variety—and if it was not removed—there would one day, he knew, be a springtime mess of white fuzzies.

A light breeze rustled the little tree's branches, and somewhere, a bird chirped.

Then, a moment of calm. The wind dropped below a whisper. The bird fell silent.

But something remained. Another sound. A low hum, faint and perhaps distant—yet at the same time seeming so near that he thought it was, at first, a mere ringing in his ears.

He turned about, but could not find the source.

He moved on to the back of the yard and leaned against the gate, looking east, then west. In both directions the woods followed the edge of the development, and in places, adjacent to the trees, an ill-defined foot trail was visible through the high grass and blooming sunflowers. The trail was more noticeable as it ran along the fence line, and just the other side of the gate it joined with a still more prominent path that disappeared into the cedars.

The sound had continued, distinct and uninterrupted. A buzzing like the beating wings of a hummingbird, seeming now more behind him than ahead.

He turned back toward the cottonwood, looking up to its top branches, then down, around the sandbox, for . . . something. Until a puff of wind stirred the trees and the bird resumed its song.

"You gonna call this home?"

The voice came from the commons.

Brad spun around. A short, smiling, elderly man now stood on the path near the gate. He wore khaki pants and a plain olive-green t-shirt tucked in around his trim waist. His full head of white hair lay parted neatly on one side, appearing combed for a special occasion.

"So, you like it?" he asked. There was an accent suggesting Texas or Oklahoma.

"The house?" Brad said. "Yeah, it's great."

The man came closer, extending his arthritic right hand over the fence.

"Paul Irvin," he said.

Brad introduced himself and, the swollen joints notwithstanding, found the old man's grip surprisingly solid.

"You come from around here?" Irvin asked.

Brad explained about the new job and the old man formed a light-hearted frown, the expression accentuating the deep crow's feet flanking his eyes.

"A lawyer, huh? Well, sorry to hear that. But I won't hold it again' ya' 'less you give me reason to."

Brad managed an ambiguous smile. "How about you? Do you live in this neighborhood?"

Irvin dropped his eyes and chuckled as if Brad had stumbled onto an inside joke.

"Well, it's like this: I've got a little garden home the other side of these trees, and the homes over there aren't as big or as fancy as the ones over here. But it's all considered the same development. You know, phase one, phase two. All that crap. And both sides share this commons. So, yeah, I guess you could say I live in this neighborhood."

"What do you think of it?"

"It's a little hoity-toity," Irvin offered. "A lot more on this side of the trees than over my way. But I'll tell you, it's safe out here. People take care of what they've got. And the property values only go up."

"Yeah, well, considering what they're asking for this place," Brad said, gesturing toward the house with his thumb, "that had better be true or my wife'll bury me here."

The old man laughed. "Oh, hell, I know they want a bunch for this. But I'm sure they'll deal a bit. As you probably know, it's been on the market a while."

Brad knew the exact number of days.

"Is something wrong with it?"

"Nothin' I know of. I'd venture to say it's one of the nicest houses out here."

"Maybe it's the yard," Brad joked, sweeping a foot through the heavy grass. "This looks like it hasn't been mowed for two weeks."

"Yeah," Irvin said, "but I come by here a lot, and I know for a fact that this was cut three days ago."

"Three days?" Brad shook his head. "You're kidding."

"I am not. Man, this yard grows like it's on steroids. I swear it. But the thing is, it doesn't all grow the same. For instance, over there," Irvin said, motioning to the west, "some of that's no big deal. But the other side shoots up like crazy. And that part," he said, pointing toward the sandbox, "is the worst. Just look at that. You could mow that every day."

Brad shook his head again, knowing this would not be at all to Sally's liking.

In the next moment, she re-emerged onto the back deck with the realtor. Brad exchanged closing remarks with the old man and started toward the house. But as the soft breeze again fell to a dead calm, he wandered off track, toward the cottonwood. And in an instant marking another pause in the avian twitter, he stopped, turning his head side to side.

"What are you doing?" Sally asked.

"Nothing," he said.

———

They had a child, a boy, six years old. At first sight, he had taken to the sandbox—which was, of course, in no condition for play. And Brad, with his new job, had no time to make it so. But he had asked the realtor to recommend a handyman, and within a few days the weeds had been eradicated and several hundred pounds of fresh sand lay in the quadrangle. Thereafter, in the spotty shade of the small cottonwood, the boy would play nonstop for as long as his mother would allow, patiently working the sand to construct forts and roads and foxholes, such projects culminating in elaborate mini-dramas involving action figures and hordes of green army men.

Sally had not initially favored the sandbox, and as the boy became more and more enamored with it, she liked it even less.

"It's full of dust and dirt," she said. "It's bad for him."

"It gets him outside," Brad countered. "He needs fresh air. The doctors say that."

"They also say he shouldn't breathe dust and dirt. It'd be better if he just had some play equipment."

"He says he doesn't want that."

"Well, he might change his mind if we got rid of that dirt pile."

But the sandbox stayed.

Typically, as the boy played, Sally would sit in a metal-frame chaise longue in the gazebo, reading a book or magazine as she watched him intermittently.

She would listen, too.

Often, even from across the yard, she could hear the rales in his chest. The seemingly inhuman chorus of rattles and squeaks that accompanied his every breath. Frequently, also, came a barking cough—or, on occasion, a collection of them strung together in an exhausting, convulsive chain. And always there was the clearing of the throat. The continual, almost desperate attempt to dislodge some obstruction that would not be moved.

At intervals, she would call to him.

"Eamon? Honey? Are you all right?"

Absorbed in his imaginary world, he sometimes failed to answer. Either way, she would eventually rise and approach. What would then follow never varied in substance from one instance to the next.

"I think it's time to go in," she would say.

The boy would protest.

"No, Eamon. You've been out here long enough. Oh, just look at you! You're a mess. Now get up."

With a disagreeable air, he would stand—a pale, undergrown stick figure with sunken eyes and a tiny voice from a gravel pit.

"It's just sand, Mom."

She would say nothing as her hands swept his clothes and skin, meticulous to remove every grain. Finished, she would pat his shoulders and kiss his pallid cheek.

"All right, honey. Let's go."

"Mom, I'm okay."

"Eamon, you're choked up. You're coughing."

"I cough all the time."

"But some things make it worse."

"Nuh-uh."

"You spend too much time in this filthy place."

"I like it here."

"It's time for a treatment."

"Mom . . ."

"We'll have a treatment, and then we'll have a big milkshake. Chocolate! How's that sound?"

She would take his hand, hauling him toward the house.

Always, he would look back, as if for something left behind.

In the spare bedroom upstairs, Brad prepared a place for himself. A sanctum where, when possible, he could work nights and weekends. He had not had such a place in Santa Monica. It would be different here.

He appointed the room with a roll-top desk and matching swivel chair, both purchased new on credit. On the desk he placed a monitor and docking station for his laptop. One of the drawers held his printer. He stocked the others with pens and sharpened pencils, legal pads and copy paper.

On the wall near the door he hung a framed copy of Dali's *Persistence of Memory*, with its melting clocks and barren shoreline. He had acquired the print several years before at an art shop in Venice Beach. He had told the clerk he had not particularly cared for the painting, but liked the title, which had evoked curious laughter. He had not laughed.

He dotted another wall with a half dozen vacation photos he had taken of Sally and Eamon on a windy shore at Big Sur. In one picture, the boy, gaunt and pasty in shorts and a flapping windbreaker, stood alone, looking blandly out to sea. In another, nestled warm and tight in his mother's arms, the child seemed imminently breakable, his pained expression passing for a smile as Sally's emerald eyes burned above him with a ghostly, deified beauty.

On a third wall he placed a work that had been done by coating a canvas with red and brown acrylic and dragging, it appeared, a finger through the paint. The effort had resulted in two circles of slightly disproportionate size, the smaller encompassed by the larger. A circle within a circle. And above the design, likewise finger-drawn and in crudely formed letters, was what seemed a nonsensical title:

MIS MUNDOS.

My Worlds.

Sitting at the desk, he tried, as he had tried so many times, to grasp the point of it. Its meaning. Its message. *Something.* Trying to remember. But he could not.

Yet the signature, scratched in black marker in the bottom right corner, was his.

He rose from his chair, running his fingers over the flourish of letters, telling—ordering—himself to remember just this much: the signing of a name—*his* name—on this now hardened paint.

But he could not do even that. It wasn't possible. Because the memory was *not* his. It belonged to another.

A predecessor.

He had a vague sense that the change had come in increments, the man he was now gradually emerging and taking control from whatever he had been before. A measured transition from one state of consciousness to another until, at last, of the former there was nothing left save fragments of dark thoughts and the suggestion of thoughts even darker. Hazy pieces of a life otherwise forgotten and, he knew, best left that way.

Why it had happened, he had no idea. He had looked for answers. But what little he had found he had not liked. Nor understood. So he had stopped looking and started trying to accept the way things were. And why not? It was a gift, really. He had been made a better man in his own image. And as that man, he had gained a wife, a child. Weren't those the things a man was supposed to have?

But always, there was the covering up. The lying. To Sally. To colleagues. To everyone. He hated himself for it. Yet those lies were so easy to tell. Easy because they were lies he himself had once believed. Lies sprung from memories that, he had come to discover, were in fact *themselves* lies. Memories of things he had never done and people he had never met. A false proxy for those lost recollections of his life before. In all, it formed a perfect backstory for one who otherwise had none. But the genesis of that story and its many fictitious intricacies, he knew, was not mere delusion, but some far greater sort of madness. It had to be. The psychological product of so badly, so desperately, wanting to completely become something other than what he had been.

And like it or not, it was a story he could never stop telling. Because without it, he was not the man he was believed to be. Without it, he was nothing.

Or something worse. Something he did not want to think about.

But what was this thing on the wall—these two inexplicable circles, his unremembered signature—if not a reminder? It had been some time since it had seen the light of day. He did not like looking at it. But somehow, like himself, it seemed to belong here, in this place he called home.

He turned his back on it and left the room, shutting the door behind.

Chapter 2

The Man at the Fence

There was an air base nearby. The big planes came and went at all hours, one after the next. It took some getting used to: the far-off sound of thunder, its rumble approaching and building to a crescendo, then falling into the distance, only to be followed by another identical storm. Going on her third week, Sally was still not accustomed to it.

But, it seemed, just as regular as the planes were the comings and goings of the old man from across the commons. Brad had mentioned his name, but she could not quite remember. Paul something-or-other.

"I guess those are bombers," she said one evening as the man ambled along the fence line.

She was likewise near the fence, having left her chair in the gazebo for a stroll around the yard. As usual, the boy was in the sandbox.

With an appreciative smile, the old man stopped and turned.

"Bombers? Nah," he said. "KC-135's. Stratotankers."

Sally cursed herself. She had previously spoken no more than sparse pleasantries to him. It unsettled her, the way he constantly hiked the commons—and loitered, she thought, far more than necessary near the Manford yard.

And now, for the sake of sociable chatter, she had attracted his attention. A full-blown conversation had become inevitable.

"I'm sorry," she said. "What did you say?"

His wide smile seemed to wrap halfway around his head.

"Those planes don't carry bombs, ma'am," he said. "They're tankers. They carry jet fuel."

"Is that right? All this time I thought they were bombers."

The smile continued. "Basically they're flyin' gas stations."

"Really?"

"Uh-huh. You see, when a plane needs fuel it just cozies up to the back of one of those tankers and a boom comes out and fills it up."

"Right in the air?"

"Yes, ma'am. Right in the air."

"That's interesting."

"Yeah, I think so, too." He laughed good-naturedly.

"Well, there certainly are a lot of them," Sally said.

"Sixty-three out at McConnell. That'd be the Twenty-Second Air Refueling Wing. Largest Stratotanker force in the world."

She scrunched her eyebrows. "It sounds like you know a lot about this."

"Yeah, I've spent a lot of time around those old tankers, startin' in the Air Force, and then with Boeing. They're Boeing built."

"So did you fly them? The tanker planes?"

"Oh, no, ma'am. I flew a Thud. F-105 Thunderchief."

She was conscious of her blank expression—and so, it seemed, was the old man.

"It's kind of a cross between a bomber and a fighter," he explained.

Her mouth gaped. "You're saying you were a fighter pilot?"

"Yes, ma'am. In a way."

"Wow. You must have a rank."

The old man chuckled. "Ma'am, ever'body in the service has a rank."

Flustered, she tried again. "I mean a *high* rank."

"I'm a colonel, actually," he said. "Retired, of course."

"That's very impressive."

He shrugged his shoulders. "Oh, I'm not so sure. But it gets me a nice pension, and at my age, that's important."

"A colonel's close to a general, isn't it?"

"One step away."

From the north, another tanker approached. Sally glanced at the sky and, as the noise grew, moved closer to the fence. She was beginning to feel less apprehensive about this guy.

"As you can probably tell," she said, "I don't know much about the military. And I know nothing at all about the Air Force. My dad was in the Army for a while, but that was before I was born, and he didn't talk about it much."

The old man shook his head, feigning a look of pity.

"A father in the Army and a lawyer for a husband," he said. "Oh, does my heart go out to you." Quickly, he flashed a smile. "No, I'm just kiddin'. I've got nothin' against the Army or lawyers, either one. We need 'em both. But that reminds me, I poked some fun at your husband's profession some time ago when you were first lookin' at the house, and I'm afraid he may have taken it the wrong way."

"Oh, no. He's not like that. He never mentioned it."

"It's just that I haven't seen anything of him since you all moved in, and we only talked the one time. I was worried he might be a little hacked off at me."

"No, he just hasn't been here very much. He's been busy getting settled in to his new job, and he's had to go out of town a couple of times. He's in Chicago right now."

At once, she caught her mistake: *What kind of idiot tells a strange man—even an old one—that her husband's away on business?*

She eyed the gate nearby. The lock that had secured it when they moved in, along with the one that had been on the other gate east of the house, was gone. Thinking them too much trouble, Brad had asked the handyman who filled the sandbox to cut them off.

The tanker was overhead. She said something as it passed. The old man pretended to hear.

For a few seconds, neither of them spoke. She was thinking of a way to break off the conversation when he gestured toward the yard with his index finger.

"Your boy really loves that sandbox," he said. "Does he do anything else?"

"Only when I make him."

"Hey, it beats sittin' in front of a TV."

"Maybe."

"I guess he's not quite old enough for school."

"He's six," Sally corrected.

"Is that right?" His voice carried traces of both embarrassment and surprise.

Sally was used to it.

"He's small for his age."

That was what she said now. A few years ago she would have volunteered more. Back then, talking about it had made her feel better. But she had grown tired of the sorrowful looks and sympathetic words. It wasn't anyone else's business, anyway.

"Well, I'm sure he'll grow a ton," the old man said, trying to atone. "Kids always do."

She responded with a perfunctory nod—and was suddenly aware of the boy's coughing.

"He needs to go in," she said, turning away. "Eamon, come on. It's time."

The boy did not answer. She started toward him, then stopped and looked back at the old man, saying something she almost wished she hadn't.

"You know, I think you're out here more than he is."

In an instant, the old man's sunny disposition began to fade, and his words came at a more calculated pace, as if read from a script.

"It's just that I don't have much else to do. And I like bein' outside. I like watchin' the planes."

Chapter 3

Evening Protocol

She kept most of the boy's medical supplies upstairs in the hall linen closet. The top two shelves held a well-ordered collection of bottles and boxes of medication, as well as several inhalers and spacers, two peak flow meters, and a finger-clip pulse oximeter. On the next shelf below were two nebulizer units, each preferable to the other depending on the drug being dispersed, and various spare nebulizer parts—tubing, mouthpieces, medicine cups—stored in ziplock plastic bags. The floor-level compartment was reserved for a therapy vest and its seventeen-pound compressor. There had been a time when she left such drugs and paraphernalia lying around for convenience, but as the child had grown older, she had begun trying, as much as possible, to keep them out of sight.

She reached into a carton on the top shelf, removed a sealed foil envelope, and tore it open to reveal a chain of plastic two-milliliter vials, each containing a measured dose of liquid corticosteroid. Snapping off a vial, she replaced the envelope and, from the same shelf, grabbed, from another box, an already opened foil pouch that held the last of what had been, that morning, four vials of albuterol sulfate.

A freshly washed nebulizer mouthpiece and medicine cup lay on a clean, folded hand towel by the sink in the hall bath. Twisting the plastic top off the vial of corticosteroid, she emptied the contents into the cup, then took the albuterol from its package and did the same, mixing the drugs. Eamon's first doctor in L.A. had insisted that she administer the medications separately—the albuterol, then the corticosteroid. But the others since, including the new one here, had said it was fine to combine them. And she had always seen it done that way in the hospital. It probably didn't save much time, but it did save a little. And when she was very tired, a little was a lot.

She fixed the mouthpiece to the cup and gently shook the solution as she walked back to the closet, where she removed a peak flow meter, one of the nebulizers, and the therapy vest. The vest fit the boy like a life jacket and, when fed compressed air, vibrated, loosening mucus.

Eamon sat on his bed in his underwear and pajama top, his short, skinny legs dangling over the side like white sticks. He was yawning as she entered, his heels tapping slowly in unison against the bed frame.

"Here we go," she said, hooking up the nebulizer. "Do you want to do this in Mom and Dad's room so you can watch TV?"

"No," he said, listless.

"Okay, then." She started to put the vest on him. "Let's do this along with our breathing treatment. I'll get the machine."

"No, I want backy-whacky."

"Eamon, that takes so much longer."

"I don't care."

"But the vest is more fun."

"No, it isn't."

The irony did not escape her: Fifteen thousand dollars for a high-tech therapy vest—and begging and finally getting an insurance company to pay for most of it—and the kid would rather have her pound on his torso.

"All right, fine." She removed the vest and handed him the peak flow meter. "Here, give me a blow."

The boy huffed into the device, moving the indicator past the red and yellow zones and just into the green.

"You can do better," she said.

He blew again, this time sending the pointer barely into the yellow—a reading, if valid, suggesting a medical emergency.

"Eamon, you're scaring me. Now *blow*."

He did, putting the indicator solidly in the green.

"There. See how easy it is? Why don't you do that every time?"

"Sometimes it doesn't work right."

"Oh, Eamon . . ."

While he used the nebulizer, she returned the vest to the linen closet.

On a chart taped to the inside of the door she recorded his peak flow. She then went to the bath to toss the empty vials and foil packaging in the trash, and, recalling a loose bowel movement he'd had in the late afternoon, gave the toilet bowl and seat a thorough cleaning. The problem, she thought, was possibly her fault. The child needed digestive enzymes with every meal and snack. Without them, the food just went straight through. But there was an art to getting the right dosage. It depended on what and how much he ate. Somewhere during the day she could well have underestimated.

That, or he had not taken what she had given him. Lately he had been doing that.

After washing her hands she went back to the cabinet and removed, from the second shelf, two bottles of nasal spray—one a steroid, the other saline. On her way to his room she heard him switch off the nebulizer.

"Done," he said, handing her the mouthpiece.

She checked the medication cup and passed him the peak flow meter.

"Give me a good one," she said.

He propelled the indicator slightly beyond his last effort—a sign the treatment had been effective.

"Good man," she said, then frowned. "Okay, let's do backy-whacky. Are you sure you don't want to watch TV."

"No, I'm tired."

"Well, you'd be ready for bed now if you'd done the vest."

Knowing the drill, the boy turned away from her and curled forward, holding the pillow against his stomach as she began tapping rapidly on his upper back with a cupped hand. Yet despite their name for it, the treatment was not confined to the back; she also thumped the boy's chest and sides, and with each change of location would give the same command.

"Cough," she would say, at which point the child would attempt to produce a gob of phlegm. When successful, she would pass him a tissue. Tonight was not too bad, but there were times he had generated such a quantity they had used a plastic cup.

"Come on, Eamon, *cough*."

"I am."

"You can do better. You've got to get that gunk out."

After, she watched as he took his nasal sprays. A shot from each bottle in both nostrils. Whether it did any good, though, she had to wonder. He'd been on the stuff for four years and still had two polyp surgeries in the last three.

She led him down the hall to brush his teeth. He seemed to be almost sleepwalking. Reentering the room, he went straight to his bed, grabbing the big floppy-eared stuffed rabbit that lay against his headboard.

"When will Dad be home?" he asked.

"I'm not sure."

"I wish he was here now."

"Me too. But hey, *I'm* here."

"I know." His voice trailed off. "I just want Dad."

He had been saying that all day.

"He'll be home soon. We have to be patient."

She pulled the covers over him and bent down to kiss him on the forehead—his skin, as always, answering her affection with the salty taste that marked his illness. *It's like kissing a margarita glass,* her mother had once joked. But that had been before the diagnosis.

"I love you, honey."

He was already asleep.

She turned off the room light and returned to the linen closet to record his last peak flow and put away the nebulizer and nasal sprays. After that, she took the peak flow meter and the nebulizer mouthpiece and cup downstairs to the dishwasher, then went to the cabinet nearest the kitchen sink for a cocktail glass, to which she introduced ice from the freezer, gin and tonic from the pantry, and, lastly, from the refrigerator, a slice of lime.

She stood at the kitchen island, savoring the bite of alcohol tempered with quinine and citrus. In these moments, she sometimes cried. And it would have been easy tonight.

Brad, this is nuts! Everything we have is here. I don't know a soul in Kansas. Neither do you. It's like a foreign country. And it's not even a better job. Why the hell are you doing this?

He had never given a real answer. Just platitudes. Drivel about quality of life and friendly Midwesterners and—his favorite—cost of living. It was all crap and she knew it.

Overhead, she heard a plane coming in. *KC . . . KC—what?* She swallowed hard and felt her memory improve. *KC-135. That was it. Stratotanker.*

Crazy old man.

She took her cell phone to the newly purchased faux leather couch in the family room, and in the gathering quiet as the plane moved on, sipped her drink and waited for Brad to call.

———————

She always put a fresh wedge of lime in every drink, but left those from before. When the phone rang, she had three green slivers in her glass.

They talked first about his trip. It would run longer than expected.

"When will you get back?"

"It's looking like Saturday."

"You're kidding."

"I'm sorry."

"Well, I know you can't help it. But he keeps asking for you."

"I'll get there as soon as I can. I promise."

"I know," she said. "I know you will."

She released a stress-heavy sigh.

"So, how was he today?" he asked.

"Really good. Another good day. And I weighed him this morning. He's up another pound."

"Wow, that's great."

"Can you believe it? That's two pounds since we got here."

"That's amazing."

"Yeah, and I sure hope he keeps it up. I don't want to have to fight with this new doctor about the . . . you know, the tube thing."

The subject of a surgically implanted feeding tube had been one of dispute with the last doctor in L.A. In Sally's mind, he had done everything but call her a bad mother. But there had been no tube.

There was a silence, each waiting for the other to speak.

"So," Brad said, "what else is he up to?"

"Oh, you know, still toiling away at the Manford Home School."

"Does he like his teacher?"

"I don't think so. She's kind of a bitch." She let loose another anxious breath. "Brad, I just worry whether this is the right thing. I mean, he's lonely. But I'd rather have him that way than the way he was last year."

"I agree."

"It's just that he's going to miss so much. And I feel like I'm the one who made the decision. It's like with the tube. I feel like I just dictated . . ."

"No, no, I was part of it."

"But I'm the one who insisted."

"And I thought it was the right thing."

"Do you still think that? I mean, it's not too late."

"No," he said. "It makes sense. The odds of him staying healthy are better this way. Way better. The doctors have said that."

"True."

"And if he keeps gaining weight and feeling good, maybe he can go back to school. Maybe next year."

Her judgment vindicated, the discussion moved elsewhere: His hotel accommodations. Something silly a politician had said. The weather.

"Oh, and I wanted to tell you," she said, "I spoke with that older man you met the day we came to look at the house. You know, the one who came over from the other neighborhood?"

"Paul Irvin?"

"Yeah. I couldn't remember his last name. He's a bit of a character."

"He's a talker," Brad said.

"He said he was a colonel in the Air Force."

"Really?"

"And a fighter pilot."

"Geez, I'll bet he's got some stories."

"I'm sure he does. But I don't know what to make of the guy. He spends half his day trekking up and down the commons."

"It's a public area."

"Yeah, but he hangs around our yard. It's weird." She paused as the sound of a barking cough came from upstairs. "Anyway," she said, lowering her voice, "I made a remark about it, and I don't think he liked it."

"What do you mean?"

"I don't know. It was just the way he acted. I probably shouldn't have said anything. But honestly, sometimes he just lurks there, next to our fence, and I have to wonder about it. Do you think he's watching us?"

"He's probably just a busybody," Brad said.

"Or a dirty old man."

"I doubt that."

"Well, he's watching *something*. He said it was the airplanes, but I thought about that, and you know, if he really spent years around those planes, you'd think he'd have something better to do now than watch one after the other fly over. And if he's really watching the planes, why can't he do it somewhere else?"

She heard the coughing again and went to the foot of the stairs, cocking her free ear toward the boy's room.

"Sal," he said, "are you there?"

"I'm just listening," she whispered. "He was coughing. It didn't sound too good."

"I'd better let you go."

"I suppose so. I'm tired, anyway. I had to mow that damn back yard again today. It grows like a freakin' jungle."

Chapter 4

The Talking Cure

It had been six years ago, near the end of an afternoon, the green window shades filtering the late-day sunlight, bathing the room in a soft teal, as he and the doctor sat facing one another in padded, high-back chairs, less than four feet of open space between.

A notepad on his lap, pen in hand, Dr. Mahindra—short and slim, a shock of black hair swept over his dark, balding head—had crossed his legs and adjusted his thick, black-framed glasses.

The room, for a moment, had seemed exceedingly quiet.

"Mr. Manford," he began, "I am happy to see you, and I am sure you are eager to discuss your reason for seeing me. But before we do that, would you please allow me to learn some things about you?"

"Sure."

"Excellent." The doctor spoke with the Received Pronunciation of the most proper Indian English. There was a comforting precision in his pace, his choice of words. "And please understand, you can tell me as much or as little of yourself as you prefer. It is totally up to you. However, understand also that the more I know about you, the more likely I am to be able to help you."

Brad nodded.

"And as we work through things today, if there is anything I can do to put you more at ease, please let me know."

Another nod.

"Very well." The doctor wrote something on his notepad. "So, please tell me, are you married?"

"Yes."

"Your wife's name?"

"Sally."

He was writing.

"How long have you and Sally been married?"

"About a year and a half."

"Any children?"

"One. A boy."

"And his name?"

"Eamon."

The doctor looked up. "Eamon Manford," he said pensively. "That has a nice ring. Eamon, I believe, is Irish, or perhaps more accurately, Celtic. Yes?"

"I think so."

"Well, it's certainly not overused. At least, not in this country. Is it a family name?"

"No, my wife just liked it. She said it sounded like the last word of a prayer."

Seeming delighted, the doctor smiled, showing large teeth.

"So it does!" he said. "It certainly does. That's wonderful." He resumed his note-taking. "How old is Eamon, Mr. Manford?"

"Just a month."

"And is he a healthy, normal . . ."

"Not really."

The doctor raised his pen. "Oh? May I ask . . ."

"Cystic fibrosis. We just found out."

"I am sorry to hear that." Mahindra wrote something quickly and placed both hands atop the notepad as if, for the time being, putting it aside. "I would imagine that has placed a good deal of stress on you and your wife."

"Yeah, but we're dealing with it."

"Certainly. But as you may know, your son's condition is one inherited from parents who are carriers of the disease. And oftentimes there is an element of guilt felt by persons who have passed on such a condition to a child. I hate to be presumptuous, Mr. Manford, but are you or your wife blaming yourselves for this unfortunate problem?"

"No," Brad said, "not really. Eamon isn't actually ours."

"Excuse me?"

"We adopted."

"Oh! Well, I *am* presumptuous."

"My wife . . ." Brad looked away. "She had an illness. She can't have children."

"I am so sorry."

The doctor, too, looked away, appearing to contemplate something other than his next question. When he spoke again, it was as if he were starting anew.

"Tell me, Mr. Manford, how are you employed?"

"I'm an attorney."

"Oh, very good. My father was an attorney. But I would imagine his law practice in New Delhi was nothing like your experience in Los Angeles."

"I don't know," Brad said. "Maybe and maybe not. The practice of law in L.A. can be pretty bizarre." At once, Brad caught himself. "Not that India is bizarre. I didn't mean to imply that."

Mahindra chuckled, looking down at his pad, then up.

"Oh, no," he said. "I know what you mean. And the fact is, India *is* bizarre. In many ways, more bizarre than Los Angeles." He sat higher in his chair, recrossing his thin legs. "But please, tell me about your work. How long have you been an attorney?"

"Going on five years."

"In what area of the law do you practice?"

"Intellectual property, mostly."

"Really?" the doctor said admiringly. "A quite complex field, I understand."

"In some ways, it is. But it has a reputation for being boring. People hear 'intellectual property' and they think about patents and trademarks and copyrights. That stuff, I know, sounds pretty dry. But it's not quite that bad."

"Not *quite?*" The doctor's emphasis on the last word was not so pointed as to seem derisive. "Perhaps we should explore that, just a little. Tell me, Mr. Manford, do you enjoy your work?"

"As much as any man, I suppose."

The answer drew a polite smile from the therapist.

"Or possibly," he said, "the better question is, does your work bring you satisfaction?"

Brad shrugged, titling his head to one side. "I don't know. Some. Maybe not that much."

"Why do you think that is?"

Brad thought for a moment. "Well, I'm not sure I can explain it, but I see my clients inventing things, creating things, and sometimes I feel like I should be doing that."

The doctor raised his eyebrows. "So you envy your clients?"

"At times."

"How long have you felt this way?"

"I don't know. I guess I would have to say as long as I can remember."

The doctor glanced at his notepad, then around the room, developing another thought.

"Mr. Manford, if you could do something else for a living, what would it be?"

"I think I might be an artist. A painter or a sculptor. Or maybe an architect. You know, somebody who creates something out of nothing."

"Have you ever tried to do that? To create something?"

Brad dropped his head, passing a nervous hand through his hair. "I made something once. It was sort of like abstract art."

"What was it?"

"A symbol of some kind."

"A symbol?"

"I guess you could call it that. A circle within a circle."

"What did it mean?"

"I have no idea."

The doctor appeared to acknowledge his arrival at a dead end.

"All right," he said, "let's go back. Your job as a lawyer. Have you ever thought about why you went into work of that type?"

"Not really."

"But as we sit here today, why do you think you did?"

Brad's head was still down. The room, again, seemed remarkably quiet.

"I don't know. To fit in, I suppose."

"Fit in?"

"You know, I . . ." Embarrassed, Brad shook his head. "I'm not sure what I meant by that."

The doctor looked at his wristwatch.

"Well, perhaps we can return to this subject a little later, but I think for now it would be advisable if we moved forward to whatever you came to talk to me about." He repositioned his notepad. "So, tell me, how may I help you?"

———————

A single light burned in the hotel room's far corner as Brad sat by the window and thought about how he had answered that question.

How may I help you?

The doctor had made it sound so easy. Like a sales clerk ready to advise a customer on a routine purchase. No doubt he had expected some garden-variety complaint.

I remember twenty-some years of a life I never lived, and almost nothing that actually occurred during the same time.

Clearly, the man had not seen that one coming.

Fifteen floors below, the Chicago River shimmered in the city lights. Brad stared at the shiny black water, contemplating whether one could strike it from this height and have any hope of surviving. But he realized it was a fairly useless thing to consider; leaning nearer the window, he could see the hotel was not as close to the river as he had thought. There was, in fact, a sidewalk café in between. Thus, aside from the question of enduring the watery impact, a superhuman long jump would be necessary to avoid splattering onto the concrete. On the other hand, if hitting the water would kill you anyway . . .

Futile speculation.

His open briefcase sat close by. Tempted, he reached into the side pocket for the envelope that had arrived two days before in the firm's mail, telling himself that he would examine it and its contents one last time, then be done with them. That he would tear them into pieces so small that all evidence of their existence would be obliterated.

The light in the room was just sufficient to show the postmark: Los Angeles, CA.

Yet he could clearly see the return address. Typed in all caps, it was strangely inconsistent with the location of posting. It was strange, too, in its deficiency. Only a single word.

MEXICALI.

But therein lay the message. Or part of it.

From the envelope, he pulled a sheet of paper folded in thirds and unfurled it to reveal a copy of a document printed in Spanish.

SE BUSCA! it proclaimed across its top.

Wanted.

And just below was a drawing of a man's face. A face with which he was intimately familiar.

Looking out the window, he could see its reflection even now.

Chapter 5

White Lies and Dark Secrets

At fifty-two, Hugh Miller had been with the firm half of his life. Affable and self-effacing, he had begun his career as a litigator, but had soon found himself better suited for other work. Now, after two decades in mergers and acquisitions, he answered only to the head of the firm's transactions department, Steven LeMark.

He had a long-standing weight problem and, for the last several years, had reconciled himself to lunching in his office four days a week on fruit and cottage cheese. On Wednesdays, though, he ate downtown at the Petroleum Club on the ninth floor of the Ruffin Building. He had a regular table on the east side of the wood-trimmed, Southwestern-styled dining room, where, along a panoramic wall of picture windows, one could see to the edge of the city and miles beyond. He came in part for the view, but mostly for the Mexican buffet—and in particular, the chicken tortilla soup, with which he had something of a culinary love affair.

"Good stuff, huh?" he said in a burble between his second and third spoonfuls.

"It is," Brad agreed.

Hugh was at the bottom of his bowl before he spoke again.

"Okay," he said, scraping out the last drops, "let's call this meeting to order." He took a long swallow from his water glass. "Bradley, as you know, the firm has appointed me your supervisor. And as your supervisor, I'm supposed to get together with you periodically to discuss your progress." He took another long drink. "So, how's your progress?"

"Good, I think."

"It sure sounds that way. Steve said things went very well in Chicago, and that you were a big part of it."

That was certainly nice to hear, but four days on the road with Steven LeMark had been a grind. Some ten years Hugh's senior, LeMark was, in virtually every respect, Hugh's polar opposite. Fastidious, humorless, and full of ego, he was as bad a traveling companion as Brad had ever endured.

LeMark had taken him to Chicago for the stated purpose of keeping track of the countless documents in what had been expected to be—and ultimately had been—an extremely complex negotiation. However, in addition to managing the records, Brad had made several suggestions that had helped facilitate a better outcome for the client. In Chicago, LeMark had taken the credit, but it appeared he had given Hugh a more honest impression.

"It did go well," Brad said. "Unfortunately, we were there twice as long as we'd planned."

"Yeah, but the important thing is, the deal got done and Steve was happy with your work. I mean *very* happy."

Hugh started on his main course of enchiladas and refried beans—a signal, Brad thought, that the business portion of this get-together was concluded.

As he ate, Brad looked out over the city. A covering of trees began just past the downtown area and stretched out high and thick into the suburbs, concealing houses and other structures beneath. Atop the canopy, fall colors were becoming apparent.

"I didn't think there'd be so many trees," he said.

Hugh looked up from his food. "Most of them were planted in the last hundred years or so. When the settlers came here, this place was nothing but prairie. Out west of here, it still is."

"Anyway, it makes for a nice view."

"Yeah, I enjoy it. But it's obviously nothing compared to Los Angeles."

"I don't know." Brad still gazed out the window. "L.A.'s impressive, but I think there's something to be said for this."

Hugh took another bite of enchilada before resting his fork on his plate and wiping his mouth with his napkin, leaving behind a more serious expression than Brad, in his short acquaintance with the man, had become used to.

"Bradley, I want to ask you a question, and I hate to seem nosey."

"No, that's okay."

It wasn't, really. Brad dreaded such inquiries. They sometimes led to dangerous subject matter, and with that came lies and the fear of discovery.

"It's just that I'm curious," Hugh said. "And I know you're young, but you've got tremendous experience, and you held several positions in L.A."

"I've bounced around a little," Brad threw in, apologetic.

"You have, but that's not really my point. And as I say, I hate to put you on the spot, but what I'm getting at is, with your background, you just don't seem like the kind of guy who would make Wichita, Kansas, his next stop. So, if you don't mind me asking, why did you?"

This again. The same question, in so many words, he had heard from Sally. And her mother. And her sister. And from so many others the day he had flown in for the interview. Hugh had been out of town that day. Yet he had no doubt heard the answer secondhand. Which meant he was after something more. Something beyond the bullshit.

But the stock response, the evasive reply—which was, in fact, the best explanation Brad could muster—had been good enough to get him here.

And it would have to be good enough for Hugh.

"I just liked the idea of living in this part of the country," Brad said.

"But why? What did you think you'd find? The Old West? Gunfights in the street?"

Brad laughed to hide his unease. "No, I knew better."

"But had you ever been here before?"

"Not that I recall," Brad said, trying to make a joke.

"Do you or your wife have family here?"

"No."

"Just wanted to get away from life in the fast lane, huh?"

"That's basically it."

Brad felt himself sweating.

"Well, that's certainly to our benefit," Hugh said, relieving the tension somewhat. "When we lost Mark Thibodeau, we panicked. I mean, we had to have somebody pronto. Somebody who knew what they were doing. Then along you came. It was like a miracle."

"It all happened pretty fast."

"I hope not too fast." Hugh glanced out the window, then at Brad. "How's your wife holding up?"

"She's . . . okay."

"Does she like it here?"

"She's getting acclimated. It's been a big change for her."

Hugh gave an empathetic nod. "Well, I hope she learns to feel at home here, and the firm wants to help her with that, because, Bradley, if your wife's happy, you'll be happy. And we want you to be happy."

Brad sensed a further drop in the stress level. The interrogation, it seemed, was over.

"And on the subject of your wife," Hugh said, "there are some people, me included, who would like to meet her. There's also a feeling that we need to give you kind of a general welcoming to the firm. So, we've planned a little dinner for this Saturday evening. It won't be anything too fancy. Just you, me, Steve, a couple other people in the firm, and spouses, or, you know, significant others."

"Gosh, I know Sally would really like to meet everyone, but . . ."

"I know it's short notice."

"No, it's not that. It's our son. Since we're so new here, I'm afraid we don't know anyone who could sit with him."

Hugh leaned forward, smiling. "Bradley, your problems are solved. My oldest stepdaughter is sixteen. She babysits all the time. She even has a car."

"I appreciate that, but Hugh, the truth is, my son has some special needs."

"Oh?"

Brad had yet to tell anyone at the firm.

"Health issues," he clarified. "Otherwise, he's a normal kid, but he takes a lot of medication."

Hugh shook his head, unimpressed. "Trust me, Alyssa can handle it. She's very mature. Whatever his problem, she can manage for a few hours."

Brad was reasonably sure of the same. Nonetheless, he thought this would be difficult. In six years, the number of non-family members Sally had allowed to sit with Eamon could be counted on two fingers, and those had been heavily vetted. To think that she would now simply hand the boy over to an unknown teenager was hard to imagine.

But the stakes were clear. This was no invitation; it was a summons. One delivered on behalf of Steven LeMark. And a failure to appear would not be acceptable.

"I'll get ahold of my wife as soon as we get back," Brad said.

———————

He was reaching for his office phone to dial Sally when it beeped to signal an incoming call. The crystal display, giving no other information, read "Unknown."

"Brad Manford."

"Well, hello, Brad Manford." A man's voice, wickedly cheerful. "Can you guess who this is?"

At once, he felt something boiling up. It was the way he felt every time he got this call.

"What do you want?"

"Did you get my little package from south of the border?"

Brad watched his open door for eavesdroppers. "Go to hell."

Phony laughter on the other end. "Oh, you can be nicer than that, can't you? After all, it's been months since we've talked, and you didn't even tell me you were leaving town."

"It didn't take you long to find me."

"Nothing to it, partner. Your firm has a very helpful website, and they wasted no time putting your handsome little mug on it." Another chuckle. "Did you really think you were going to shake me by moving to the middle of nowhere?"

"That's not why I came here."

The voice turned nasty. "Don't lie to me, Manford. A young hotshot like you? Living it up in SoCal? Why else would you just up and move to the sticks?"

"That's none of your damn business."

"It's *all* my business."

"I don't have anything to say to you. I'm hanging up."

The tone changed again—sugary and foppish: "Oh, dear Brad, please don't."

"No, I'm done playing your game. I was done the last time."

"But Brad, I've got frightfully large bills to pay, and I'm planning a simply marvelous trip to Cancun."

With the phone cord stretched to its full length, Brad moved around his desk and extended a hand just enough to reach the door and swing it shut.

"Look, I don't have any money."

"Then get some."

"It's not that easy. I've got bills, too."

"You should have planned ahead, my friend. Now listen, I want five thousand in cash next week."

"I can't do that!"

"Then you'll be sorry."

Brad knew that might be true. Then again, it might not. But five grand in so short a time was out of the question. It could not be done.

"I can get you a thousand. That's the best I can do. I'll pay the rest later."

"How much later?"

"First week of November."

There was a silence, the offer under consideration.

"All right. You send a thousand. But I want the rest in three weeks. Understand?"

It was like being tied up and kicked. Neutered. Over and over. And begging wouldn't help. He knew that. He had begged so many times.

And yet he begged.

"Ron, if I pay you, will you please leave me alone?"

"Partner, I'm afraid that's not part of the deal."

"Let's *make* it part of the deal."

"Well, you're going to need a lot more than five G's for that. But hey, old buddy, I don't want to be too rough on you. You just pay the five and we'll talk about it."

"I'll try."

"I hope you do better than that. I'd sure hate to have to ruin your miserable life."

Chapter 6

Lawn Service

Before the move to Kansas, Sally had scarcely mowed a blade of grass in her entire life. She had grown up in a pillbox of a house with a postage stamp of a yard—a space covered with far more dirt than weeds, and more weeds than grass—and to his death, her father had attended to the very minimal needs of what could only jokingly be called "lawn care." He could cut the whole thing in the time it took him to smoke a Marlboro.

Now, however, she had a back yard large enough, by itself, to hold her childhood home and its surrounding real estate three times over. It was the biggest yard in the neighborhood—a neighborhood where many of the affluent residents employed a lawn service. And after closing on the home, Brad had renewed his suggestion that he and Sally do the same. Losing that debate, he had again argued for a riding mower. But she would have none of it. She saw no reason to pay more than the price of a decent walk-behind, self-propelled model. And she would be the one using it. She had made that very plain.

I need the exercise, she had said.

And now she was getting it. She was getting it in spades.

On average, she found it necessary to cut the back yard every third day. With a short break or two, the job took about an hour and a half—longer if she caught all the clippings. But, as a rule, she bagged only around the sandbox. She usually trimmed as well, running a weed whacker around the house, fence, hedge, gazebo, sandbox, and pear trees. That took another fifteen minutes. The much smaller and slower-growing front and side yards needed far less attention, and she cut them only every other time she did the back, but with trimming, edging, and sweeping the drive, the work involved required, at a minimum, another thirty minutes.

The back yard, though, was the issue. The whole issue. The thing was out of control and she could not begin to fathom why. There had been no rain for some time before they had moved in and the ground was quite dry, prompting her, during the first week, to run the sprinkler system every day. However, noting the rampant growth in the back yard, she had reduced watering that area to every other day. Then every third day. But to little effect.

She also came to realize that while most of the yard behind the house sprouted up like a science experiment gone wrong, there was a portion of it—the part furthest to the west—that seemed more ordinary. The growth there was similar to the front and side yards. But just east of that, the grass grew considerably faster and more robust. Left uncut, much of it, in the space of only a few days, could become as high and thick as two weeks' growth in spring.

Yet there was something even more peculiar. Something that had taken her longer to notice.

From the west fence line, the farther one went to the east, the more remarkably developed the growth became until, in the vicinity of the sandbox, its intensity reached a pinnacle. And from there, in every direction, its lushness, and the richness of its color, diminished progressively the farther away it lay. To some degree, this aberration covered most of the yard, and, to a lesser extent, spilled over into the commons and the empty lot to the east. Its boundary—where the density of the grass declined and vivid green became a shade less noticed—was ill defined. To the south, its periphery was interrupted where it met the house. Nevertheless, the pattern was unmistakable.

It was a circle.

———

The afternoon was humid and eighty degrees. In the calm October air, jet contrails traced the blue sky and hung undisturbed as a parade of KC-135's rumbled from north to south, directly overhead.

Sally wheeled the mower into the back yard through the side gate.

Stopping several feet inside the fence, she called toward the sandbox.

"Eamon, time to go in."

"What?" The boy was indignant.

"I need to mow," she said, walking over. "You can't be out here. You know that. It'll choke you up."

"No, it won't."

"Yes, it will. Besides, you have school work."

"I don't go to school," he said.

Angered, she stepped into the sand, standing over him. "You certainly do. Now, get up." She gave him an unusually quick, less-than-thorough brushing off. "All right, now, *get* inside. And go straight upstairs and do your reading and math."

The boy looked down at the ground with his big eyes, hesitating before heading toward the deck stairs.

"Don't mess with my fort," he said.

"I won't. I never do."

He looked back. "I worked hard on it. It's my best one ever."

"It'll stay just like it is."

He started forward, then again looked back.

"Go," she said, less demanding.

She watched until he had entered the house and shut the door.

———————

The store had touted the mower's reliability: *Starts On The First Pull, Every Time!* And Sally had found the claim to be true—as long as she got a death grip on the cord and yanked with all 124 pounds moving in the same direction.

Her iPod helped pass the time. She had loaded a variety of music, from grunge to show tunes. But a guy she had dated—a body builder—had told her that AC/DC was music to sweat to. The sound equivalent, he had said, of an adrenaline rush. At the time, she had dismissed the notion. After all, these were geezers who had been screeching and banging strings longer than she had been alive. But two weeks ago, she had given the boys from Down Under an audition, and damned if that muscle-head hadn't finally been right about something.

She pulled up "Highway to Hell," cranked the volume, and began, cutting first between the east fence line and the walkout patio that lay below the deck, working out from the house as far as a line flush with the landing of the deck stairs. She then did the same on the west side of the deck before moving north down the fence. By that time, she had gone through "Rock and Roll Damnation" and was into "Love at First Feel."

She went around the outskirts of the yard four times, which left her far enough from the fence to make 180-degree turns while mowing successive strips east and west. And as she made a series of passes near the house, Bon Scott bragged of "Big Balls," and Brian Johnson told of "Givin' the Dog a Bone." Partway through the latter, she started laughing—first in her head, then out loud—because, boy, her sister Eva sure didn't listen to this stuff.

No, because Eva had religion. And the collected works of the Gaither Family.

Then too, Sally thought, the song titles alone would probably give the old broad a coronary.

Cutting a swathe just south of the sandbox, she glanced up at Eamon's bedroom window and wondered what the chances were that he was doing what she had told him. Fifty-fifty, she figured.

What concerned her far more, though—and it always did when she had to mow—was the child being in the house alone. She thought about stopping to check on him, but a moment later, there he was in the family room at the big picture window, giving her the thumbs up. She had instructed him to do that from time to time, just to ease her mind. More often than not, he forgot. But the kid was learning.

And as the job wore on, she began to think that she, too, was improving. At the pace she was setting, this was going to be a record. And there would be no breaks. Not today.

She felt the sweat soaking her bra and t-shirt. It rolled down her forehead and behind the lenses of her sunglasses. She stopped just long enough to wipe her stinging eyes with the collar of her shirt.

"Hells Bells" took her onward. Brian Johnson shouting. He was thunder. He was rain. He was the energy of pure evil.

Row after row, she kept pace with the mower, deviating from a straight line only to cut around the sandbox, the gazebo, and the pear trees. As always, she had planned to bag the environs of the sandbox, but, knowing it was past time for Eamon's afternoon snack and treatment, decided, this time, to leave the clippings.

North of the sandbox and gazebo she began to crave a glass of water.

But the end was in sight. The remaining uncut strip lay wide open, inviting a dash to the finish. Going east to west, she covered the last ribbon of turf, then, seeing a grassy fringe along the evergreen hedge, reversed direction and let the mower scrape the bushes, chopping away what would otherwise have been left for the weed whacker.

At the end of the hedge, with "Night Prowler" blasting, she let the drive lever drop and dragged the mower back toward the gate that opened to the commons. There, she pushed the machine into the gap in the hedge, rattling the wrought iron as she cut as close to the gate as possible.

That was the last of it.

She released the safety lever, killing the engine as Bon Scott signed off: *"Shazbot. . . . Nanu nanu."*

She took out her earphones and turned off the iPod. The sudden lack of noise seemed like a return from another world.

Removing her sunglasses, she pulled up a shirtsleeve and used it to mop the sweat from her face. She rubbed her eyes and, gazing indiscriminately at the wall of cedars in the commons only a few yards away, batted her eyelids to bring things back to focus.

She glanced to her left, then right. Along the open commons, the combination of grass and weeds—particularly that which fell within the same circle of growth that enveloped most of the back yard—was high and heavy. But through the vegetation, in each direction, she could discern the trail that she had come to associate with Paul Irvin. Certainly, others used it. But they were, in essence, mere interlopers. Borrowers, at best.

Oddly, she had not seen the colonel all day. And for a long while, there had been plenty of planes to watch. But no more. Somewhere during the course of her work, the procession of aircraft had come to a halt. Even the network of contrails had dispersed.

Time to get in, she told herself. There was trimming to be done, but it would have to wait.

She turned and took hold of the mower to push it toward the side gate, but had no sooner started when a sound from somewhere beyond the cedars—a rustling of something in a thicket—jolted her to a stop.

She wheeled about and froze.

A rabbit, she thought.

No, too big.

She judged the commotion to have come from just past the spot where the trail along the commons led off into the trees. She fixed on the one big cedar where the path went round and disappeared. The tree fairly well concealed its other side. Yet she detected, through its branches, a shifting shadow. A dark form distinct from the foliage.

And suddenly—eerily—she felt herself on display.

"Hello?" she said, her voice shaking.

There was the sound of crunching dry sticks. A single, stealthy footfall.

Leaving the mower, she took several slow steps toward the house. Then ran.

Chapter 7

Father and Son

It had become a wasted day. He was buried in work and had tried to buckle down, but after the call from Ron, it was useless. He did not have the strength. Not even to call Sally.

His suit coat slung over a shoulder, he entered the kitchen from the laundry area. She was loading the dishwasher, but looking, as he came in, out the window above the sink.

"I thought you'd be later," she said. "I went ahead and ate with Eamon."

"That's okay."

"You should've called. I would've waited."

He pecked her on the lips. "No big deal."

"Is something wrong?"

"No," he said. "Why?"

"You look like something's wrong."

"I'm fine." He glanced around the kitchen. "What'd you have?"

"Me? Scrambled eggs and toast."

"What about him?"

"Macaroni and cheese," she said, unenthused, "with extra cheese."

Brad nodded as if to say *of course*. For Eamon, there was always extra: Extra cheese. Extra butter. Extra bacon. Another dip of ice cream. Sally fed him like a grown man.

And so little of it stuck with him.

She shut the dishwasher and leaned against the counter.

"So, how about you?" she asked, again looking out the window. "Eggs? Or mac and cheese?"

Brad appeared to have sampled something disagreeable.

"Eggs," he said. "Definitely."

He loosened his tie and moved into the family room, dropping his coat over the arm of the new couch before making a check of the living room and glancing down the basement stairs.

"Where is he?" he asked.

Still at the sink, Sally briefly turned his way and gestured toward the yard. "Where do you think?"

From the picture window in the family room, Brad could see the boy playing in the sand under the little cottonwood tree, not quite a shadow in the mustering twilight.

"He's out late," he said.

With Brad keeping vigil, Sally went to the refrigerator for three eggs and to the cabinet for a mixing bowl.

"I thought fresh air was supposed to be good for him," she said wryly.

"It is, but it's cooled down a bit."

Using only her right hand, she cracked the first of the eggs into the bowl. "He has a jacket."

"Yeah, but it's probably time for him to come in, don't you think?"

"Then you tell him," she said, cracking the second egg, "because he's going to pitch a fit, and I'm not very happy with him as it is."

"Why?"

"Because he's been a pain all day, and at dinner I caught him trying to hide a couple of his enzymes in his napkin."

He spoke without thinking: "And you let him go outside after that?"

She cracked the third egg, but stopped short of dropping its contents. "Well, I guess I'm just a bad mother."

"No, Sal, I'm just saying we shouldn't let him . . ."

"Brad!"

Commanding the floor, she took a deep, aggravated breath, green eyes fuming.

He waited.

"I fight this every day," she said. "I fight it all day long. I'm a doctor. I'm a nurse. I'm a pharmacist. I'm a dietician. And now I'm a goddamn first-grade teacher. I *live* for him. But sometimes I get tired."

Deftly, her fingers parted the hemispheres of the shell.

The egg landed in the bowl with a plop.

"I'm tired now."

But he knew that was only part of it. In California, she'd had family and friends. A circle of support. Here, there was none of that. At least, not yet. And the days did not pass quickly for her.

"I'll take care of it," he said.

———

His dress shoes on the wood deck and stairs echoed like gunshots in the evening still. The air hung heavy, on the verge of dewfall, and in the west, a splash of crimson marked the last of a brilliant sunset.

"Eamon?"

He marched toward the sandbox, trying to seem stern, as he thought a man should be in this situation. But the child, sitting with his legs crossed, was oblivious.

Sunken brown eyes gazed up in anticipation. "Hi, Dad. Wanna play?"

"Eamon, your mother tells me you tried to throw away some of your pills at dinner."

In an instant, the boy's demeanor changed. He stared down at the sand, slowly positioning a green soldier.

"No, I didn't," he said, low and raspy.

"Yes, you did. She found two of them in your napkin, and they didn't get there by themselves."

The boy said nothing.

"You put them there, Eamon."

Not looking up, the boy turned loose of the green soldier. The phlegm rattled in his throat as he expelled a deep, guilty breath.

"I guess I did."

"I know you did."

The child fumbled for an excuse. "It was an accident. I didn't mean to. I thought I took them. I thought I did. But there were too many."

"Weren't there the same number you always take at dinner?"

"Yeah," the boy said, raising his voice. *"Too many."*

With a sudden fury, he snatched the green army man and flung it against the thin trunk of the cottonwood tree.

Brad realized the time had come for action—to speak with authority and send the boy inside. He had promised as much.

But there was something in the calm of the coming night that dis-

tracted him. Something that caught his ear and stole his train of thought.
For several seconds it held him in thrall—a sound he had heard before in
this very place. A peculiar hum that rode the air, it seemed, just below the
level of random noise.

A convulsive cough broke the quietude, returning his attention to the
child pouting in the sand. He squatted beside the boy and, dropping all
pretense of menace, laid a hand across the skeletal shoulders.

"E, look, you need those pills. If you don't take them, you won't be
strong and healthy. You know that, right?"

"I guess."

"And without those pills, your stomach will hurt, and you'll have to go
to the bathroom all the time. You know that, too, right?"

"Uh-huh."

"That's no fun, is it?"

"No."

"So you have to take the pills. All of them. Just like Mom and I say.
Okay?"

The boy, looking down, made no reply.

"Okay?" Brad repeated.

"Other kids don't have to take pills."

"Some do."

"Not like me. Not all the time."

"But so what? You just swallow them. There's nothing to it."

"That's easy for you to say."

The child had a point.

"Eamon, I'm not going to argue with you. The fact is, you need to take
those pills, and whether you like it or not, your mother and I are going to
see that you do. And that's really all there is to it."

Struggling to clear his throat, the boy nodded. But within the gesture,
not particularly well hidden, dwelled something less agreeable.

Brad patted him on the head and stood up. Through the kitchen window he could see Sally spooning his eggs on the stove.

"It's time to go in," he said.

Seeming in a trance, the boy lifted a handful of sand and let it drop,
spilling it slowly like the measured fall of grains in an hourglass. In a pen-
sive silence, he watched as the last of it trickled away.

"Eamon?"

The child spoke with a belated whisper. "Yeah?"

"I said it's time to go in."

It was then the boy raised his head. And somehow, Brad knew what was coming.

"Dad?"

"Yes?"

"Will I always be sick?"

In his immediate panic, it occurred to Brad that he might be no better at truth-telling than a six-year-old. But there were some things that could not be spoken.

"Always sick? You're not always sick. You're not sick today, are you?"

"A little."

"But you're not in bed. And you haven't been to the hospital for several months. You've been having lots of good days."

"But I'm never really well. Not all the way. Will I ever be like that? Well? All the way?"

What could he say?

"I hope so."

"Is there something that can make me well?"

"You mean like medicine?"

"Uh-huh."

With a pained expression, Brad pressed his lips together and ran a hand through the child's fine hair. "I don't know, E. But I believe somewhere, sometime, there might be."

"If there is, will you get it for me?"

"I'll sure try. I'll try my best."

The western sky had faded to a stale gray-blue. The stars were popping out, and Brad was about to again prompt the boy to go in. But in the hush before he could speak, it returned: The faint, smooth drone that seemed to emerge only when nature itself took a pause. A sound audible only in the absence of all others.

Brad wondered about his son. Did he hear it?

The boy looked up at his father, smiling.

Chapter 8

Man and Woman

The discussion with Sally did not go as expected. And that was a good thing.

"Sure," she said. "We could use a night out."

"It'll just be for a couple of hours or so."

"Yeah, fine. Where?"

"Steven LeMark's country club."

"Sounds good. Who's paying?"

"The firm."

"Even better."

"And Hugh's stepdaughter has had a lot of experience babysitting," Brad added. "She's very mature."

"Says who?"

"Hugh."

"Don't know the man."

"He's a good guy."

She turned up one side of her mouth, mocking him with a wary half-grin. "Just the same, I think I'll keep my phone handy."

———

In suits and cocktail dresses, the five couples gathered in the club lounge for drinks before dinner. Among the group, Hugh's wife, Charlene—Charley, as she was known—was clearly the dominant social force. She advanced on Brad and Sally the instant they entered the room, her teased, platinum blonde hair shining like a big hat.

And she was to the point. Few pleasantries had been exchanged before she turned to a meatier topic.

"So, what brought you two together?"

Sally was quick to answer: "Jeans."

Charley narrowed her eyes. "What, now?"

"Once upon a time," Sally said, "I did some modeling, and the agency sent me to model a new brand of jeans. Anyway, Brad's firm was representing the jeans company, and don't ask me why a lawyer needed to come to a photo shoot, but guess who showed up."

"It was strictly business," Brad chimed in.

"Not for long, it wasn't," Sally said, poking him in the side.

"Oh, I'll bet it wasn't!" Charley crowed. "What happened to your modeling career?"

"It wasn't much of a career," Sally said.

"Well, you could always get back into it."

"Fat chance," Sally said. "And I do mean fat."

"Sally thinks she's lost her figure," Brad said.

The squatty Charlene stepped back and, feigning indignation, looked Sally up and down.

"Honey," she said, "I should lose things so easily."

Steven LeMark looked his usual self: Graying hair styled to conservative perfection. Thin moustache clipped precisely to follow the contour of his upper lip. Tanned face with dark eyes divulging little emotion.

As Brad introduced him to Sally, however, LeMark displayed a boyish enthusiasm as surprising as it was unnerving.

"Well," he said lustily, sandwiching her hand between two sets of caressing fingers, "it is certainly *lovely* to meet *you*."

Sally politely replied. Small talk ensued as LeMark maintained his embrace. But he had no sooner turned his attention elsewhere than Sally caught Brad's eye with a furtive look as if to say *yuk*.

Moments later, at LeMark's suggestion, the group drifted out to the patio. They watched as the final golfers of the day, a foursome, approached the eighteenth green in the dusk, each driving his own cart. One of them struck an iron shot from well back in the fairway, the ball invisible against the darkening sky before landing on the green with a thump and stopping close to the hole.

"Hell of a shot," LeMark said to no one in particular. He waited until the golfers had parked their carts greenside, then called out: "Hell of a shot there, Thompson."

"You'll see more of that tomorrow, Stevie," Thompson said as he walked to mark his ball.

"You'll need it," LeMark answered.

Several in the group chuckled dutifully.

"That's Rod Thompson," LeMark said to Brad. He rattled off the name of a local company Brad knew to be a client. "Chief financial officer. We play almost every Sunday."

"Is he good?" Brad asked. "Or just lucky?"

"He's good," LeMark said, dropping his voice. "But he only beats *me* when I let him. And sometimes, I do. Good for business, you know."

Brad stood between LeMark and Sally, the former watching with interest as the golfers finished the hole. Sleeveless in the evening chill, Sally folded her arms across her chest.

"Want my jacket?" Brad offered.

"No, I'm fine."

But as he put his arm around her, touching the cool flesh of her shoulder, she leaned closer for warmth. He could sense then, very distinctly, the floral scent of her perfume. And there was another smell. A smell that was all her own. Something equally apparent. And alluring. He found himself moving toward it, his lips at the curve of her ear.

"Hey, boy," she admonished in a whisper, pretending to watch the golfers, her green eyes lost in the dark.

"Hey, yourself."

With little fanfare, Thompson holed his putt.

LeMark announced it was time for dinner.

A round table for ten had been set in a small, private room. On the way, Charley Miller latched on to Sally, and, as Charley had no doubt planned, they sat together. Hugh then sat next to his wife. Bill Jaylan, a partner for ten years, sat beside Hugh, and Bill's wife, Jill, sat next to her husband. And next to Jill sat Natalie Boettcher, a rather newly made partner. Natalie's significant other, Tom Fair, was thus sentenced to a chair beside Steven LeMark's third wife, the painfully thin and abnormally blonde Tiffany Le-Mark, some twenty years her husband's junior.

"God, don't ever get stuck next to her," Charley murmured to Sally, her lips barely moving. "It's like talkin' to a bag o' wood chips."

Brad, naturally, was given the seat of honor beside his command-er-in-chief, at which point, on LeMark's signal, dinner was promptly served.

The meal—from the Caesar salad tossed tableside, to the beef Welling-ton, to the desert of frozen chocolate-covered cappuccino crunch cake—was exquisite. Throughout, a wine steward hovered nearby. And LeMark, though a conversational bore, was nevertheless a gracious host, standing to honor Brad with a wealth of flattering comments: . . . *the hero of our recent negotiations in Chicago . . . couldn't have done it without him . . . expecting even greater things . . .*

"You know, it's interesting," he said, concluding. "This firm is on the cutting edge of contemporary legal practice. But in some respects, we still do things the old-fashioned way. We don't seek out job candidates. We let them seek us. But when Mark Thibodeau had his very unfortunate accident, we needed someone right away, and we needed someone with solid experience. So, we did something we've never done. We *advertised.*" He emphasized the word in such a way as to let his audience know they should be humorously amused.

"And we not only advertised, we advertised, of all places, on the in-ternet. And do you know that the very next day after we posted our shameless little advertisement—the very next day, mind you—we received a call from this wonderfully talented young man." He glanced approvingly at Brad. "I know many of you will call that luck, but I'll tell you, I think it was more than that. I think it was what the mystics call *kismet.* It was fate. Something meant to be. And I, for one, couldn't be happier."

LeMark raised his wine glass in a toast, and as applause rose from the table, Hugh gave Brad a look and a nod. And the message was clear: *You got it made.*

———————

The table talk went as Sally had hoped it would not.

The day before, she had called Charley Miller under the pretense of introducing herself, but more for the purpose of probing the babysitting competence of Charley's daughter. At the same time, she had given Charley the details on Eamon—not only to avert misunderstandings about the child's medical needs, but also to avoid, to the extent possible, awkward questions at dinner. Inevitably, though, such questions arose.

With four children between the ages of seven and fourteen, Jill Jaylan was obsessed with the facts of family life, both hers and others—but somewhat more the former.

"Our oldest, Jeremy, he's the basketball player," she recounted. "Started every game last year at Collegiate. And our next is Jason. He's twelve and quite the musician. Guitar, trombone, piano. And he also plays sports. Then there's our daughter, Jordan. She's nine and does piano and dance and soccer and softball. And basketball. And then our youngest, Jimmy—Lord, we don't know what to think of him, but he may end up being the best athlete of the bunch, and he's in the gifted program, so . . ." She took a much-needed break for air. "I guess you have a son?"

"Yes."

"And he's how old?"

"Six."

"And where does he go to school?"

Sally knew she could not answer that question without an explanation. And she knew just as well that providing that explanation would bring on the usual response.

Which it did.

"Oh, I'm so sorry," Jill said, scrunching her face into its most compassionate facade. "That must be so hard for you and Brad."

Not to mention, Sally thought, the kid who's spent the last half dozen years trying to take a decent breath.

She could see Bill and Jill on their way home, her telling him about the poor little Manford boy, and both of them thanking God that none of their children were like that. Their healthy, talented, perfect children. So free of any defect. They wouldn't dare have one any other way.

Sally sliced violently into her desert, clanking steel on china.

"You okay, Sal?" Brad asked.

"My fork slipped."

———

Alyssa performed beyond expectations. She had arrived early with Happy

Meals that she and Eamon ate on the deck while Brad and Sally readied themselves for the evening. After, she had played with the boy in the sandbox until dark, then played Xbox with him, then fixed cinnamon rolls. She had, as Sally instructed, made sure he took his enzymes. She had him ready for bed when Brad and Sally returned.

And she had left the house spotless.

Brad was opening his wallet to pay her for a job well done as Sally ushered Eamon upstairs.

"She's so much fun," the boy said in his room. "She's even more fun than Tina."

Tina, Eva's oldest, had done her share of babysitting. She and Eamon had always gotten on well.

"Gosh, if you like her better than Tina, she must be *really* fun."

"She is. She's my new best friend."

My new best friend. It had been a while since Sally had heard that one. Not since Larry Felding. That had been almost two years ago. Larry, an outgoing, kindhearted ten-year-old, had been like a big brother to Eamon in the pediatrics ward. But when Eamon had left, Larry had stayed. He had promised to keep in touch, but the prognosis was poor. The end, Sally learned, had come soon after.

She had told Eamon that Larry moved away. Far away. For a time, the boy lamented hearing nothing from his friend, but then turned his attention elsewhere. Or so it seemed.

Several weeks ago, as they had prepared to move, the child had asked what initially sounded like an offhand question.

"Mom, is Kansas far away?"

"Pretty far."

"Do you think I'll see Larry there?"

———————

Brad undressed in the master bedroom closet. He hung up his suit pants and coat. He hung his tie on his tie rack, his belt on his belt rack, and placed his shoes on his shoe rack. He slid his shirt and socks down the laundry chute.

Wearing only his boxers, he went from the closet to the bath, brushing his teeth in front of the big mirror above the double-sink vanity.

Catching a glimpse of himself, he looked away.

Naturally, there had been questions. But nothing out of the ordinary.

So, where did you do your undergrad?

You went to law school where?

And what took you to Los Angeles?

Without fail, he'd had the answers. All of them. But then, he always did. He had the facts down pat. Places and people, dates and descriptions. A history of Brad Manford fashioned from memories of events only imagined. If pressed, he could go on and on.

Lie after lie.

But what else could he tell them? The truth? And what was that? A wanted poster written in Spanish? Sins from a life he could not remember? No, if that was truth, it belonged to someone else. A monster, perhaps. But it was not his truth. Not now. He had been separated from it.

There was, though, another truth. A truth that was his alone. And of all things, it had its origin in that seemingly innocent little story. The one about the jeans. Sally had always liked that story. Liked it the way women like to hear and tell of chance meetings, and romance, and love at first sight. She told it at every opportunity. But there was so much more to it than she knew or could ever comprehend.

And yet, in another way, it was very simple.

It was about her eyes.

He entered the bedroom to find her standing at the dresser mirror, removing her earrings. He sat behind her on the edge of the bed.

"I think Alyssa wore him out," she said. "He went to sleep before I could even fix the nebulizer. But I guess he can miss a treatment. He's been doing pretty well." She looked at him in the mirror, those eyes catching him, holding him. "You feeling okay?"

"Yeah."

"You look like you ate too much or something."

"Something."

She started to unbutton her dress, her gaze still locked on his. "You know, they're crazy about you."

"Who?"

"Those people at your firm."

Buttons being released, slowly, all the way down.

"You're their golden boy," she said.

"I don't know about that."

"Oh, you are."

The dress slid to the floor. Her bra followed.

"You're *my* golden boy."

She turned to face him, her bare breasts so close he could feel their heat.

And from above, from green eyes on fire, came that look. That look she had given him that day in those jeans. That very first look. The one that said he was the only man in the world.

"Hey, boy," she whispered.

He cupped his hands to her flesh and she crushed into him, moaning soft and hungry.

Chapter 9

Neighborly Ways

Charley Miller had recommended the local zoo, and it proved a good way to spend a Sunday afternoon. They stayed until closing, and only near the end did Eamon show any sign of fatigue. In the hours before, he had, for the most part, dared his parents to keep pace, often running to the next exhibit. There were, of course, a few coughing fits. But Brad thought, on the whole, it had been quite a while since his son had lived a better day.

Sally agreed.

"Could you believe him?" she said, gesturing behind her, where the boy slept in his safety seat. "It was like we couldn't keep up."

Brad turned the SUV onto the expressway. "He was excited."

"Yeah, but I haven't seen him like that since . . ." She paused. "I don't know. A long time. Anyway, he obviously felt good."

"Oh, he did. No question."

"You know, recently, he's just really been improving. He's gained even more weight."

"I know."

"And he's got more energy. He's stronger. Brad, I really think he's getting better."

Brad glanced back to make sure the child was still asleep. "Well, they've always said he'll have good days and bad days."

The air seemed to leave the vehicle.

"Meaning what?"

"Meaning that lately he's had some good days. And this was one of them."

Stiffening, she turned away. They went several miles without speaking.

"I have a surprise for you," Brad said, taking the exit.

"Surprise me."

"I saw the back yard needs mowing."

Her eyes flared and, with a twist of her head, caught him in their glare.

"I skipped a day," she said, snapping her words.

"Which is fine. I'm just saying, it's a little shaggy, and when we get home, I am going to mow it." He looked over, touching her leg. "And I am going to mow it *real good.*"

Slowly, her scowling face broadened to a dimpled smile.

And then, for just an instant, there it was again: that look.

"Brad Manford," she said, "you are my hero."

Brad wheeled the lawnmower through the side gate to find Paul Irvin idling about the commons near the fence. With evening coming and the size of the job ahead, he knew there was little time for small talk. Yet he could see some manner of neighborly discourse would be required. The old man was veritably waiting for him.

"There's Mr. Manford," Irvin chirped. "Haven't seen you since you moved in."

His gray hair was parted just as neatly as the day of their initial meeting, and he wore what looked to be the same khaki pants and green t-shirt. With the addition of a camouflage jacket, he blended well against the cedars behind him.

Brad left the mower and went to the fence. As he shook the old man's arthritic hand, the firmness of the latter's grip evoked memories of a disparaging comment on the legal profession and a remark about the yard being on steroids.

"Colonel Irvin, how are you?"

"Colonel? I bet your wife told you that. I knew I shouldn't have shot my mouth off. You call me Paul, ya' hear?"

"All right, as long as I don't have to be Mr. Manford."

"It's a deal," Irvin said. "It's Brad, right?"

"Right."

"Well, nice to see you again. So, where have you been keepin' yourself?"

"The office and, oh, here and there, working."

"Boy, that's too bad. It's a shame when work keeps a man away from home so much."

"Yes, it is."

A rumbling grew in the north as a military plane approached. Still unaccustomed to the passing aircraft, Brad looked at the sky.

"Your wife thought those were bombers," Irvin said.

"Honestly, so did I. But she set me straight after she talked to you. She also said you used to do some flying yourself."

"That, I did."

"She said you flew a fighter of some kind."

Irvin issued a modest grin. "Yeah, I've flown fighters, and about everything else with wings. I did a couple of tours in 'Nam in an F-105. I'll tell you, that was hairy. Then I caught on with Boeing as a test pilot, and that was a little hairy, too. So, yeah, I've kinda sampled everything."

"Well, it looks like you came through in one piece," Brad said, raising his voice as the plane closed in. Taking a slow step in the direction of the lawnmower, he was ready to end the conversation. Irvin, however, was not.

"One piece? Yeah, I guess." He chuckled at an unspoken thought. "Anyway, that sort of craziness is for young guys who don't know any better. And my wife was a nervous wreck. So I gave it up and basically spent my last twenty years at Boeing just hangin' out with engineers and goin' to cocktail parties. And the pay was fair. But I'll tell you, when you get too old for the game, it's hard watchin' somebody else play it."

"You must have enjoyed it," Brad said. "Flying, I mean."

"Oh, hell yes! Man, there's nothin' in the world like straddlin' twenty-five thousand pounds of thrust. Makes you feel like God himself."

Brad watched the plane as it moved to the south.

"Good ol' KC-135," Irvin observed. "Been around forever. You know, they're bringin' in a new model here soon. Gonna phase out those old Stratotankers. But there was never a better plane. Many was the day a shot of juice from one of those babies kept my ass out of the Hanoi Hilton."

"As big as they are, they must carry a lot of fuel."

"Only about two hundred thousand pounds."

"Geez." Brad pondered the number. "I can't even imagine how much that is."

"I guarantee you it's a butt load," Irvin said, laughing. "You damn sure don't want to smoke around it."

Brad found himself laughing as well. This old man talked a lot, but he seemed all right.

"Paul, I hate to run off, but I've got to do some mowing, and I need to get done before dinner."

"I hope you're plannin' on eatin' late."

"Yeah, I know. This may take a while."

Brad had gone several steps toward the lawnmower when the old man called after him.

"I didn't lie to you about how this yard grows, did I?"

"No, you didn't. But you know, I remember you said that it doesn't all grow the same. I guess I didn't appreciate it then, but I can see now what you were talking about. I mean, most of it's pretty bad, but around that sandbox, it's scary."

"It'd be even worse if that sandbox wasn't there."

"Lucky thing it is."

Irvin shook his head. "Nothin' lucky about it. That thing is where it is for a reason." He pointed at the sandy square. "That's ground zero. Worst spot in the yard. What used to grow there looked like somethin' from a sci-fi movie. The folks before you put that sandbox there to cover it up."

"I guess I should thank them," Brad said.

"You ever met 'em?"

"No."

"Well, they're assholes," Irvin said. "But that's another story, and like you say, you need to get to work."

"Right. Talk to you later."

Brad was at the lawnmower and about to pull the starter cord when Irvin called again.

"Hey, Brad?"

Hearing another tanker moving in, Brad raised his eyes, following the aircraft. "Yeah?"

"I'm just wonderin', has your wife ever said anything about me comin' by here so much?"

"No."

"I know I spend a considerable amount of time around here, but I don't mean to be a pest."

"Oh, no problem."

"It's just that I live alone, and I get restless sittin' around the house. And as old as I am, I still like seein' the planes come and go."

Brad watched the tanker as it flew over.

The old man remained at the fence, looking into the yard.

Chapter 10

Rear Window

Sally was setting the kitchen table as Brad came in from the garage.

"Finished?" she asked.

"I am."

"I don't suppose you bagged any of it, did you?"

"Should I have?"

"It wouldn't have hurt. Especially around that sandbox."

He shrugged, frowning. "There really wasn't time."

"There might have been, if you hadn't stopped to chat with Colonel Creepy."

"That's your name for him?"

"It fits."

Brad glanced down and saw his shoes covered with grass. Quickly, with Sally turned away, he slipped into the laundry room and removed them.

"I don't think he's all that bad," he said, continuing the conversation.

She blew out a mouthful of air with a scoffing sound.

"Anyway, it was only for a few minutes," he said. "I was just trying to be a good neighbor."

Sally opened the oven and pulled out a baking dish of pork chops and scalloped potatoes.

"I wouldn't call him a neighbor," she said, putting the dish on the kitchen island.

"Close enough. He lives just the other side of the commons."

"How do you know? Have you been to his house?"

"You know I haven't."

"Have you even been *through* the commons?"

"Have *you?*"

"With that weirdo out there? Are you kidding?"

As she dished up the meal, Brad went around the corner to wash up in the half bath.

"He told me he lives alone," he said over the running water. "He's probably lonely."

"Yeah, I'll just bet he is."

Brad dried his hands and stepped into the family room, where Eamon, half asleep, lay on the couch watching *SpongeBob.*

"E," Brad said, "time for dinner."

The boy hardly stirred as Brad moved toward the room's big window and gazed out to the back yard. The sun had set; darkness was gaining, but the freshly mown lawn remained dimly visible.

"Sal," he said, "have you ever noticed how some parts of this yard grow a whole lot faster than others?"

She came in from the kitchen. "Boy, are you master of the obvious."

"Huh?"

She put a hand on his shoulder. "Brad, whose yard is this?"

"Well, it's our . . ." Mid-sentence, he understood. "It's *your* yard, dear."

"That's right," she said. "It's mine, baby. I am queen of this yard. I know every inch of it. And I know that most of the west side grows fast, and the east side grows even faster."

"Yeah, that's what I'm saying. One side grows different than the other."

"And I know also that it grows fastest of all around that damn sandbox."

"I know that, too."

"Of course you do. But with your limited experience in lawn care, one thing you may not know is that while it grows fastest around the sandbox, it grows slower the farther away you go. And it does that in every direction, equally."

"So?"

"So, it makes a circle. A perfect circle. Did you know *that?*"

Vaguely incredulous, Brad shook his head. "No, I didn't." He looked into the yard, straining his eyes. "Why is it a circle?"

She seemed suddenly indifferent. "Heck if I know." She turned around and gently shook Eamon, still on the couch. "Come on, honey. Time for dinner."

Her effort had more effect than Brad's. The boy pulled himself to a sitting position as she went to the kitchen. She brought back a glass of water and four enzyme capsules.

"I'm going to watch you take all of these," she said, handing him the glass and passing him the pills in succession. "That's it. . . . Honey, don't spill the water. . . . Okay, let's eat."

The child rose and trudged to the kitchen.

Brad, still looking into the yard, again felt Sally's hand on his shoulder.

"Can't stop admiring your work?" she asked.

"What? Oh, I guess not."

"Well, you did a good job." She kissed him on the cheek. "Thanks."

"Sure."

He was about to remark on the anomaly of the grassy circle when something else caught his attention.

"That tree," he said, pointing to the cottonwood in the sandbox. "It's grown."

"Yeah, what of it?"

"No, I mean it's grown *a lot.*" He assessed the tree against the darkening backdrop of the commons. "I honestly think it's grown a good four feet."

She laughed. "Since when?"

"Since the first time I saw it, when we were over here with that realtor. What's it been? Six weeks?"

"Oh, Brad . . ."

"No, it's true. I swear. That tree has grown *four feet.*"

She pushed him good-naturedly on the arm. "Get out of here."

"Sal, I'm serious."

"Me too. That tree has not grown four feet."

"Well, three, at least."

"Brad, please."

He was getting irritated. "Sally, I'm telling you, it *has.* You just haven't noticed."

"No, I haven't. But maybe Eamon has. Let's ask him. Eamon?" she called into the kitchen. "Has the tree in your sandbox grown a whole bunch?"

The boy had seated himself at the table. "I don't know."

"But that's my point," Brad said. "*You're* out there all the time. *He's* out there all the time. When you see something all the time, you don't notice how it gradually changes."

"I'll notice when it grows into the clouds and a giant comes climbing down," Sally said, walking away. "Come on, Jack. Chow time."

Brad was slow to leave the window.

"Dad," Eamon said, "is there such a thing as magic beans?"

Chapter 11

A System of Measurement

"It's probably a fairy ring."

Brad cackled. "A *what?*"

His legal assistant, the frumpy and bespectacled Sharon Hubert, sat in one of the two captain's chairs facing his desk. A Monday morning meeting to discuss assignments had gone off topic.

"A fairy ring," she said. "That's what they call it. It's caused by a kind of fungus that grows in a ring, and over time the ring just gets bigger and bigger."

Having heard the conversation from his office next door, Hugh sauntered in. "What are you talking about?"

Sharon, who also worked for Hugh, had been with the firm over twenty years and was as much at ease gabbing with senior partners as she was the lowest minion. She spoke to Hugh as she would a sibling.

"Hugh, for God's sake, we're in an important meeting here."

"I doubt that," Hugh said. "What's the issue?"

"Brad's got strange grass in his back yard."

"Try mowing it."

"That's what we've been doing," Brad said. "It's not the answer."

"You know, you probably don't need to worry about it," Sharon said. "I've heard those things are hard to stop, but as big as you say yours is, it won't be long before it'll be somebody else's problem."

"Come again?"

"What I'm saying is, the really green part where the grass is thick will keep expanding. It'll go over to your neighbors, then they can deal with it."

Brad shook his head. "You don't understand. There is no really green *part*. It's *all* really green. A big green circle. And the grass inside it grows like nothing you've ever seen."

"Like I said," Hugh iterated, "mow it."

"And like *I* said, we *have* mowed it."

"How often?" Hugh asked.

"Every three days."

Sharon had a quizzical expression. "Three days?"

"I'm telling you, it grows fast," Brad said.

"Who does your mowing?" Hugh asked.

"My wife, mostly."

Hugh guffawed as Sharon lowered her eyebrows.

"Bradley," she said, "for shame."

"Hey, I've tried to talk her out of it, but she won't let me hire anybody."

Hugh and Sharon exchanged skeptical looks.

"All right," she said, "I guess I *don't* understand. Because what you've described is not a so-called fairy ring. A fairy ring is a thin ring, and the ring itself is all lush and green, but the grass inside it is nothing special."

"Well, my grass is plenty special. It grows like a rain forest."

"You know," Sharon said, "some people would kill to have a lawn like that."

"Not Sally Manford," Hugh said, heading back down the hall.

Not long after, Hugh called Brad to his office. The room had a small conference area with a round four-person table, where Hugh, with a concerned expression, was sitting as Brad entered.

Hugh motioned to the chair nearest his own and Brad sat down, an open three-ring binder lying between them.

"I hate to do this to you," Hugh said, "but you're about to get buried up to your ears in work."

Brad shrugged. "You're the boss."

"Yeah, well . . ." Hugh did not appear to enjoy the compliment. "The fact is we've suddenly become a little short on manpower around here."

"Why's that?"

"Jenn Baker. She was let go . . . let's see . . ." He looked at his wristwatch. ". . . about ten minutes ago while we were BS'ing in your office."

Jenn had been with the firm several years, but in his short time, Brad had not learned much about her.

"What happened?"

"I'm not at liberty to say. But you know how it is. Sometimes if you piss off the wrong people, little things become big things." The manner in which Hugh frowned and shook his head gave an indication that he had not agreed with Jenn's dismissal—a decision made, almost certainly, by Steven LeMark, who was known to have something of a hair trigger when it came to firing subordinates. "Anyway, I'm not going to dump her whole caseload on you, but she had a few things I'd like to get you involved in."

Hugh closed the binder, which held perhaps a hundred pages, and slid it toward Brad. The label on the spine read *RightLine Chemicals*.

"This," Hugh said, tapping the cover, "is job one. It's an acquisition Steve and I are handling. Jenn was helping with the due diligence."

"I assume this isn't all of it," Brad said.

"Oh, God, no." Hugh laughed, acting more his usual self. "Take this and multiply by several thousand. We've scanned a bunch of it, but we've still got a roomful of paper. For now, though, just use this to get yourself started."

Brad reopened the binder and turned through the first couple of pages.

"This is everything in a nutshell," Hugh said. "The CliffsNotes version. Just know this front and back before you get there and you'll be fine."

"Get where?"

"New Jersey. Newark. You leave day after tomorrow."

Brad did a poor job of looking excited.

"Okay," Hugh said, "if you don't like this one, I can send you to Lubbock on a patent infringement."

"No, this'll be fine."

"Good, because this is the biggest thing we've got going and I want you on it. And anyway, that's your part of the country, right?"

"Actually, it's Vermont."

"Yeah, I know. But you have to understand," Hugh quipped, "here in Kansas, as far as we're concerned, everything east of Chicago is pretty much all the same."

"They think the same way in Vermont," Brad replied, "about anything west of the Adirondacks."

Hugh laughed again, louder than before. "You know, I've never been to Vermont. But from the way you described it the other night, I'd really like to see it."

"Oh, you should," Brad said.

He had told them at dinner of his sleepy little hometown in the Green Mountains. The one straight out of a Norman Rockwell painting. And as he and Hugh spoke a while longer, he told even more. Recounting minute details. Talking about it the way he always did. The way that made people believe.

———

Late in the day, Brad stopped at Sharon's cubicle.

"Following up on this morning," he said, "one more question." He waited for her to look up from a stack of paper. "What do you know about cottonwood trees?"

"Well, let me think. They're made of wood. They have leaves. They drop seeds that blow into every nook and cranny. And when I was a kid I fell out of one and broke my arm in two places."

"How fast do they grow?'

"Pretty fast."

"Can a cottonwood tree grow four feet in six weeks?"

"No," she said categorically.

"How about three feet?"

"I seriously doubt it. Why do you ask?"

"I have a cottonwood tree in my back yard that has grown three feet, and maybe four, since the day I first laid eyes on it, which was about six weeks ago."

Sharon wasn't buying.

"Have you measured it?"

"Not officially."

"Well, believe me, it hasn't grown any three or four feet."

"How do you know?"

"Because, first off, cottonwoods grow fast, but not *that* fast. And second, this is fall, so even if a cottonwood could grow like you say, it's not going to happen this time of year."

"You're sure?"

"I'm positive. And speaking of fall, whatever the deal is with your yard, you won't have to worry about it much longer, because the grass here doesn't need mowing much past the end of October, and we're nearly there."

"Okay. Thanks, Sharon." Brad took a step into the hall, but, at once, retraced. "Sharon, just out of curiosity, if I *was* going to measure my tree, how would I do that? With a stepladder or something?"

"Lord, no, boy. Don't you know anything?"

"I guess not."

"All right, listen close." Sharon rolled her chair around, facing him. "First, you get a tape measure and a yardstick. Then," she said, demonstrating, "you put your right arm out straight and use the yardstick to measure the distance between your right eye and the knuckle of your index finger. Got it?"

"Uh-huh."

"Then, with your arm still sticking straight out, you hold the yardstick vertically—up and down—and you make sure that the part of it that's above your hand is the same length as what you measured from your eye to your knuckle. Still with me?"

Brad nodded.

"*Then,*" she said, "you close your left eye and put yourself at a distance from the tree where it looks like the base of the tree is on top of your fist and the top of the tree is right at the top of the yardstick. Then you put the yardstick down to mark where you're standing and use the tape measure to measure the distance between the yardstick and the tree, and that'll tell you how tall your tree is."

"That really works?"

Sharon dropped her head and gave him a long stare over the top of her glasses.

"Brad, trust me, I'm a country girl."

Chapter 12

A Quiet Evening

In the dining room, sitting at their new oak table, Brad and Sally worked on plates of spaghetti. He had been very late, but she had waited.

"Five pounds," she said. "Five pounds in six weeks." She had taken Eamon to the doctor that morning for a routine checkup. The child had received a glowing report. "And he's grown a whole inch."

"In six weeks? That's incredible."

"His lungs are clear too." She was quick to amend: "Well, not totally. But better than they've been for months. Or maybe years. I wish I knew what was going on."

"It's the clean Midwestern air," he said.

"Could be."

"Or maybe it's the dust and dirt."

About to take a bite, she stopped the fork short of her mouth. "I hardly think that damn sandbox is therapeutic."

"It hasn't hurt anything, though. You've got to admit that."

"Okay, okay." She resumed eating. "You were right. I was wrong. The sandbox hasn't sent him to the hospital."

She described the rest of her day: Eamon had returned from the doctor with such energy he had whipped through his schoolwork in half the usual time. They had then spent the better part of the afternoon outdoors, taking a long walk through the neighborhood before settling into more customary activities in the back yard. The Colonel had made no appearance, his absence enhancing her enjoyment of the time outside.

"Sounds like a perfect day," Brad said.

"Yeah, sort of."

With a small sigh, she stirred her pasta. She had almost forgotten.

"Eva called," she said.

"Oh? How'd that go?"

"How do you think?"

So, do you still want to come back?

No.

That wasn't what you said last time.

Yeah, but I'm starting to get used to it here. Things are getting better.

In Kansas? I find that hard to believe.

"Did she say how your mother's doing?" Brad asked.

"The same."

Between them, the answer was code: Margie was still hitting the sauce.

And what about Eamon? Sally, that child needs quality care, and you took him away from the best doctors in the country. And now who's treating him? Some hillbilly sawbones?

Eva, that is just ignorant. They have good doctors here. And good hospitals. That's true in a lot of places. But you wouldn't know because you've never been east of San Bernardino.

Oh, so now you're a world traveler.

No, I'm just saying you don't know what the hell you're talking about.

Sally, dear, don't cuss.

Boy, that had done it, Eva scolding her.

"You okay, Sal?"

She was staring past him, clenching her teeth. "Yeah, I'm fine."

She hated it most when the subject was Brad.

You've always let him run your life.

He does no such thing.

Oh really? He dragged you to the middle of nowhere.

Yeah, well, Sally had wanted to say, at least I had a man to do the dragging. You ran yours off with a load of Bible quotes and hallelujahs.

Eva, you don't know crap!

Sally . . .

Look, I love him. And I want to be with him.

To the ends of the earth?

To anywhere.

Well, then, praise God.

That's all you have to say?

Isn't that enough?

That was how Eva always did it, playing religion as some kind of trump card. It had, as usual, brought Sally to her boiling point.

And for your information, in the few weeks he's been here, Eamon has never felt better in his life.

Praise God for that as well.

Sally had held the phone at arm's length, conflicted on whether to throw the thing or just hang up.

Oh . . . stuff it!

She had lost all love for her sister. She had lost it years ago. Eva had apologized profusely, and afterward they had pretended everything was fine. But it wasn't. And it never would be.

So, the Lord will not bless you with a child?

Guess not.

I hope you see now, Sally, that actions have consequences.

I was sick, Eva.

Yes, and we both know why. And so does God.

"Sal?" Brad said softly.

"Yeah?"

"Are you here?"

"Sorry, I was just thinking of something." Her dinner unfinished, she pushed back from the table. "You know, I'm not that hungry."

"I thought you were."

"I lost my appetite."

With a portion of his own meal remaining, Brad promptly placed his fork on his plate.

"That was delicious, but I think I'm done, too," he said, rising to gather the dishes and silverware.

"I'll get those," she said.

"No, I got it."

Carrying the water glasses and paper napkins, she followed him to the kitchen sink, tossing the napkins in the trash and setting the glasses on the counter.

"Here, let me see those," she said, grabbing the plates and utensils, and, with a fork, furiously scraping the leftovers into a plastic container. She put the food in the refrigerator and returned to the sink, where Brad was rinsing the skillet and saucepan she had used for the meal. "I'll do that," she said, moving him out of the way.

He stood by silently as, with her face turned away, she rinsed everything and loaded it into the dishwasher. After, she remained at the counter, her teary eyes aimed out the small window above the sink, into the dark.

"Are you okay?" he said.

He put his arm around her. She did not seem to notice.

"You know," she said, "while I was out there this afternoon, I took a look at that tree."

"The cottonwood?"

"Yeah. And you're right. It *has* grown. A lot."

There was, naturally, no way of knowing exactly how much. But assuming the legitimacy of Sharon's method, the tree now stood just above fourteen feet.

He had gone out after dinner. The light on the deck had been sufficient. And Sharon's system seemed to render a valid result, confirming his visual estimate. So, he wondered, what had it been six weeks ago? At the time, he had thought ten feet. But then, that was such a standard approximation. A little like the casual way in which people describe the passage of time.

How long does it take to brush your teeth?

Five minutes.

How long before we get there?

Oh, about five minutes.

Indeed, five minutes could be five minutes. Or it could be less. Or more.

And ten feet might be closer to nine. Or eleven. But the fact was, the thing had definitely grown.

He told Sally as he entered the bedroom.

"Fourteen feet?" she said, in bed watching television. "Yeah, I suppose so. But that sure is a whacky way to measure a tree."

"My legal assistant is a little whacky, too. But she knows what she's doing."

He prepared for bed and lay down beside her, propping his head on two pillows as he studied the RightLine binder. He would hit Newark mid-afternoon Wednesday and spend the rest of the week interviewing

---

officers and other employees of a key distributor of the company being acquired. It would be tedious work. "Due diligence" always was. And the more diligent you were, the more tedious it became. Like walking through a field and looking under rocks. But you had to look under every one. Investigate every conceivable avenue. Because you could never tell where the deal breakers—the potential liabilities, the questionable patent and licensing rights—might be hiding.

Thankfully, though, Jenn Baker had done most of it, and this little excursion to the East would mark the end of the information-gathering stage. After that it would boil down to data analysis and negotiating a purchase agreement. Of course, in principle, the deal had been done for weeks. But the firm's client was expecting this acquisition to nearly double its net worth, so there was far too much at stake to take anything for granted. Not that Brad thought otherwise. He had done this enough to know that the last step in the process could be just as critical as the first.

Still, the job would be drudgery, and at this late hour, the dry pages of the binder—the letter of intent, the nondisclosure agreement, the endless spreadsheets and memos—made for torturous reading.

He knew he did not have to settle for this—this grunt work. He was capable of far greater things. But to do more, to be more, was to move further into the spotlight. And in that light, things could be so easily exposed.

With heavy eyes, he slogged on through the binder. He was sleeping soundly when Sally turned off the TV and took the book from his hands.

"Mis Mundos."

The voice came in a whisper, and before him, a finger traced a circle in soft clay, and, completing its revolution, formed another ring within the first.

Then, from a sharp rise, he looked out over a grassy plain, its tall leaves waving in the gusty furnace of a sweltering summer's heat. In the distance, a man approached, his shaven head and bare, sun-blistered torso floating above the bluestem. Over one shoulder hung a leather knapsack; over the other, a bison's bladder that had not for a day held water.

He carried something in his arms. A child. A small girl, limp and lifeless.

With an unsteady gait, he staggered to the foot of the slope, stopping there on a huge slab of reddish-pink stone, the rock tapered like an arrowhead, its tip pointing to the one who stood above.

Gazing up, the man seemed faint—and afraid.

He spoke through lips burnt and bleeding: "I have come far. I have traveled The Way of Stones."

"I know."

"Are you The Keeper?"

"I am. And I am That Which Is Kept."

The man shuddered. "You are both?"

"We are one."

"How is that possible?"

"In this place, all things are possible."

A surge of wind raked the prairie, and with it came a roaring din. But as the clamor dwindled, in the dying breeze there remained a gentle hum. A low drone that seemed to come from every direction and carry with it yet another voice, speaking a name.

"Brad . . ."

He felt a hand on his shoulder.

"Brad . . . Brad . . ."

He raised his head and looked about. The room was dark. His thoughts floundered.

"What is it?"

"Brad . . ."

"Eamon?"

"No, he's fine."

"You're sure?"

"Yes! Brad, listen."

He sat up in the bed, his neck and back resisting the effort.

"I was checking on him," she said, her voice shaking. "I looked out the window."

She stopped to catch her breath.

"Sally, *what?*"

"Brad, someone's in the back yard."

Chapter 13

Night Light

He took the stairs at a sprint and stormed through the dark of the dining room and kitchen, narrowly avoiding a collision with the island and, on bare feet, sliding to a stop at the French door that led to the back deck.

Sally fell in behind.

"Exactly what," he asked, pausing to breathe, "did you see?"

"A light."

"You mean like a flashlight?"

"Maybe."

"Where?"

"Well, first by the sandbox. Then just kind of, I don't know, all around."

He shot her a puzzled look. "All around?"

"You know what I mean."

"Not really." Straining his eyes, his nose touched one of the door panes. "Did you ever see an actual person?"

"No, but there had to be one."

The waxing moon, near its first quarter, had set. There was no light, save for the diffuse glow of the city and a smattering of anonymous sparkles through the trees of the commons, their sources far to the other side.

He could not see clearly even to the end of the deck.

"I'm going out."

"Are you crazy?"

"Do *we* have a flashlight?"

"No."

"It was worth asking."

He flicked on the deck light and spun the door's dead bolt.

"Brad, don't."

Wearing only his boxers, he opened the door and stepped into the nighttime chill.

The deck light revealed a portion of the yard's middle—the same place he had stood hours before, measuring the cottonwood. Beyond that, partially masked in a hint of fog, was a poorly lit fringe. And farther out, the night remained unaffected.

Through light and shadow he scanned the yard for movement, shapes out of place.

He did his best to muster a tough disposition. "Who's out here?"

The question unanswered, he repeated it, louder and more demanding.

A slight breeze arose. Enough to stir the leaves in the trees. Nothing else.

He was suddenly conscious of the cold wood beneath his feet, while behind him, in slippers, arms folded against an oversized t-shirt, Sally shivered at the door's threshold.

For a time shorter than it seemed, they stood unmoving, inspecting the scene.

Brad started down the steps of the deck.

"Where are you going?" she said in a dire whisper.

He continued his descent.

"Brad, let's just call the police!"

At the landing, he took the stone path toward the gazebo. The stones, too, were cold—more so than the deck. For a moment he considered opting for the grass, but, thinking conditions might be even worse there, stayed on the path.

He went slower as he neared the gazebo. There, the light from the deck was thinly dispersed, scattering the jumble of shadows cast by the latticework. The ambiguous mix of form and shade seemed to expand the possibilities of what might lie in wait.

Tightening her arms against her chest, Sally moved onto the deck with a grimace, watching anxiously as Brad patrolled the gazebo, then crept behind it, out of view.

Now in the grass, Brad felt the intense cold of the night's near-frozen dew. In the almost pitch black, as best he could, he explored the yard's west side. But an intruder, he thought, could be lurking here totally unseen. Could be, in fact, standing right before him. And with his icy feet aching for relief, he easily concluded that it was best not to prolong things in this place.

He turned down the fence line next to the commons, and as he headed east along the evergreen hedge, Sally could see him again, a silhouette drifting in the mist. She saw him stop briefly at the break in the hedge, and heard a clang as he jiggled the gate to ensure it was latched, before continuing toward the far east side of the yard—another very dark spot.

"Brad, don't go over there!"

He went part of the way, but not quite out of the light, before looking over with an exaggerated shrug of his shoulders.

"There's nobody here, Sal."

"I *saw* something."

"Yeah, but through a window." He was moving his feet up and down, marching in place in a kind of dance that relieved one freezing appendage at the expense of the other. "It was probably reflected light."

"From where?"

He started briskly for the deck, then stopped, glancing toward the side of the house. From her position, she could not see it.

"What?" she asked.

"Nothing."

"No, *what?*"

There was no use pretending. He had given it away.

"The side gate's open," he said.

He hurried to shut it and ran up the deck stairs.

"Brad, I'm sure I didn't leave that gate open," she said. "Did you?"

"You know, I think I probably did, after I mowed yesterday."

"I didn't notice it today."

He ushered her into the house. "Let's just go back to bed."

"Brad, I'm telling you, I don't think that gate was open today."

He prepared to follow her in, but, before entering, stood for a moment looking into the darker parts of the yard and commons.

He felt certain someone was looking back.

Chapter 14

Due Diligence

Carrying pen and legal pad in one hand, Sharon reached through the doorway of Brad's office with the other and knocked on the wall.

"I got your message."

"Come on in."

He sat with his back to the door, paging through the RightLine binder that lay on the credenza behind his desk.

"Do you have everything you need for your trip?" Sharon asked, sitting down.

"I think so." He took a last look at the notebook and turned to face her.

She raised her eyebrows. "I hope you don't take this the wrong way, but you look like you missed a night's sleep."

"Part of one."

"What kept you up?" At once, she raised a hand and dipped her head. "Sorry, I shouldn't have asked."

"I assure you, it's nothing embarrassing. Let's just say I had a late-night visitor." He tore off a sheet from a legal pad and began writing. "Anyway, I've got a little project for you, and I'm afraid it's one of those good news, bad news deals."

"What's the good news?"

"The good news—and I know you'll like this—is that I want you to snoop around on somebody."

"Sounds like fun."

"It might be," he said, still writing. "On the other hand, the bad news is that this project isn't billable."

"That's okay."

He looked up. "Yeah, but the thing is, it isn't even work-related. It's personal. And I know the firm has a policy about that. But all I can tell you is that if you keep your mouth shut, I'll make it worth your while."

"A mink coat would be nice."

"I was thinking more along the lines of a gift card to Chili's." He reached over the desk to hand her his scribblings. "I want you to check this guy out."

She tilted her head back, perusing his notes through her bifocals. "Paul Irvin?"

"Right."

"You say he lives . . . where? I can't read your writing."

"The Gardens at Meadowbrook. It's the development next to mine."

She nodded and read on: "Approximately seventy-five years old. Five feet, seven inches. A hundred and fifty pounds. Blue eyes." She lowered the paper and feigned a serious tone. "Any tattoos or other identifying marks?"

"I was just trying to give you a general picture of the guy."

"And I appreciate that." She folded the paper in half. "So, why are you nosing around on this fellow?"

"Because he has some very odd habits."

"Does he keep you up at night?"

Brad shook a finger at her. "You know, I think you're too smart for your own good."

"Nobody's *that* smart." With a self-satisfied grin, Sharon folded the paper into quarter sections. "But we digress. What else can you tell me about this Mr. Irvin?"

"He's supposedly a retired Air Force colonel. He says he flew in Vietnam, and that he worked for Boeing after that."

Sharon had begun taking notes. "Married?"

"At one time, I think. But probably not now. He claims to live alone."

"Kids?"

"I don't know."

"And what, pray tell, are we looking for?"

Brad let out a tired breath and drummed his fingers on his desk. "Honestly, I'm not sure. I'm just wondering about him. I'm wondering if he's legit. If he was really in the Air Force and all that. And whether he's got any problems that might be following him around."

"Such as?"

"Nothing specific. Look, just check the guy out. Get the dirt. Check the court records. Google him. Talk to people you know who used to work at Boeing. Etcetera, etcetera." He swiveled away from her, returning to the materials on his credenza. "Just dig. I'm turning you loose on this."

"That could be dangerous."

"I'll take the risk," he said over his shoulder.

She rose from her chair.

"Remember," she said, "mink."

"Chili's," he replied.

Whoever or whatever Paul Irvin turned out to be, Brad thought the old man was right about one thing: It was a shame when work kept a man from home.

Facing another three days away, he had, for once, left the office along with the secretaries. He had made a brief stop at a hardware store. When he walked into the kitchen, Sally was fixing dinner. He kissed her with one arm conspicuously at his side.

"What have you got?" she asked.

He held up two new combination locks. She nodded with approval as he made for the back door.

"Don't let him see," she said.

Slipping a lock into each of his front pant pockets, he stepped onto the deck to find the boy scuttling about the sandbox.

The child glanced up. "Hey, Dad, what'cha doin'?"

"Just taking a walk."

Brad went down the stairs and across the yard to lock the side gate as the boy, unobservant, assembled opposing lines of green army men and plastic artillery. Heading next for the commons gate, Brad stopped at the sandbox.

"What are *you* doing, E?"

"Havin' a war."

"That doesn't sound good."

"It's just pretend, Dad."

Brad looked around the sand for any trace of a shoeprint from the previous night's intruder, but if such a thing had ever been present, it had been obliterated. The boy who had once played here so docile had become far more active, relentlessly razing and rebuilding every inch of his imaginary world.

Brad had ceased to understand the child's fascination with it. He thought that, by now, the newness should have worn off. True, the boy had never before had a sandbox—or, for that matter, a yard. But to want to spend every minute here seemed nothing short of obsessive.

Perhaps, he thought, Sally had been right: Maybe the kid needed some play equipment—which, he reminded himself, they couldn't afford. Not until that matter of five thousand dollars was cleared up.

The child again lost in fantasy, Brad secured the commons gate and wandered down the fence to the west.

Darkness would come early tonight; a bank of thunderheads blotted out the setting sun. Overhead and to the east, the sky remained clear, but the cloudless expanse was being fast covered by the approaching storm.

He had reached the northwest corner of the yard when the back door opened.

"Hey, you two," Sally called. "Dinner in five minutes." She ducked inside, then popped back out. "Eamon, get in here and take your enzymes."

Just short of launching his green army melee, the boy, ignoring his mother, stood surveying the order of battle.

"Eamon . . . now!"

He took several dawdling steps before increasing his pace and bouncing up the deck stairs like a very average six-year-old. Sally met him at the top to brush away the sand. "Take off your shoes, honey," Brad heard just before the door shut.

He, too, started toward the house, but lingered at the sandbox, pausing to admire the boy's organization of military might. The two sides were of equal number, with each army divided into subgroups, some set to attack, others to defend, while behind the lines of both forces, rows of artillery awaited the start of a make-believe barrage.

Every piece seemed arranged with absolute precision. Every soldier stood straight. Every cannon sat faultlessly positioned. And within each army, the separate companies had their own symmetry, those on one side being arranged in triangles, those on the other in squares. It was, Brad thought, something of a masterpiece. A world created to angular perfection.

With one exception.

A soldier with a mounted bayonet and a gung-ho expression had tilted over and was leaning against the trunk of the cottonwood tree. Feeling the need to correct the anomaly, Brad stepped cautiously into the sand and, half-squatting beside the tree, put the green man upright.

And as he did, in the heavy, static air, he heard it again.

That sound. That soft, elusive vibration that came like the seldom-heard moan of a finicky ghost. A thing that refused to manifest itself under anything less than optimal conditions. Conditions that seemed to demand the utter stoppage of the world itself.

Beside the cottonwood, he stood and froze, enveloped by the unwavering murmur. On past occasions it had seemed to come from . . . well, from somewhere. From left or right. Front or behind. But here, in the very center of the sandbox, it literally came from *everywhere*.

Then, like the blast of a jet engine, a clap of thunder from the west.

The back door swung open.

"Little boy," she said with a dry impatience, "are you going to quit playing in the sand and come to dinner, or am I going to have to put you in time-out?"

"Sorry."

Mindful of the armies below, he maneuvered his way to the grass, then hurried up the stairs much as Eamon had, pausing at the top to remove his own sandy shoes.

———

From deep in the commons, under cover of the cedars, the old man watched Brad enter the house. He remained, watching, listening, for some time after, until night fell and sprinkles of rain spattered the trees.

In the dark, he turned and headed back the way he had come, down a short but steep trail he knew as surely as if he had carved it himself—which, in large part, he had. The path wound through cottonwoods and Osage orange to a shallow, stagnant creek, where a flat, reddish stone of epic size stretched from one bank to the other. Chipped and worn, the slab was reminiscent of an arrowhead, its jagged tip pointing up the path toward the Manford home.

In the wet season, with the channel flooding its banks for long periods, the rock could grow mossy and slick. But tonight, even with the rain, there was no such concern.

Knowing each step by heart, the old man went to the stone's midpoint and dropped to a knee, sliding a hand over the hard surface to find once well-defined grooves that had, through the effects of water, wind, and time, all but faded from recognition. He slid his fingers over the undulations as if scanning a text in Braille. Feeling marks made by the hand of one dead and dust millennia before the first stone laid at Giza. Marks from an age unremembered. Unimagined.

The rain was getting heavier. It was soaking his jacket and pants. He pulled his hand back, about to rise and move on, but on impulse returned his fingers to the rock. To feel again the ancient glyphs, wondering, as he always wondered, what they meant.

Those two circles.

PART TWO

RAINY DAYS

Chapter 15

First Confession

D r. Mahindra had tried so hard to appear detached—the consummate professional. But the quickened pumping of his chest. The way he held his lips tight, as if struggling to hold something in—or keep something out. These were the signs of a man disturbed.

He had not written on his pad for some time.

"Is there more?" he had asked, seeming to fear the answer.

Brad's eyes shifted about the room.

"Mr. Manford?" The doctor leaned forward, waiting for his patient's gaze to meet his own. *"Is there more?"*

"There is. But I think you get the gist of it."

"Yes, I believe I do."

Mahindra adjusted and readjusted himself in his chair, unable to find a satisfactory position, and, for an extended time, said nothing.

"Mr. Manford, have you ever told anyone else the things you have just told me?"

"No, none of it."

"Does it feel somewhat, shall we say, liberating to do so?"

"Not really."

The doctor had obviously hoped for something different.

He took a deep breath.

"Mr. Manford, as I said previously, you are under no obligation to tell me anything. You may tell me as much or as little as you please. But I must ask you something."

He slid to the front of his chair, moving very slow. Abnormally

89

slow. As if to forestall his own inquiry.

"You have described to me, for want of better words, horrible things. Things in which you have participated. Indeed, in many of these doings—in fact, in all of them, I believe—you are the primary participant."

"Yes."

"Or shall I say, the *only* participant."

"Right. Other than the people I . . ." Brad stopped. ". . . that I hurt."

"Yes." Mahindra, too, took a pause—a nervous one. "And my question is, these things you have told me, are they things you have actually . . . *done?*"

The room had grown perceptibly darker. The sun, it seemed, had dropped behind a building, divesting the green window shades of their backlight, and the room of its comforting hue of teal.

"These are things . . ." Crossing his arms, Brad put his head down, speaking toward the floor. "It's just that I can't stop thinking about them."

"Do you think about them all the time?"

"No. At night, mostly. It's just that they seem so real."

"They *seem* real," Mahindra said, seizing upon the verb. "So are you saying that these things you have described—these acts on your part—are merely images in your mind?"

Receiving no answer, the doctor nonetheless fell back in his chair, relieved. Greatly and unreservedly relieved.

"Ah! So these are dreams! You have dreamed these things."

"Well, I don't know . . ."

"But do you have these thoughts during the day as well?"

"Sometimes. But they come and go, and it's like I can't stop them."

"Obsessive thoughts," Mahindra said with a confident nod. "Daydreams of an unpleasant variety."

"They do come more at night, though."

"Yes, because that is when we are most vulnerable. When we sleep, our guard is down, so to speak. All the easier for unwelcome thoughts to creep in and become the substance of our dreams. And some dreams can be quite troubling."

"But these don't really seem like dreams. Or even daydreams."

"No? What do they seem like?"

Brad hesitated.

"Memories."

Chapter 16

Housebound

It had been pouring all morning. And before that, all night.

From the picture window, the boy gazed into the back yard, watching the hard rain puddle in the sand. The storm had brought devastation. Roads had been wiped out, trenches caved in, walls and towers melted into shapeless mounds.

His miniature world had been washed away.

"When will it stop?" he asked.

From the kitchen, Sally peeked around the corner.

"I don't know," she said, swinging a dishtowel onto her shoulder, "but you need to finish those math problems."

He scampered to the coffee table and held up two sheets of completed work.

"Then start on your handwriting."

He held up another sheet.

"Well, aren't you Mr. On-The-Ball." Smiling, she came into the family room. "Feeling good again today, huh?"

"Yeah."

Together, they looked out the window.

"I wish it would stop," he said.

"It will. Eventually."

"But if I can't go out, there's nothing to do."

"You could play video games."

"I don't want to."

Two months ago he had not wanted to do anything else.

"Or you could play with toys," she said, "or we could play a game."

He was still looking out. "I don't know. Not right now."

"Well, it's almost noon, anyway. We need to do your breathing treatment, and we need to do therapy, and we need to have lunch. And after that you'll have more schoolwork. So, we can worry later about other stuff."

The boy remained at the window as she went upstairs for his late-morning treatment—a simple dose of albuterol—and brought it down with a nebulizer. She made a second trip for the therapy vest and its compressor.

"Can I have backy-whacky?"

"No," she said, out of breath, "do the vest while you're taking the treatment. I'll make lunch. It'll be faster."

Less than pleased, he sat on the couch as she helped him put on the vest.

"I don't need this," he said, as if telling a secret.

"Eamon, you know that's not true."

"No, it is. I don't need the vest and I don't need the treatment."

"You may think that. But the doctor says you need them even when you're feeling good. That way, you're more likely not to start feeling bad."

"But I'm not going to start feeling bad. I'm fine."

"You are, but . . ."

"I could go to school," he said, insistent.

"Oh, I'm sorry, honey, no."

"Why can't I go to school?"

"Eamon, you know why. You know what happened last year, how sick you got."

"But it's different now."

"Honey, it may seem that way, but it really isn't."

"It *is!*"

His words came angry and impulsive. A long-building overload of frustration had reached its tipping point.

She stepped back, startled by his belligerence.

"Don't you yell at me," she said, pointing a rigid finger. "I won't stand for it."

He took several halting breaths, struggling to fend off a wave of tears. Her own flare of temper abated as she watched him toughen against his emotion, not giving in. She switched on the vest and nebulizer and stood beside him for a moment, trying to find something to say. The right thing. Anything.

Pretending to ignore her, his watery eyes at last glanced her way. She ran a hand through his hair and kissed his forehead before grabbing the remote to turn on the TV. She tuned in Cartoon Network and went to the kitchen, thinking all the while that something about that kiss had not tasted quite the way it used to.

———

"It's raining," she said. "It rained all day and it's supposed to keep on raining."

"Well, that's no good."

Sitting at the end of the couch, she held her cell phone in her right hand as she turned off the TV with her left and tossed the remote onto the far seat cushion.

"It's killing him that he can't get outside to that damn sand pile."

"Sand*box*," Brad corrected.

"Whatever." She reached toward the coffee table for her gin and tonic. "It's been a rough day."

"How's he feeling?"

"He feels great. That's the problem."

"If that's a problem, I'd say it's a good one."

"It is," she said. "It definitely is. But Brad, what the kid really needs is a friend. Someone his own age. And to get away from this house for a while. And I could probably say the same for his mother."

"I wonder if it would help to get out in the neighborhood a little more. That realtor said there were lots of kids around. And young couples."

"Brad, I've hardly seen anyone, young or old, since the day we got here."

"There's that playground down by the entrance. You might take him down there."

"I've never seen anyone there. Not a soul."

"But you could take him down there and maybe people would come along. You know, kids and their parents."

She knew he was just trying to help. Wanting to make things better.

Her tone softened. "Yeah, I may do that. But it's got to quit raining first." She took a sip of her drink.

"Not to change the subject," Brad said, "but speaking of people young or old, have you seen anything of Paul Irvin?"

"Colonel Creepy? I think he took a rain check." She watched as the bubbles in her glass rose and clung to the three floating slices of lime. "You think he's the one that was in the yard the other night, don't you?"

"Not necessarily."

"Well, I do."

"Sal, I really doubt anyone was there. Like I said, I think it was a reflection or something."

"Or *something*. So, it's just a coincidence you bought those locks?"

"Call it a precaution."

"Yeah, well, anything to keep those nasty reflections out of the yard." She stopped for another drink. "Brad, why don't you just admit it? You think someone was out there."

"Sally . . ."

"And I'll bet anything it was that old man. And you know, I hope it was. What's he going to do, anyway, talk me to death?"

"I thought you were scared of him."

"I'm not scared of anything," she said. "I can handle myself. You know that."

"Yeah, but keep the doors locked."

"I will." She had already checked them twice.

"But really, Sal, I'm sure there's nothing to worry about."

"Who's worried?"

"And keep the deck light on."

———————

She lay awake in bed. The rain had stopped. On and off, the big planes cruised overhead, setting up their usual rhythm as the sound of each, in turn, approached, climaxed, and receded. In the spaces between the last and the next, was nothing. A noiseless void she expected to be filled by, at the very least, an occasional cough or throat-clearing rattle from down the hall.

But there was only silence.

She had never known a time like this. Strangely, it distressed her. Over the years, through the nights, the child's coughing and gargled breathing had been an audible sign that, at a minimum, he was still there. Still inhaling and exhaling. Doing the one thing he needed to survive. And she had so often been able to discern subtle changes in the sound and frequency of what she heard—enough to know whether he was resting or miserable. But with such indicators now totally lacking, she could not help but fret, at times, whether he was even alive.

After a sleepless hour, she went to his room. Through the louvered blinds, the light from the deck below revealed his shadowed features. There was indeed an inanimate quality about him. An almost motionless serenity the romantic poets would have reserved for the cool calm of death. But his slow, deep breathing eased her fears. His chest steadily rising and falling, reminiscent of the comings and goings of an endless line of tanker planes, and without a single disruptive crackle.

She wondered about this. It did not seem right. But then, she knew even the sickest have their days of inexplicable remission. It had been that way with her father, wasting away with cancer. There had been good days that sometimes followed those that were very bad. Yet nothing quite like this.

But why question? *Just be thankful,* she told herself.

Her concerns assuaged, she left the room. She was not at all drowsy. Perhaps another drink would help.

Near the bottom of the stairs she heard a voice in her head. Eva's or her own. She couldn't tell.

You'll end up just like Mom.

Maybe, she thought. But at least I'm drinking better stuff.

The deck light shining into the kitchen led her to the pantry, where she pulled a dwindling liter of Tanqueray from the back shelf and thought that, at this very moment in a California trailer park, her mother was very likely doing the same with a bottle of McCormick.

She mixed her drink and stood looking out the panes of the French door into the dimly lit back yard. Nothing was stirring in the lighted area just beyond the deck, but with the vast balance of the yard in deep shadows, she could only imagine what might be lurking in its darkest corners.

And what the hell was she going to do about it?

Turning away from the door, she gulped her drink and set the glass on the granite counter. It was funny how she never wanted one of those during the day. Or, for that matter, at night—unless Brad was gone. Then it was all different. And she would spend her evenings counting limes.

It had been some time since a plane had passed over. It seemed they were done for a while. She almost missed them—their reliable, comforting commotion.

He would not be home till Friday. Another night like this. God.

She went back to the pantry for what she told herself was the last time, then sat at the kitchen table, in the glow of the light from outside, drinking and listening to the utter silence of the house, soon broken by the patters of another rainstorm.

Chapter 17

Financial Need

The ringing of the room phone stirred Brad from sleep. He lurched toward the nightstand, groping for the receiver.

"Hello?"

"Hello there, Brad." The voice, snakelike, was unmistakable.

"Hello, Ron."

"How's things in Jersey, partner?"

"It's late."

"Not for me. Here in La-La, the night is young."

"I'm hanging up."

"Oh, you always say that."

"I'm hanging up."

"There you go again. Don't you want to know how I found you?"

"I don't care."

"You should. You know, that sweet piece of yours in Kansas shouldn't be so quick to give out information."

Brad ground his teeth. "I don't think she did any such thing."

"Oh, she did. When your old college buddy called to see if you were coming back for the big game this weekend, she couldn't wait to tell him right where you were. In fact, she said she'd just gotten off the phone with you. And she was sure you couldn't make the trip, but she knew you'd want to talk to old Skip Sellers. We had so many good times back in school."

The fake laughter that followed was purely intended to intensify the pain. It did.

"Yeah, good old Skip," he said. "You told me all about him. Remember?"

"Yes."

"Yeah, Skip was such a swell guy." Exhausting his sarcastic streak, Ron turned to business. "All right, Manford, now goddammit, it's been a week and I haven't seen any green. And you don't know how close I came to giving that little perky-boobed wife of yours some very unsettling news about her sweet hubby."

Thinking of the many ways he would enjoy killing this bastard, Brad could scarcely get out the words: "I sent the money."

"When?"

"Today. This morning."

"Regular mail?"

"Yes."

"A thousand?"

"Yes."

"Cash?"

"Yes."

"What took you so long?"

"Look, you don't know how hard this is!"

"That's not my concern."

"Ron . . ."

"What?"

Brad wanted so much to turn the tables, to make the other suffer, to make *him* worry, if only just a little.

"Ron, have you ever thought about what would happen if you actually went through with these threats?"

"It's pretty simple, Manford. You're a dead man."

"Probably. But what do you think would happen to you?"

"Not a damn thing."

The guy was insufferable.

"I guarantee you, Ron, you're wrong. If I go down, you go down."

"How's that?"

"Because I'm going to take you there. I'm going to tell them about these calls, and the money I've paid, and why I paid it."

"Manford, get real. That money was paid in cash. All of it. There's no trail from you to me. And you know just as well there's none from me to you."

That was true, Brad thought. There was nothing in print anywhere to suggest what Ron was doing to him. No evidence of anything passing through the mail. And the bastard used only stolen or prepaid cell phones.

"I don't care," Brad said. "I'm just telling you, if you ever turn me in, I will nail you. I swear it."

The responding laughter was brief, but, this time, genuine.

"Well, then, you just go ahead and burn me, partner. I'll do my year or so in the county and send you a postcard wherever you are. And that'll be, let's see, San Quentin, or maybe somewhere back East, or—oh, I know— Mexico! Yeah, some Mexican shit hole. That's where you'll be, after the extradition."

It was useless. He couldn't beat this prick.

"But enough chitchat," Ron said. "I'll be watching my mailbox. And don't forget, four thousand in two weeks."

"Ron, I can't. Not in two weeks."

"Sorry, bud. I'm not waiting any longer."

"But just give me a little more time. Please. Look, what if I get you another thousand in two weeks and you give me till Christmas to send the other three?"

"Christmas! Oh, partner, no can do."

"Then how about Thanksgiving?"

Ron expelled a breath, expressing his irritation. "Manford, I don't get how you think you have any leverage to renegotiate this arrangement. I mean, what are you offering that I won't get anyway?"

"I'm offering to *pay* you. I'm telling you that I can get you the money *if* you give me the time. Otherwise, I'm sunk. I can't do it."

For a long moment, the line was quiet. Ron was thinking.

"Got yourself a problem, don't you, Manford?" Another lengthy pause. "Okay, I'm a nice guy. You get me another grand in two weeks and send the rest by turkey day. But that's it. Understand?"

"Yes."

"Now, Manford, say thank you."

Brad started to hang up.

"Say it."

Fighting a violent urge, he turned away from the receiver.

"Thank you."

———

He thought the next thousand would be relatively easy. He always with-held a portion of his paycheck for spending money, keeping some and giving some to Sally. Next payday he would take his share, then, a day or so later, add to it by making a withdrawal from the checking account. If Sally happened to notice, he would say he had needed the extra money for repairs on his car, and that he had misplaced his debit card and the shop wouldn't take a check. Money was always tight, but, for just the one time, he was sure they could get by on a little less than usual.

No, the next thousand would be no problem.

Today's payment, though—dropped in the mail as he had left town—had been somewhat harrowing. There had been some recent, unforeseen expenses, leaving just enough in the checking account to pay the remainder of the month's bills, buy gas and groceries, and keep Eamon's prescriptions filled. But no bother, he had thought. He would simply pull cash from his credit cards. He had two. On one, Sally was a secondary cardholder; on the other, she was not, but only because he had never gotten around to having another card issued. They had used the card they both carried to buy the majority of the new home furnishings, so that one, he knew, was near the limit. He was certain, however, that the other was good for two or three thousand dollars, and was therefore shocked to learn, upon calling for the balance, that he was a mere $531.43 from maxing out. (He had forgotten that he'd used that card for the purchase of the roll-top desk and chair he had placed in the spare bedroom—the room and its intended purpose now more or less also forgotten). So, as it turned out, he was able to pull only around $680 from both cards combined.

He had then combed his car, the couch cushions, and all of his pants pockets, collecting random bills and coins, which, together with the cash in his wallet, totaled just over fifty dollars. Still short of what he needed, he had been ready to just send Ron what he had and hope for the best when, on Monday, the trip to Newark had come along. That had sparked an idea, and by the following day he had worked up the nerve to ask Hugh to authorize a three hundred dollar advance for meals and other minor expenses. Such a thing was not normally done; the firm provided a credit card for traveling attorneys. But Hugh, being the accommodating person he was, had arranged it.

In the end, he had managed to assemble $1,032.68—meaning he had exactly $32.68 on which to subsist during a three-day trip. Thus, he was resigned to the fact that, for the most part, he would be working on an empty stomach.

But as difficult as it had been to make this most recent payment—and considering that he would be out yet another thousand to Ron within the next couple of weeks—pulling together an additional three grand by Thanksgiving would be even more problematic. He took some consolation in having negotiated the extra time. However, with his bills and credit situation being what they were, when the final payment came due, he would be in even worse financial shape than he was now.

Got yourself a problem, don't you, Manford?

Before, he had always had enough income or assets available to get the bastard off his back. But not this time. He simply did not and would not have the cash on hand to make this thing go away.

Unless, that is, he won the lottery. Or made a quick killing on a penny stock.

Or committed a criminal act of some kind. And quite frankly, that seemed a fairly attractive option. The lottery, the stock market—you couldn't count on them. But there was always money in the register at Quik Trip. And there was a nice big liquor store not far from his house.

Then too, there were more conventional methods. A home equity loan, for instance. With all the money he'd put down on the house, he was reasonably sure he could qualify. But there was a hitch: Sally was on the deed. She would have to cosign. There might be questions.

On the other hand, if he left the house out of it—just asked for a standard personal loan—he could keep Sally out of it as well. And yes, with two cards capped out, his credit score had to be awful. And aside from the home equity, he had no collateral to speak of. (He didn't even own a car; he leased.) Still, it wasn't as if he would be asking for that much. A bank might very well not even require security.

Yet there was some risk in going to a bank. The fact was, he worked for a prestigious law firm. Every banker in the city knew his employer. Many of those bankers were clients. No doubt some were even friends of Steven LeMark and Hugh Miller. And it would be all too easy for those friends to let slip a few bits of gossip about the new kid who was begging around for money. The young lawyer who, in less than two months, had managed to bankrupt himself. Prestigious law firms were not fond of such lawyers.

There were, however, other ways to get a loan. You could apply online and never have to look a soul in the eye—which, in the last week, he had done numerous times. He'd had no luck, but that had been with the more legitimate lenders. The sharks were still out there, waiting for him in cyberspace with their three-digit APRs. They would be his absolute last resort. And not far ahead would be the local payday folks with their own usurious rates. The high-interest crowd worked fast, though. You could get your money today and they didn't give a damn about who you were or your state of financial decay. There was something to be said for that. But he did not want to have to go to those people.

If he could just get another credit card. There was no good way out of this, but of all the bad ways, getting another card seemed the least potentially ruinous. But it would take time, and it was no cinch. He might get approved, and, just as easily, he might not.

And if not, well, there was always that criminal thing. There was something to be said for that, too. It would be faster, cleaner. No application, no waiting period, no monthly payments.

But was he the kind of person who could do that?

No, he told himself. Absolutely not.

And yet, lying awake, listening to his empty stomach growl, he thought—and feared—that maybe he was. That maybe he was *just* that kind. Or worse.

Much worse.

Chapter 18

Across the Commons

Sipping a cup of tea, Paul Irvin stood looking through the glass of the sliding door that led to his patio, watching the steady downpour. Only last weekend the so-called meteorologists could not stop talking about what a dry fall it had been. But in the last three days, the city, and most of the state, had been hit by a season's worth of rain. The soil was so completely saturated that the water had begun ponding at the end of his back yard and running downhill in rivulets, past an assortment of trees and all the way to the shallow creek that marked the commons' lowest point. Over the last twenty-four hours the usually unimpressive stream had become a gushing torrent, and through the trees, here and there, Irvin could see white water moving far outside the confines of the natural channel, carrying along dead branches and various items of human refuse—beverage cans, newspapers, plastic grocery bags. And still the rain kept on, unrelenting.

It was no day for a walk through the woods.

He went to the kitchen, where he had tomato soup heating on the stove for lunch. On the small TV on the counter, CNN was reporting the same tired stories he had been hearing since early morning. For a few minutes, he surfed the dial, but there wasn't much else on. Fox and MSNBC were showing the same stuff, and on the Weather Channel the news was all bad: nothing in sight but more rain. Before turning the thing off, he tried the History Channel, but found only a man haggling with a hoarder over a barnful of junk.

He sat at the breakfast bar with his tea, a bowl of soup, a box of saltines, and a buttered slice of Roman Meal, listening to the rain pound the roof. After his father died, his mother had often said how she hated it when the sun went down, to be the only one in the house all evening, no one to talk to, going to bed alone. He, too, hated that. All of it. But for the same reason, he also hated mealtimes. Sometimes he just didn't eat. It was a bother to cook, anyway.

Now and again he thought about getting a dog. Just something to provide a little companionship. He'd had one growing up on the farm. A big black and tan coondog named Buster. Then little Dickie had wanted a dog, so he and Linda had gotten a nice white Lab. The boy had loved that dog. He had loved him even after he had left for Texas Tech and started calling himself Richard. But the animal had suffered one malady after the next. A bad hip had finished him. They had put him down just short of thirteen years. And by then, Dickie was gone too.

Irvin thought that he himself was a little like that old broken-down Lab. Aching joints by the bushel and no one left to care. It was so unfair about Dickie. He had been such a good kid. He would have looked after his old dad. Damn right, he would have.

Carol was different, though. He and Carol had never really gotten on. Three years younger than her brother, she had always been quick to claim he was the favorite. And the worst of it was that she had been right. She was down in Dallas now and he heard precious little from her. Just a call every month or so. More often when she needed money. He tried to be generous with her, and with the grandkids. But it never seemed to buy much.

He put away the saltines and took his tea cup, soup bowl, spoon, butter knife, and bread plate to the sink, where they joined last night's dinner dishes and the juice glass, spoon, and cereal bowl he had used for breakfast. Loading the dishwasher was another annoyance. He refused to do it until it was absolutely necessary.

He took the soup pan off the stove and, as it contained almost another bowlful of fine Campbell's product, put it in the refrigerator. Maybe he would have it for dinner. That would be the easiest thing.

He went back to the sliding door, noticing, as he did, how the sound of the rain against the house was shifting to a lower pitch and drops were hitting the patio with less regularity. He thought he might be able to get out today after all.

But he knew the problem wasn't so much the rain. It was the creek.

The big arrowhead-shaped stone probably lay under two feet of murky water, but he was confident he could find it. He could find it with his eyes closed. But in crossing the rock, he would, even then, be up past his knees in the rushing flood—and over his head if he were swept off and into the channel. Either way, he would find himself very wet, and, in the latter scenario, someone might well find *him*—downstream, just another piece of waterlogged debris.

A bad way to go, he thought.

You've lived too long to have it end like that. Better give it a rest today.

Besides, it was obvious he was not too popular over there. Well, actually, Brad was all right. He didn't seem to be around much, but he had been pleasant both times they had talked. And that wife of his wasn't any too hard on the eyes. But she was tired of the ever-present Colonel Irvin. No question about it. She had said as much a couple of weeks ago when he had told her the lie about watching the planes. He knew she had not swallowed that. She hadn't said much since, just a cursory hello or good morning. Nothing more. Trying to be courteous, but clearly not wanting to talk. By now, he figured, she and Brad were probably both through being friendly. Even so, they were a hell of an improvement over the last occupants.

Yeah, better give it a rest.

But this made three days running. Three days since he had crossed the rock.

A lot could happen in three days.

He sat down in a chair near the sliding door, watching the creek and wishing it would drop just a foot or so.

Sally sat at the desktop computer in the basement, reading and answering emails. There were several from friends in California. There was one from Eva, too. But that one would have to wait; she just wasn't up to it.

She had a nagging fatigue and a stabbing pain behind her left eye, both compliments of a now empty bottle of Tanqueray. She hated herself for drinking like that. No decent parent alone with a child chronically ill would do such a thing. But she had always held herself at two limes. Three, at most. She could handle three. These last couple of nights, though, with Brad gone, and the weather, and Eamon sleeping so well . . .

So well, that is, until this morning.

With the pain building in the back of her eye, she had awakened in the dark to the sound of him clearing his throat. For quite a while after, there had been nothing. Then she had heard it again. And then, a cough. And another.

She had been waiting for this. The resumption of life as usual. But she had been more disappointed than concerned. He had not seemed terribly congested. No more than typical. To be sure, his condition had changed, but only, she thought, from the exceptional to the ordinary.

But as the day wore on, his breathing had become more labored. The nebulizer had not helped. His peak flow had deteriorated. And there had been an all too familiar but disconcerting rattle in his chest.

He had been sluggish with his morning schoolwork, then dropped off for a nap after lunch—something he had not done since their first days here. And now, even as she sat two stories from his bedroom, his barking coughs came loud and deep. And constant. Bellowing down the stairwell. The same repeating chorus she had learned all too well in darker times.

Chapter 19

Miles to Go

Brad had just enough left for a bowl of clam chowder before heading to his gate. It was six o'clock and he had not eaten all day.

In the waiting area he took a seat at the end of a row of connected chairs. He set his briefcase on the floor and his luggage on the empty seat beside him. With half an hour until his plane boarded, he thought about tracking down a newspaper or magazine, but decided against it. He propped his feet on his briefcase and slid down in his chair to rest.

There was a boarding announcement for a flight to Pittsburgh, and another for Boston. It occurred to him that he had never been to Pittsburgh. Or had he? He could not be certain.

Boston, though—he had been there. He remembered that one. For sure.

But today it would be Dallas, then, after a short layover, home.

The seating at the gate was filling up. He moved his luggage so a woman could take the chair beside him. She was young and shapely in jeans and a tight green sweater, and she reminded him, in many ways, of Sally. But not the eyes. Only Sally had those eyes. Those eyes that could take you and hold you and make you forget what you were. Make you believe you were something you were not.

Yet even those eyes had lost their power to enforce a belief in what he knew to be a lie.

There was a final call for Boston.

———

Officially, it had been a business trip. But not much of one. Just a flight in on Thursday, a half-day's work on Friday, and a whole weekend to find his way back to L.A. He had booked an extra ticket for Sally. They had been married just a year. She had never seen Boston.

On Saturday, in a rented car, they had driven inland. It had been she who suggested it—and just as quickly, questioned herself.

"You know, we don't need to drive all the way over there," she had said. "We can do something else."

"No, it's okay. I'd like to see it again. Really."

"It won't upset you?"

"Why would it?"

He had so often talked of the quaint village where he had grown up. Of its town square and stone courthouse. Its white, steepled Congregational church. The simple red-brick elementary school he had attended. And of the yellow, two-story clapboard house with blue trim where he had lived with his mother, and, for a shorter time, his father. A house that had stood since 1874.

Brad had described his parents as pillars of the small community. His father had been the only physician for miles around. Tireless and willing to make calls at any hour, his life had ended on an icy road one December night as he drove to reach the home of a woman suffering a dangerous labor. Brad had been only eight. His mother, a stalwart in the church, had lived another twelve years until her own untimely death by stroke while he had been at college.

The day was overcast and a drizzle began falling as they sped north up I-91. The rain became heavier as they crossed into Vermont until, near Brattleboro, visibility grew challenging, the conditions further aggravated by a host of big rigs kicking up walls of water. They spoke little as Brad concentrated on driving and Sally sat with her arms folded, nervous as the vehicle swerved and skidded atop the wet road. The situation remained the same for twenty miles, the windshield wipers whacking away on high. Finally, just south of Bellows Falls, the storm slackened and became a gentle shower as they left the interstate and headed west on roads less traveled.

For the most part, the fall colors were at peak.

"The trees are so beautiful," Sally said.

"I've seen better." Brad tapped the brakes as they approached a tight turn. "Overall, I'd say this is a pretty so-so year for foliage."

"I still think it's beautiful. It must have been wonderful growing up here, seeing the leaves like this every year."

He nodded with a smile. "It was nice."

Coming into the village, there was a moss-covered rock fence running along the right side of the road for perhaps sixty yards, a big golden-leaved sugar maple growing near its far end.

"Folks around here say that fence has been there since before Washington crossed the Delaware," Brad said. "No one knows who built it."

"Gosh," she marveled. "How neat."

To the left sat the town square, the stone sides of the courthouse dark with rainwater. The absence of vehicles around the structure left no doubt as to the day of the week. And across the empty green, cradled in the midst of spiky pines blotched with yellow birch and red maple, lay a long, thin pond, raindrops dotting its surface.

"I used to play hockey on that pond," he said. "In the winter it freezes like a rock."

She sounded surprised. "You played hockey?"

"Yeah." He assumed a look of pretended conceit. "I was pretty good."

"Get out." She pushed him playfully. "I suppose you think you were as good as ... as ..." She laughed at herself. "I can't think of any hockey players."

"How about Bobby Orr? Greatest ever for the Boston Bruins."

"Okay, him."

Brad shook his head. "I was no Bobby Orr."

The streets were empty save for an approaching pickup, its white paint splashed with mud. The driver, nondescript in a baseball cap, waved as he passed. Brad reciprocated.

"Friend of yours?" Sally asked.

"Could be."

Along the street was a post office, a town hall, a general store, a couple of art galleries, an inn with a restaurant. There was little else.

Three blocks past the courthouse, the pavement turned to gravel, and there, on the left, looking just as Brad had described, was the spired church. On a hill beyond was a cemetery filled with craggy trees and bordered by the same style of rock fence they had passed coming in.

And across the road from the church stood a yellow, two-story clapboard house, its shutters and front door painted a light blue—the last house before the road wound around the cemetery, out of sight.

Brad pulled the car to a stop. The rain had become a slow mist. The wipers, still running fast, squeaked for lack of moisture.

"That's it," he said, looking at the house.

She smiled, happy for him. "I knew it. It's just like you said."

He turned off the wipers, lost in thought.

"You should go up and say hi," she said.

There were no vehicles in sight, but, as he knew, the stand-alone garage to the rear could hold a couple of cars or trucks. The house had a nice coat of paint, as did the short, white picket fence that ran the length of the yard. The lawn and shrubs were well kempt. Wind chimes hung on the front porch and a wicker chair sat near the door.

After his mother's passing, he had sold the place to a couple with young children. The Franklins. Maybe they were still here. Maybe not. But somebody was.

"I'll check it out," he said.

He left the car and walked hesitantly up the brick sidewalk that led to the fence gate. He unlatched the gate and, knowing the trick, raised it slightly—enough to swing it open without the pickets dragging the uneven walk.

He shut the gate the same way and continued toward the house. At the front steps he paused before climbing up to the big porch, which extended to his left along two windows that looked out from what he knew to be the parlor. The drapes were pulled, but parted just enough to reveal a light from inside.

He pressed the button for the doorbell and heard the familiar ring. Footsteps advanced from within.

The door half opened and a tall man of retirement age stood in the threshold.

"Can I help you?"

"Sir, I'm sorry to bother you, but I'm wondering if there's a Tim Franklin here."

"No," the man said, shaking his head. "This is the Garrett residence."

"I see. Well, I know some time ago there was a family named Franklin that lived here . . ."

The man cut him off. "No, son, you're mistaken. No such person has ever lived in this house."

"Oh?" Brad tried to make sense of it. "Well, I just assumed they lived here, at least for a while. They bought the house, anyway."

"Bought the house?" The man seemed almost offended. "No, as I said, you're mistaken."

"I don't think so. I sold it to them."

A look of disbelief. "Son, I'm telling you, you've got the wrong house. The people you're looking for aren't here. They've never been here. And you most certainly didn't sell this house to anyone."

"The hell I didn't!"

Brad took an impulsive step toward the entrance as the man quickly swung the door to within inches of closing, keeping himself behind it.

"I *lived* in this house," Brad said.

"You did no such thing. Now get off this property."

Seeing the effect of his outburst, Brad retreated, raising his hands.

"I'm sorry. But please, just listen. This house used to belong to my parents, George and Eileen Manford."

"Who?"

"Haven't you heard of Doc Manford?"

"Not since I've lived here."

"And how long has that been?"

"Forty years!"

The door shut with an angry finality.

Brad lingered on the porch, pacing several agitated circles before looking back to see Sally hanging out of the car window.

"Brad, what's wrong?"

Tossing up his hands, he stomped down the front steps and swung open the fence gate, letting the pickets scrape the bricks.

PART THREE

TWO WEEKS

Chapter 20

A Brief History of
Col. Paul T. Irvin, USAF (Ret.)

It was late morning before he got to the office. He had stayed longer at the hospital than he had planned.

As anticipated, a mountain of mail was waiting on his desk. Last week in New Jersey he had promised himself he would come in Saturday to whittle away at it, but, as it turned out, that had not been possible. And Sunday, he had not thought much about it.

He had just arrived when Sharon came to the door with a stack of files. She found him in his chair, unpacking his briefcase.

"Hey, stranger. Welcome back."

"Thanks."

"Took our time getting in today, huh?" she teased.

With one foot, Brad pushed the briefcase far enough away to allow room for his legs under his desk.

"Well, yeah. But I should probably tell you why," he said. "Have a seat."

Briefly, he explained about Eamon, Sharon's cocky smile becoming a look of humble apology.

"Brad, my God, I had no idea."

"I know. But I wanted you to be aware of the situation, because when he's in the hospital my life tends to get a little crazy."

"Oh, but I feel terrible. And even worse for your little boy."

"I appreciate that. But I'm sure he'll be okay. It's just going to take some time." He tapped his fingers on his desk, ready to change the subject. "Anyway, what do you have?"

"These are contracts Hugh's working on," she said, half rising from her chair to hand him all of the folders but one. "He wants your input."

"I hope he doesn't need it right away."

"Just the one on that thing with Cessna."

"I suppose that's the nasty one."

"It is."

"Figures."

"But," she said, turning bubbly, "I've got something else that might pick you up a bit."

She held out the remaining folder so he could read its label: *Paul Irvin.*

"That's the one I want," he said, reaching.

She pulled the file back, beyond his grasp.

"Not just yet," she said, settling into her chair. "Allow me the pleasure."

She opened the folder to reveal a collection of copy paper and hand-written pages from a legal pad.

"Paul Travis Irvin," she said, referencing her notes. "Born Pampa, Texas, February 8, 1940. Direct descendent of Colonel William Barrett Travis, Defender of the Alamo."

She paused for effect as Brad pulled himself closer to his desk.

"Air Force Academy," she continued, "class of sixty-two. Graduated top ten percent. Varsity football, second team halfback, one letter. Thereafter . . ."

"Jet pilot?"

"Yep. Attended flight school at Laredo Air Force Base. First in his class. Married Linda May Harper of Laredo in 1963." She looked up from her notes. "After that he moves around between several bases, here and overseas. Then Vietnam. Two tours."

She pulled out a printed copy of an internet page, raising it to show Brad.

"From Wikipedia," she said, "but I've cross-referenced."

"Good idea."

"This is from an entry discussing the leading U.S. fighter pilots in Vietnam. It says that in 1968, during then-Captain Irvin's second tour, he was credited with shooting down three enemy MiGs, all on the same day, all within five minutes."

Brad opened his mouth wide.

"*Three in five minutes?* In two tours he must have shot down dozens."

"No, just the three. But here's the deal," she said, raising an index finger. "Irvin flew an F-105D Thunderchief. It was what they called a fighter-bomber. But it was really more bomber than fighter. It could carry nukes. In fact, it was built *specifically* to carry nukes—although it could carry conventional bombs, too. Like fourteen thousand pounds' worth. And it had terrific power. It could go twice the speed of sound. On the other hand, it was a big, heavy plane. The joke was that when it landed, it came down with a thud. And that's what they called it, the Thud. It was not supposed to be able to outmaneuver a MiG. Yet over Hanoi on July 12, 1968, Captain Irvin did just that. Three times. For which he was awarded the Air Force Cross, a decoration second only to the Medal of Honor."

Amid his astonishment, Brad could not help laughing. "Sharon, you should be on television."

"But this is incredible! In the entire war, there were only about two dozen MiGs shot down by Thuds. And there were two guys who got two each. But only *one* man ever shot down *three* MiGs while flying an F-105D."

"Our man, the Colonel."

"Exactly."

Sharon passed the Wikipedia page across the desk. Brad's eyes danced over it:

In one of the legendary aerial incidents of the conflict . . . wingman's plane badly damaged . . . outnumbered three to one . . . considered some of the greatest flying and fighting in the history of jet warfare.

"My God," Brad said, "I've met Chuck Yeager."

"Well, not quite."

"How so?"

"Remember when you told me last week that this was sort of a good news, bad news thing?"

He fell back in his chair. "I don't like the sound of that."

"But just let me say, his military career, as far as I can tell, was exemplary to the end. And he made colonel, just like he said. And he went to work for Boeing, just like he said. And he retired from Boeing, just like he said. Now, after that . . ." She paused, pulling out what looked to Brad like a copy of a document from a court file. ". . . a guy by the name of Michael Renner . . ."

The name registered.

"That's the guy I bought my house from. Irvin said he was an asshole."

"He may be. But it appears Mr. Renner had similar sentiments toward Colonel Irvin. About a year and a half ago, Renner tried to have Irvin charged with criminal trespass. It looks like nothing ever came of that, but there was a companion civil suit where Renner and his wife asked for a restraining order, which was granted."

"What was the cause of the ugliness?"

"The allegations are vague, but Irvin supposedly came onto the Renner property a couple of times and was told to leave, and when he did it again, the Renners got fed up."

"Do you have a copy of the order?"

"Of course," Sharon said smugly.

She handed him the court document. It was a mere two pages, stating, in pertinent part, that *Paul T. Irvin shall not enter his person* on the Renner property, *nor come within four feet of the same.*

"Why was Irvin on the property?" Brad asked.

"I have no idea, but it looks like he lost his wife about that time, so . . ."

"She died?"

"Yeah. The obituary requested donations to a hospice." Sharon turned up one side of her mouth, wincing. "I'm guessing cancer."

"So what do you think was going on?"

"I don't know. But they'd been married fifty years. Maybe he flipped out."

Brad shook his head. "Something tells me that's not what happened. And I'd also be willing to bet that this restraining order didn't solve any problems."

"Aren't we perceptive." She flipped through the folder, referencing another handwritten page. "The fact is, even after the order, the Renners called the police twice to report that Irvin was in violation, and when nothing came of that, they filed suit for nuisance and harassment."

"How was Irvin harassing them?"

"According to the petition, he was just standing at their fence, watching them. Weird, huh?"

Brad had a queasy feeling. "Yeah, weird. What happened to the lawsuit?"

"It died on the vine after the Renners left town."

"I think they went to Alabama," Brad said, largely to himself. "Anything else?"

She paged through the folder and handed him one last document—a grainy black and white copy of a photograph printed from a website. It showed a group posing for a picture at an apparent social occasion.

"This," she said, "was taken at a MUFON convention in Kansas City just last February."

"A *what* convention?"

"MUFON. M-U-F-O-N. It stands for Mutual UFO Network. It's a sort of club."

"Why the hell is Irvin involved in that?"

"Who knows? Maybe he saw a flying saucer in Vietnam."

Brad stared at the blurry picture. "Is he in this?"

Sharon stood up and leaned over the desk, pointing with a long, red-painted fingernail. "Right here. Second from the end. I should have circled him."

"I'll let it slide," Brad said, lowering the paper. "Boy, Sharon, you did a job on this guy. I mean it. I definitely owe you one."

"Nah, forget it. I love to pry. And what would I do with a mink coat, anyway?" She put the rest of the file on his desk and, stepping back, turned somber. "Brad, I want to say again how sorry I am to hear about your son. I'll certainly be praying for him, and for you and your wife."

"Thanks, Sharon."

"So, anything else?"

He did not have to think long.

"One thing: Michael Renner. I don't know him. I've never met him. But I'd like to talk to him. Can you get me a number?"

"I'm on it."

Chapter 21

In Hospital

The doctors were calling it a "clean out." The term was nothing new. Since he was a toddler, Eamon had been through the ordeal, on average, once or twice a year. And it was always the same: Stepped-up breathing treatments and physiotherapy. A host of needle pokes. Loads of antibiotics. And hours of tedium.

The bulk of medical personnel had the habit of comparing the procedure to an automobile tune up—something periodically necessary to prevent the machine from falling into irreversible disrepair. But Brad preferred the analogy given by one of Eamon's pulmonologists in L.A., who had likened it to flushing out the pipe in the bathroom sink. Over time, he had said, the gunk builds up to such a level that the thing nearly ceases to function, so every now and then, you have to use a little clog remover.

In the past, however, it had been clear, well in advance, that the boy was headed for the medical profession's version of a Drano application. He would gradually become more congested than normal. He would cough more. Wheeze more. His medications would be adjusted, but to no avail. Then came the hospital. The clean out. In all, it would be several weeks from the first sign of trouble to the day of admission.

This time, though, had been different. Only days before, he had felt so well. Better, perhaps, than ever. Then, literally overnight, things had changed. The doctors wouldn't admit it, but they didn't understand. The kid had been in for a checkup the preceding Monday and everything had been fine. Must have picked up a nasty bug somewhere, they said.

Well, what else could they say?

It would be two weeks, Brad thought. It always was, give or take. And in that time, for the boy and his mother, the pediatrics ward would become a virtual cellblock. Given the germs he might contract, as well as those he possibly carried, Eamon would, naturally, have a private room. And Sally would spend every night there. Even during the day, she would not leave the hospital campus unless someone took her place. In L.A., Eva or Tina had played the substitute when Brad could not. But now the job was his. Alone.

During past hospitalizations, Brad had, on occasion, also stayed the night. But doing so had little value other than as a show of support. And Sally was constantly shooing him away.

You've got to earn a living, she would say. *You need a decent night's rest.*

Indeed he did. But getting one was another matter. He so often had things on his mind.

———

Brad spent the better part of Tuesday afternoon at the hospital while Sally went home to shower and change clothes. He worked on his laptop in Eamon's room as the boy, in jeans and a t-shirt, sat in bed playing the Xbox that had been brought from home and hooked up to the hospital's small, cheap television.

Brad was working on one of Hugh's contracts when the email arrived: *Hey, partner, when's payday?*

He made a sound that drew the boy's attention.

"What's wrong, Dad?"

"Nothing. Just something silly."

The address was an amalgam of seemingly unrelated letters and symbols. Possibly a covert account the bastard had set up to avoid detection—or, just as likely, he was pirating someone else's computer.

Brad dispatched a reply: *Ron—Mine Friday. Yours after.*

"Dad?" Eamon said, his eyes on the TV.

"What is it, E?"

"Can I have some water?"

"Sure."

There was a half-filled plastic cup with a lid and straw on the over-bed table. Brad stood and pushed the table within the boy's reach, and, putting his game on pause, the child quickly created a slurping sound at the straw's far end.

"Want some more?"

"No." The boy put the cup back on the table and placed his controller beside it.

"Done with your game?"

"For a while." He touched his arm where a transparent dressing covered the insertion point of his PICC line. "My arm kinda hurts."

"You should let it rest."

"And it itches." He started to dig at the dressing.

Brad took gentle hold of the child's hand. "E, you know better than that. You could pull the tube out."

With the line going up a vein in the boy's arm and into his chest cavity, Brad worried, as he always did, that the jostling of it might cause some internal injury.

"But it *itches.*"

"Let's try not to think about it."

"I hate this stupid tube."

"Me too," Brad said. "But if you mess with it, you'll just end up making things worse."

The boy lay back in bed, pouting as the laptop signaled the receipt of another message: *Who's Ron?*

Brad smiled. The cocksucker didn't like seeing his name. Well, that just made this the perfect time to turn up the heat. To throw the list of his crimes in his face and let him sweat at the thought of all that very damning information floating around in cyberspace.

"Dad?" Eamon said, sounding less agitated.

Brad was typing. "Yeah?"

"Can we take a walk?"

"We can go around the hall or to the playroom. Do you want to go to the playroom?"

"I don't care."

"Okay, just let me finish what I'm doing."

For a few moments, the boy lay quiet.

"Dad?"

"Uh-huh?"

"Am I gonna get to go trick-or-treating?"

Brad stopped typing and looked up. Surely, he thought, Sally had covered this.

"Well, no, bud. Halloween's this weekend, and you'll still be here."

The boy looked hurt. "But can I trick-or-treat when I get out of here?"

"No, we just get to trick-or-treat on Halloween. That's the rule."

"But that's not fair for kids like me."

"I know it's not. I'm sorry."

It occurred to Brad that the boy had missed Halloween last year, too. And for the same reason. Only the hospital had changed.

"A kid should be able to trick-or-treat any time he wants," Eamon said.

"Yeah, but people won't always have candy."

The boy mustered a mischievous smile. "Then they should get tricked," he said, showing his teeth.

Brad began to laugh just before his son joined in, the two of them, for a time, laughing together. And Brad thinking all the while that *he* wanted to trick somebody.

He wanted to trick cocksucker Ron.

"Hey, Dad?"

"Yeah."

"Will there be snow here at Christmas?"

"I don't know about Christmas, but there will be sometime. Everyone says so."

"For sure?"

"I think so."

"Do you promise?"

It seemed a safe bet. "Yeah, I promise. There's going to be snow." He went back to his email and finished just as the boy spoke again.

"Dad, can we go?"

"Yeah." He clicked on Send.

Suck on it, Ron.

The boy flipped over and slid out of bed on his stomach. Brad helped him put on his slippers and then the mask he was to wear whenever he left the room.

"I hate this thing," Eamon said.

"Pretend you're a doctor."

"Whatever."

"Wouldn't you rather be a doctor than a patient?"

They had walked only a few steps out of the room.

"Dad?"

"Yeah?"

The little voice was muffled behind the white swathe. "I didn't think I was going to have to go back here. I thought I was getting better."

Chapter 22

In the Club

Wednesday brought another lunch with Hugh at the Petroleum Club. Brad hadn't seen him since returning from New Jersey. They sat at Hugh's usual table as Brad offered a quick summary of his trip.

"Sounds good," Hugh said. "Get me a memo, would you?"

"I've got one in dictation."

"And copy Steve."

A waitress came by to take drink orders. As she left, Hugh looked as if he was about to suggest they hit the buffet, but Brad spoke first.

"Hugh, I've got a bit of a problem."

"What's that?"

"You know that three hundred dollars you authorized?"

"Yeah?"

"I spent it."

Hugh laughed. "Forget it. Work on the road can be expensive. Just turn in your receipts."

"But that's the problem," Brad said. "The bookkeeper's asking for them and I can't find them. I was sure I had them, but when I unpacked, they weren't there. They may turn up, but . . ."

Hugh shook his head, unconcerned. "Don't sweat it. Just fill out vouchers for what you can remember and I'll explain things."

"But I don't want the firm to be out anything."

"We won't. We'll bill the client for reimbursement on the next statement like we'd do anyway. They won't give a rat's ass. Bradley, this deal is

worth millions. You could've spent three *thousand* dollars and they probably wouldn't care."

A mere extra hundred, though, would have been enough, Brad
thought—if only he'd had the guts to ask for it. He kicked himself, thinking of how hungry he had been those three days.

"Come on," Hugh said. "Let's eat."

The club was serving the usual Mexican fare. Hugh doubled up on the
chicken tortilla soup and followed that with hefty portions of enchiladas
and refried beans.

"Man," he said, placing his silverware on his plate, "I'm stuffed."

From the big window that ran along the table, Brad took in the view.
Back East, the fall colors had been past peak. But here, some were still in
transition. Beyond downtown, in the residential areas, lay a striking carpet
of red, orange, and yellow.

"Nice out, today," Hugh said. "Love to be on the golf course."

"You should."

"Yeah, but I'm afraid that's going to have to wait." He folded his napkin and dropped it on the table. "Bradley, we've got to push this RightLine
thing through. The client wants it done by the end of the year, and I don't
think the negotiations are going to be that easy."

"You think the deal could go south?"

"No, I'm not saying that. But we haven't even started on a purchase
agreement. And you know how that goes. We draft one and they don't
like it. So, they redraft. Then, we redraft. And it goes back and forth for
weeks. And we're dealing with some difficult people on the other side.
Hell, our people aren't all that agreeable either. I just think this could be
messy. And as I say, it can't go past December."

"What do you want me to do?"

"As you know, we have a rather enormous collection of documents
on this. I need you to plow through everything, make sure there's nothing
there that can backfire on us, especially stuff related to the intellectual
property. Jenn Baker more or less already did that, but Steve's not satisfied.
He wants you to do it all again. Every scrap of paper. After that, we'll bring
in our people and talk about terms. Then you can get busy on a purchase
agreement. We'll need a draft before Thanksgiving."

From the start, Brad had known he would be seeing this matter to conclusion. No surprise there. But re-examining every document? That, in itself, was a month-long project, for which he would have, realistically, about two weeks.

"I'm sorry to do this to you," Hugh said, looking contrite. "I know you already have all you can handle, and with your son in the hospital, this is a terrible time to start snowing you under. But I don't have a choice."

Brad was trying not to seem as glum as he felt.

"Hugh, I'll give this my best. You know that. But honestly, it sounds like I'm going to have to live at the office for a while, and my wife simply has to have someone stand in for her at the hospital from time to time. If she doesn't, she'll never leave. And right now, I'm the only one."

"I understand." Hugh, the great solver of problems, thought for a moment. "Say, what about Charley? She can help out."

"Your wife?"

"Sure, what else has she got to do? She hangs around the house, goes to lunch, gets her nails done . . ."

"But Hugh, she's got kids of her own to take care of."

"Nah," Hugh said, flippant. "Alyssa takes care of herself. And other than her, there's just Audrey. She's twelve. And Alyssa can take care of her, too."

"But Hugh, your wife isn't obligated . . ."

"Yep, yep," Hugh said, "that's what we'll do. I mean, Sally likes Charley, doesn't she?"

"Yeah."

"And you know, Alyssa could also stay with him some."

"He really likes Alyssa."

"Great. See? You're all set."

"I guess so."

Just as with Hugh's babysitting proposal of two weeks ago, this plan would need Sally's consent. But Brad saw no reason to believe it wouldn't pass muster.

It was just the thought of all that damned work. Grunt work. And being away from her. And Eamon.

And home.

"You know, Bradley," Hugh said, "Steve is already pretty crazy about you. But if you get the job done on this thing, he'll love you forever."

"Forever's a long time."

"Indefinitely, then. He'll love you indefinitely. How's that?"

Brad took a stab at a smile and looked out the window.

Chapter 23

Incoming Call

He had not thought about the back yard all week. And leaving every morning before daybreak and returning well after dark—in between making visits to the hospital and working twelve hours—he'd had no real opportunity to observe it.

Friday night at the hospital, however, Sally had raised the subject. Charley Miller had spelled her for several hours that afternoon. Sally had gone home to shower and do laundry, and had been passing the window in the family room when she noticed it.

"I've never seen anything like it," she said.

"I'm sure it's pretty bad."

"*Bad?* Brad, it's a forest! I swear, around that sandbox it's over a foot high. And the rest of it's not much better."

Only then it occurred to him that it had been nearly two weeks since it had been mowed—the Sunday before he had left for New Jersey, when he had cut it himself. A week of rain had followed, and the past week had been relatively mild and sunny. All in all, great conditions for growing things.

With one exception: It was November.

November, and his yard was still popping up like spring. Sharon had promised something different.

"Look, Sal, I don't have time to deal with it and neither do you. I'm just going to hire somebody."

"They'll probably charge a fortune."

"So be it."

He knew they didn't exactly have the money lying around. But this time of year, the lawn-care business was no doubt on the decline. Maybe, he thought, he could get a bargain rate.

———————

Saturday morning he spoke with a lawn service and scheduled the job for Monday. On Monday afternoon he was in his office, surrounded by piles of RightLine documents, when his desk phone rang with a nameless call from a number he did not recognize. He thought at first it might be a certain someone from the West Coast, but the area code was local.

"Brad Manford."

"Brad, hey, this is Paul Irvin. You know, from across the commons?"

Brad found himself taken aback. "Sure, Paul. How can I help you?"

"Well, actually, I'm tryin' to help *you*," Irvin said with a chuckle. "You see, there's a guy here at your house to mow your yard and he can't get in."

"Can't get in?" Brad spent a moment in confusion. "Oh, the . . ."

"Locks on the gates."

"Right! Gosh, I forgot about those."

"Yeah, well, you've got a combination lock on the gate out here by the commons and another one on your side gate. 'Course, I just happened to be passin' by and saw the problem. Anyway, I told this guy that I thought I remembered you sayin' where you worked, and that I'd try to get 'hold of you and get the code for one of these so he could get in. The side gate would be best."

Without thinking, Brad nearly spouted off the numbers, but stopped himself. "Paul, thanks very much for calling. Is the guy from the lawn service close by?"

"Well . . . yeah."

"Could I talk to him, please?"

Irvin seemed a bit put out. "All right."

Brad could hear the rustle of the afternoon breeze, then Irvin calling the man to the phone. There was the sound of the phone changing hands.

"This is Bob with Splendor in Your Grass."

"Bob, this is Brad Manford. I'm sorry you weren't able to get into the yard."

"No problem."

"Listen, I'm going to give you the combination to the lock on my side gate."

"Okay, sir, just let me get over there."

There was a pause. Bob was walking.

"Bob?"

"Yes, sir?"

"Is that guy who called me following you?"

"No, he's still out by your other gate."

"Let me ask you, just confidentially, was he at my house when you got there?"

Bob didn't seem quite sure how to take the question. "Well, sir, when I first walked from your driveway back here to your side gate to try to get in, he was where he is right now."

"And you say he's standing at my fence?"

"Yes, sir."

"Is he looking into my yard?"

"Yes, he is."

"What's he looking at?"

"Hard to say, sir," Bob answered. "Your tree, I guess."

Chapter 24

Outgoing

"Hello?"

"May I speak to Michael Renner, please?"

"This is Mike."

"Mike, this is Brad Manford. I'm the guy who bought your house in Wichita."

On the other end, a momentary silence. "Well, hi." The voice had risen in pitch. "I sure hope everything's okay."

"It is. We love the house. No complaints."

"Good, good." The sound of relief. "We loved it, too. I wish we could have taken it with us."

"I guess you're in Alabama now?" Brad said.

"Yeah, Huntsville. You know how it is. Up the ladder."

"Right."

"And as I recall, my realtor mentioned that you came from California."

"Santa Monica," Brad said. "You know how it is."

Responding in the affirmative, Renner apparently thought he did.

"Anyway, Mike, I don't want to keep you, but there's something I want to ask you about."

"Sure."

"You only lived in the house a little over a year, right?"

"Yeah, we built it and no more got settled when this opportunity here came up. Then we moved and it just sat there. The market wasn't all that great." Renner laughed. "I can't tell you how happy I was when you came along."

"Me too. But what I'm wondering is, while you were here, did you become acquainted with a guy who lives across the commons named Paul Irvin?"

There was another silence—then a sharp, disgusted exhalation of breath. "Oh, I'm acquainted with him. Believe me, I'm acquainted."

"What can you tell me about him?"

"He's a flake. A nutcase. I mean, the whole time the house was going up, there he was, milling around the site. The guys on the construction crew got sick of him. And the day we moved in, there he was again."

"Standing at the fence?"

"So you know what I'm talking about."

"I'm afraid I do."

"And he would go away," Renner said. "He'd go up and down the commons, wearing out a path. But he always ended up back at my fence. He claimed he was watching the planes, the ones that go in and out of McConnell. But that was bullshit. I never even saw him look up. All he ever did was stare into my back yard."

"I know he was an Air Force officer."

"Yeah, some kind of old-time flyboy hero. And I don't know the story there, but as far as I'm concerned he should've been discharged on a Section Eight."

The animosity was thick.

"But let me ask you, Mike," Brad said, knowing the answer, "while he was hanging around, did he ever actually come onto your property?"

"Hell, yes. I caught him red-handed. One night I was up a little later than usual and looked out the window, and there he was, just strolling around the back yard in the moonlight."

"What did you do?"

"I went out and asked him what the hell he thought he was doing, and he gave me . . ." Renner broke for a contemptuous laugh. "He gave me some cock-and-bull story about seeing something in my yard. And I'm like, '*Something?* What the hell does that mean?' Of course, he didn't have much of a comeback. He claimed it was a light of some kind. That's all he would say. Anyway, I told him I didn't ever want to see his sorry ass again, and the next day I went and got some locks for the gates to keep the silly bastard out for good."

"Did that work?"

"Well, it kept him *out*. But it didn't keep him away. He kept coming back. Morning, noon, and night. It pissed me off. Finally, I called the cops and made a complaint, and then I hired a lawyer to try to make his life miserable enough that he would leave us alone. But none of it did any good. The guy just kept coming back, right up to the time we moved."

"Did you ever find out what he was after?"

"Not really. But he had the chance to tell us a couple of times under oath."

"What did he say?"

"He admitted he'd been on the property the time I caught him—and how many times he was there before that, we'll never know. And he told the story about seeing this supposed light and, according to him, he followed it into my yard to investigate. He claimed that was why he was so interested in my yard. He said he kept seeing this light. Then he got off on all sorts of weird stuff, ghost lights and, I don't know, St. Elmo's Fire . . ."

"Do you think there's anything to that?"

"God, no. The guy's either delusional or some kind of Peeping Tom."

Brad recalled that Sally had put forth the latter theory.

"Mike, I know I'm kind of grilling you here . . ."

"No, that's fine."

". . . but I'm wondering, do you think he's dangerous?"

"Who knows? I can tell you that I, personally, never felt threatened by him. But with someone like that, you can't say for sure."

"Did he ever act like he wanted to get into the house?"

"To be honest, I can't say he did. As far as I know, he was just in and around the yard."

"Well, since he likes it so much, maybe I should ask him to mow it," Brad joked.

"Now that's an idea," Renner said. "That yard's a pain, isn't it? Like I say, I loved the house. But that yard and crazy Paul Irvin are two reasons I'm glad I'm out of there. I truly wish you the best of luck with both."

"Thanks a lot," Brad said, falsely sarcastic.

"Really, though, I do hope you and your wife enjoy it there."

"We do. And so does our son. We can hardly drag him away from that sandbox you built."

"My kids liked it, too."

"So, Mike, I've got to ask, did you plant the tree or was it already there?"

"What tree?"
"The cottonwood. The one in the sandbox."
"Huh?"

———————

Brad stood on the deck, looking into his back yard at the tree. It seemed like no other within sight. Save for the cedars, the trees in the commons had all turned and most were starting to thin out. And the pear trees to the yard's west side had become, for the most part, a reddish-purple; leaves of the same color blew about the lot. But the cottonwood had not, it appeared, dropped a single leaf. Its very top had turned a somewhat dusty yellow. Below that, though, it remained wholly a deep spring-green.

All of which was strange enough. But if Michael Renner was to be believed, last year at this time there had been no tree.

And yet, just two weeks ago, it had measured fourteen feet.

Was there any way, in less than a year, it could have grown like that? The answer, Brad thought, was no. A source online said that the reported all-time record growth for a cottonwood in its first year was only thirteen feet, and that had been under exceptional circumstances: the most favorable soil conditions, optimal moisture and weather, etc.

Which appeared to leave only one possibility: The tree had been planted—and why or by whom, he couldn't imagine—when it was already good-sized, after the Renners had left, and had subsequently grown to its present height. And that explained it.

Only it didn't, really, because he could not deny what he himself had witnessed. And whether it had been four feet in six weeks, or three feet, or something else, the fact was that the tree's rampant growth was beyond dispute. And that suggested a very different, albeit less rational, conclusion.

But then again, it seemed a conclusion no less rational than what he observed at this very moment, judging the tree, as he had those two weeks ago, against the backdrop of the commons.

He went inside and, returning with a yardstick and retracting tape measure, went down the deck stairs to the east side of the yard. He held out his right arm and, with the yardstick, measured the distance from his right eye to the knuckle of his index finger; then, with the same length of yardstick above his fist, held the stick vertical and moved toward the tree until he had framed it between the top of the stick and the top of his hand.

He put the yardstick on the ground to mark where he stood and began walking backwards toward the tree, letting out the metal tape. There was supposed to be sixteen feet.

He looked back to avoid tripping as he stepped over one of the wooden poles bounding the sandbox. He looked back again to ensure he didn't run into the tree. Ultimately, though, that was not a concern.

The tape ran out.

PART FOUR

INDIAN
SUMMER

Chapter 25

By the Grave of Ezra Billups

"I think my time is probably up," Brad had said.

Dr. Mahindra had offered an assuring smile.

"That's quite all right. You are my last appointment. But do excuse me for a moment." Leaving his pen and pad in his chair, the doctor rose, stretching his arms and back. "One gets quite stiff from sitting. Would you like to stand?"

"No, thank you."

The doctor went to one of the windows, lifting its green shade enough to see out.

"Some weather moving in," he said.

It was then Brad realized that what he had taken for the sun dropping behind a building had involved, instead, a storm cloud.

The doctor made a short study of the darkening sky and returned to his chair.

"Let's talk a bit more about this man in Vermont," he said. He pulled a clean handkerchief from his back pocket and, unfolding it to the size of a quarter section, spoke as he wiped his glasses. "You say this man was living at the house you believed had once been yours."

"Yes."

"And he claimed he had never heard of your family."

"Right."

Mahindra put his glasses back on and refolded the handkerchief, returning it to his pocket. "Was that the point, Mr. Manford, when you first began to question certain things about yourself?"

"No, not right then. At the time, I thought he was just a cranky old man trying to get rid of me."

"This gentleman, his name was what?"

"Garrett, I believe."

Mahindra began writing. "That was his surname?"

"I assumed it was."

"Did he tell you his given name?"

"No, and I didn't ask him for it."

"What else was said between you and him?"

"I asked him about the Franklins. Tim and Janelle. I told him they had once owned the house, but he said that wasn't the case. I then told him I knew for a fact they had owned it because I had sold it to them, at which point he got testy."

"And said what?"

"That I was full of it, in so many words."

"Because?"

Brad put a hand to his forehead. "Because . . ." Vise-like, he squeezed his temples. "Because he had lived there forty years."

"Do you know that to be true?"

"I was told it was." He dropped the hand to his lap, a restless thumb running back and forth over his fingertips. "You see, after I talked to the old man, we stopped at the local inn. My wife had suggested we rest and have lunch. I hadn't told her what had happened, just that the guy was a jerk and had ordered me off the property. But she could see I was upset. Anyway, at the inn, I took the manager aside and asked him about this Garrett fellow, and he said that, as far as he knew, the guy had lived at the house—my parents' house, if I can call it that—for just as long as he claimed. And he'd never heard of the Franklins. And . . ."

He stopped abruptly.

"And what?"

"And . . ." Brad looked at the floor. ". . . he had never heard of Dr. George Manford. Or Eileen Manford. Or . . ." He made a face as if struck by a sudden discomfort. ". . . Brad Manford."

"But you had been away several years," Mahindra said. "Perhaps this man at the inn came during your absence."

Brad shook his head. "Said he'd lived there all his life."

"And he claimed he did not know you, but did you know *him?*"

"Maybe," Brad said—then reconsidered. "I don't know. I really don't."

The doctor mulled things over. "Did you think this man was lying to you?"

Brad lurched in his chair. "I thought he *had* to be! That, or he was some kind of idiot. I mean, it made zero sense. This was where I grew up. I lived there for eighteen years. My parents knew everyone. Everyone knew *us*. I mean . . ." He threw up his hands. "What else could I have thought?"

The doctor nodded analytically. "What do you think now?"

"Now . . ." Brad let go a heavy sigh. "I don't know what to think."

"But surely you made some further inquiry into this, shall we say, conundrum."

Slowly came a grin—nearly a grimace. "Oh, yes. I made further inquiry."

"Tell me about that," Mahindra said, leaning forward.

Brad covered his face with his hands, rubbing his eyes. He was tired, and the room had grown humid and stuffy—a prelude to the coming storm.

"After we left the inn, I was totally confused. Who wouldn't be? But I still didn't have any doubt about my own sanity. Because I knew what I knew. I mean, we all have things we know are true. We know where we grew up. We know the street we lived on. We know who the people were that raised us. Those things are facts. We don't question those things. And people can tell us otherwise, but we aren't going to believe them."

He looked squarely at Mahindra, then toward the windows.

"I'd been going to do it anyway," he said. "It had been a long time—at least, I thought it had—since I'd been up there. But by then, I wasn't thinking about that. I was thinking more of just somehow proving—not to myself, but to . . . well, I don't know who—that Garrett and the guy at the inn were liars or kooks. Anyway, I went to the cemetery."

For a long moment, he stared blankly into space, saying nothing.

The sound of thunder crossed the city.

"It's up on a hill, and the road is steep and really just a washed-out path, big tree roots growing in the tire ruts. I parked at the bottom and we walked up. It had quit raining, but it was wet and muddy, and a couple of times Sally slipped and almost fell. But we made it."

"And was the cemetery as you remembered it?"

"Yes and no," Brad said, hinting at something. "It's a small ceme-tery. And very old. Some of the graves go back well into the seventeen hundreds. A lot of them you can't even read, the names and dates worn off. But you know what family they belong to because you recognize the names on the stones around them. They're the names of the families that have always lived there. Generation after generation. 'They're bred there, and they're dead there.'" Brad chuckled to himself. "That's what my dad . . ."

With a sudden fright, he stopped mid sentence.

"What about your father?" the doctor pressed.

"I was going to say, 'That's what my dad used to say.'"

"Do you distinctly remember him saying that?"

"No, but I remember being *told* he said that."

"By whom?"

Brad looked about, agitated. "My mother. I could swear."

"Very well."

Mahindra had not written anything for some time. He sat at the front of his chair, his pad and pen on the seat behind.

"So you and your wife were in the cemetery," he said, prompting.

Brad gathered himself as another rumble rattled the windows.

"We were the only ones up there. It was cooling off. Getting cold. Sally had just a light jacket and she was huddled against me. We walked down several rows of tombstones. But I wasn't wasting time. I was going right to it. I knew right where it was.

"In one corner of the cemetery there's a big, fancy marker for a man who got rich running the local mill after the Civil War. *'Ezra Billups. Born June 25, 1831. Died July 25, 1894. Loving Husband and Father.'* That's what it says. And I looked for that stone. Because it was right there . . ."

Brad shut his eyes and drew a deep, trembling breath.

"It was next to Ezra Billups where I stood as a boy when they put my father in the ground. And I stood there when they put my mother in. I *know* I did. And that day with Sally, I went to that very spot, and . . ."

Hanging on the halted thought, Mahindra sat as motionless as a still photograph, his thin face twisted in morbid expectation.

There was a flash of lightening, the window shades flickering vivid green.

"And *what?* What did you find?"

"Two graves."

A wave of rain smacked the building.

"Whose?"

Brad opened his eyes.

"The names were Charles M. and Faye Anne Windsor. They'd been dead a hundred years."

Chapter 26

Homecoming

It was not two weeks. But twelve and a half days was close enough. By its end, Eamon was a fussy, fidgety mess, hating everything about the hospital and letting everyone know it; and Sally, her attitude little better, had the haggard look of a woman who had served hard time.

It was always that way. Regardless of the hospital, the succession of days and nights on the pediatric floor never failed to produce, over time, an unhappy transformation of mother and child. Physically, the boy would improve, but emotionally, he would go another direction. In the process, Sally, too, would become disheartened, her state of mind made all the worse knowing that somewhere in the future waited yet another hospital room.

But she tried to find encouragement, and, in a transitory way, there was good news. Eamon had left the hospital with a relatively clean bill of health. According to the doctors, his cultures were clear, his lung function had returned to a satisfactory level, and his weight was holding steady. All was again well, they said—or as good as could be expected.

However, there were certain things the medical profession could not measure. Things for which it could not test. And Sally could see that there was something—something indefinable—that had been in the boy before his recent illness that was now missing. It was, simply put, an energy. A unique sort of vitality. The sickness, she reasoned, had sapped it away. But she thought that perhaps, in time, it would return.

It would.

The night before Eamon came home brought the first hard freeze of the season, and the next few days were cold and overcast. Sally had not thought the weather conducive to the continuing recovery of a child just released from the hospital; she had kept her son inside. And with a kind of sulking lethargy, the boy took many glances into the back yard, pining for the box of sand that had, in his time away from it, become a disordered, misshapen lump.

But then, quite out of place, came days like those of the previous month. The skies cleared. Temperatures rose well into the seventies. It became a November more common to Southern California.

In the warm afternoons the boy was discharged from the house, and, with a gradually renewed vigor, he restored his sandy world to its previous complexity. He began slowly, moving about with seemingly little purpose, a cold engine off to a sputtering start—but within several days, gaining momentum, running hotter and faster until, in a single afternoon, a network of roads emerged, and in another, buildings of impeccable design sprang up on every street.

To Sally, things seemed as before. The days were calm and sunny. Eamon was happy and hard at work. The hospital was far in the rear view mirror—at times, almost forgotten. (And maybe, she deluded herself—even while knowing better—never to return.)

Other things, too, were the same. The back yard, while having shown recent signs of waning growth, was once more sprouting at full strength, and with strains of AC/DC battering her ears, Sally resumed the task of taming it. Meanwhile, in the commons, a man watched from the trees as she mowed row on row. He watched also as she sat in the gazebo and the boy played in the sand. And he watched long after night had fallen, and in the twilight before dawn.

"Does he ever say anything?" Brad asked.

"No. Not a word."

It was nearly ten. With his tie loosened, he sat on a stool at the kitchen island eating the last of the chicken fettuccini Sally had fixed for dinner. She was unloading the dishwasher.

"It's like he's hiding. He hangs back in the trees, but I can tell he's there. It's weird."

"Well, keep the locks on the fence."

Pulling out the silverware basket, she gave him a heated look. "Brad, I'm tired of it."

"I don't blame you."

"But if what that Renner guy said is true, then that old man is some kind of whacko, and we need to do something about it."

"What do you suggest?"

"Tell him to go away."

"Renner did that."

"Tell him like you *mean* it."

"But Sally, the guy's not breaking any laws. He's in the commons, and he has a right to be there."

Shaking her head, she began an aggressive transfer of knives, forks, and spoons to the nearby silverware drawer. "What about three weeks ago? He was in our *yard,* wasn't he?"

"Maybe. But we didn't actually see him. And Renner went after him tooth and nail. It didn't do any good."

Handfuls of utensils were being treated violently. "Brad, he's *stalking* us."

"Sal, I really don't think he is. I think it's something else."

"God, what a fruitcake!" He could scarcely hear her over the clanging of metal. "I wish we'd have known about him before we bought this damn place."

With a mouthful of fettuccini, Brad quit chewing. "You want me to talk to him?"

The clanging stopped.

"Didn't I say that?"

"Okay, first chance I get."

Chapter 27

T.C.B.

The new credit card had him worried. He had applied online, and somehow, by a stroke of grace—and with the aid of a few less than truthful representations—been approved on his first and only request. But the plastic had not been forthcoming. He had checked twice with the issuing bank and been told both times it was on the way. However, he was suspecting more and more that either it had been misrouted or the bank was having second thoughts. Something had to happen soon, though; Thanksgiving was a week away.

He had been assigned a credit limit of three thousand dollars, which seemed like some kind of miracle—until it occurred to him that the cash advance limit was bound to be less than the total line of credit. It was that way with his other cards, and, sure enough, the fine print in the letter verifying his approval confirmed it was the same with this one. The total cash advance was restricted to one-half of the credit limit. But there was also a daily limit on cash withdrawals such that, if the card was not delivered by Saturday, he would not have time to drain off all the available funds before it became necessary to send payment to L.A.

And there was a further concern: Even if he got the card in time, the bank might very well think something was fishy about it being used for a succession of maximum daily cash advances and shut down the account before he could complete the withdrawal process.

In any event, though, the card would, at most, give him only half of what he needed. He figured that was nothing a payday loan couldn't fix, but the catch there was that the payday people would no doubt want their money back, plus a load of interest, on the date of his next paycheck. Consequently, next month he would be desperately tapping some other source to cover the resulting shortfall.

It was never ending.

If only Ron hadn't shown up, he would be getting by. *Just* getting by, but getting by, nonetheless. But the demands of that blackmailing bastard had, in a mere month, taken him to the edge of financial ruin.

He could not, however, blame it all on Ron. He wanted to. Over time, so much hard-earned income had been paid to that son-of-a-bitch. But Brad knew he had set himself up for this. Sally had been right. The house was a bit much. The mortgage alone—not to mention the furnishings— was a drag on his solvency. And there was absolutely nothing in reserve. Sally still did not suspect that, but it was only a matter of time.

He knew the only sensible thing was to sell. To get something smaller with a manageable payment. Or maybe that apartment she had been ready to settle for. But such things were simply not options. Because he knew also that what he had must be kept; to lose it was to lose himself.

Yet the house—the physical structure—was not the imperative and never had been. It had style, to be sure. And prestige. But had it been just as nice and down the block, he wouldn't have had it. No, it was not the dwelling, but rather, the *place*.

It had been like bringing an object in a lens to perfect focus. It had started after the events in Vermont. Whenever he had gazed at a map of the country, his eyes had moved instinctively to its center. To folks on the West Coast, it was a wilderness. And Wichita, they said, some hick town. But his eyes would go there. Be drawn there. And he felt as if something were drawing *him* there. And finally, the pull had become too strong, and it had taken him to the end of that quiet cul-de-sac, to the plush colonial and its sprawling yard. And cost had been no deterrent. He had wanted the place regardless. He had wanted it because . . .

He could never complete that sentence. He did not know how. Not any more than he could explain why he had uprooted his wife and child and moved them over a thousand miles to a place he had known almost nothing about. But he was here. And now, after only a couple of months, he felt he had been here forever. And he wasn't going anywhere.

Unless, of course, Ron spilled things. If that happened, the house would be gone overnight, and with it, Sally and Eamon. But he was not going to lose any of it. And if more lies were necessary, then more lies it would be. He had reached the point where another deception, another misdeed, really didn't matter. He had long ago filled that bucket to overflowing. In that respect, he thought, he was very much like the man in Los Angeles, who, for six years, had held him hostage.

———————

The card came in Friday's mail at work. Just before noon, he went to a nearby ATM and made a withdrawal, then drove to a payday loan office on the south side of town—far from the firm and where he might run into anyone he knew.

"How long have you lived in Wichita?" the woman asked.

"About two months."

"Well, we generally require that you be at the same residence for three months."

She was rough-looking and, even separated from him by a glass partition, smelled of cigarettes.

"But I'm employed," Brad said. "I'm an attorney. I work for a law firm."

"How long have you worked there?"

"Since I moved here."

"Which was two months ago?"

"Uh-huh."

"I'm sorry, sir, but like with your residence, we require that you be at the same job for three months. And you also need to have had the same checking account for three months, and I'm assuming . . ."

"Here," Brad said, passing a copy of a pay stub under the glass. "That's what I make every two weeks."

Her heavily mascaraed eyes grew big. "You get paid this twice a month?"

"Yes, that's my salary."

"Just a minute."

She took the stub back to a blubbery man sitting at a desk. They spoke for a moment. He gave Brad a long look and said something else, after which the woman returned to the counter and slid the stub back across.

"I'm sorry, sir, but we can't help you today. Like I say, we have rules."

Brad cursed and pushed the stub back at her. "Now look, it is obvious I can repay a loan. I only want fifteen hundred dollars."

"You couldn't get that, anyway, sir. The state only lets us loan five hundred at a time."

"Then I'll take five hundred!"

Startled, the woman looked back to the man at the desk. He stood up, watching Brad closely.

"Sir, I'm sorry," she said.

This had to be a sign of something. Couldn't even get a damned payday loan. Three months? What a load of crap. Yeah, maybe those were the rules. But rules could be bent. He was no transient.

He should have lied, he thought. Just like on the credit card application. And everywhere else.

But would that really have done any good? Clearly, something else had been amiss. He had read it all over that woman. And as he drove back to work, it struck him: A man in a suit. A well-paid attorney. Begging for a paltry fifteen hundred dollar—okay, five hundred dollar—high interest loan.

What had been wrong with that picture?

Undoubtedly, she and her lard-ridden boss had either deduced a gambling problem, a drug problem, or both. But whatever, they weren't going to make it their problem.

He had just returned to his office when Sharon came by.

"Did you get my message?" she asked.

"I don't know. About what?"

"You got a call. Your secretary was at lunch, but since I don't engage in such frivolities, they funneled it to me."

Brad looked at her indifferently. "Who was it?"

"A Mr. Sellers."

"Skip?"

"Yeah. Didn't leave a number. Said he just wanted to check in, and that he'd be back in touch with you soon."

"Terrific."

"Kind of a funny guy. When I told him you weren't here, he asked if you were out 'takin' care of business.'"

Chapter 28

Where Credit is Due

The initial draft of the RightLine purchase agreement was due the following Monday. It was, at best, half finished. And numerous other projects badly needed attention. But he could not bring himself to focus. He spent the better part of the afternoon alternately looking out the window and doodling on a legal pad. He found himself drawing mostly circles. Circles within circles.

Circles he had hung on a wall in a room whose door had remained closed ever since.

Circles whose meaning he could not fathom.

Mis Mundos, he wrote mindlessly at the top of the pad. *My worlds.*

Two circles. Two worlds. A world within a world? And how did that make sense?

He went home early.

He drove with a perilous inattention, lost in the same thoughts that had plagued him all afternoon. There had to be a way out of this. But what was left? Try another payday dealer? Hock something at a pawnshop? Sell his soul to some online loan shark? There were still possibilities, but no good ones. Then again, there never had been.

Even so, he knew that not going to a bank had probably been a mistake. But every time he had considered it, something had held him back. It was the fear, he had told himself, of his fiscal predicament somehow getting back to the firm. Endangering his job. And yes, that was part of it. But he knew there was more. He was, after all, a man of supposedly unimpeachable standing. And such a man simply did not present himself at a respectable financial institution pleading for a trivial sum of money. What would a bank officer think?

Well, most probably, that officer would think much the same as had a tobacco-soaked employee at a certain payday loaner.

There was, however, clearly a way to avoid such ugly supposition. It would take only a sad tale about the overwhelming expense for the gravely ill child at home. That, he thought, would be a tearjerker guaranteed to produce some cash. But it would also be the most disgusting lie of all. He could not sink that far. Not even to save himself. A man did not do that.

In any event, it was too late. Bank loans took time to process, and time was a commodity of which he was in short supply. He would just have to make do with whatever funds he could scrounge from the new credit card and less conventional sources.

But the exasperating thing was that the credit card itself, with its remaining limit of twenty-seven hundred dollars, was, when joined with the three hundred he had already withdrawn, enough—if only he could find a way to convert all of the former to cash.

And yet what was cash? Just something you could spend. Something you could use to buy things. And in that respect, well, a credit card was just like . . .

It was just like cash.

So why wouldn't Ron be satisfied with a nice fat piece of plastic? He would never take a check, because checks were traceable. But a credit card? Hell, as slithery as he was, he could bleed the thing dry before anyone would have a clue.

And then the real genius of it hit him: Report it lost. Not right away. Give it time. Time for Ron to squeeze out the last dollar. Then make the call. *I seem to have misplaced my card . . . What? . . . Oh, no, those aren't my charges.*

Then the bank that issued the card—the one that took so long to get it here—would eat the loss. And a new card would be sent. One, Brad thought, that *he* could use.

He was feeling like a man reborn as he pulled into the drive and hit the remote to open the garage. And entering the house, he had a rhythm in his step that had been missing for some time.

———

Carrying his suit coat, he came into the kitchen, hearing the television from the family room—then, abruptly, not. Going several steps further, he could see her on the couch, sitting before a blank screen.

"Hey, Sal," he said cheerily.

"Hi." She did not seem to share his excitement. "Did you have a good day?"

"I did. At the end, anyway." He wandered toward the couch. She did not get up. "You okay?"

She crossed her arms and looked off. And in the change of light angle, on the side of her cheek, he saw the glint of a tear.

"I need to talk to you," she said.

That quick, the life went out of him—and a single, terrible thought struck his mind.

Ron.

"What . . ." He began to choke. ". . . is it?"

"I got a call about an hour ago . . ."

No, no, no . . .

". . . from Eva. My mom's in the hospital."

His knees about to fail, he dropped onto the far end of the couch, his suit coat falling to the floor. His sense of reprieve was such, he had to consciously form the words: "What's the problem?"

"Oh, you know." There was a small, mournful frown. A shrug of her shoulders. "The way she lives. It's caught up to her."

No doubt the drinking, he thought. But the smoking, too. A quart of gin and three packs a day did not make a healthy blend.

"I have to go out there," she said. "And I'll take Eamon. I know with all you've got going on, you can't take off work to look after him. And he should see his grandma. It'll probably be the last time."

"She's critical?"

"It looks that way." More tears seemed imminent.

He slid down the couch, putting an arm around her. "When will you leave?"

"Sunday, I suppose. And I'm sure we'll be there through the week, which means you'll be here alone."

"That's okay."

"It's Thanksgiving."

"I'll be busy."

"I know, but still." She touched his leg. "I'll miss you."

"I'll miss you, too."

She curled into him. He stroked her hair.

"I never see enough of you," she said. "And now, this. A whole week."

"You don't have any choice. You've got to go. Look, I'll take care of getting your plane . . ."

Again, he almost choked.

. . . *tickets.*

At about five hundred dollars a pop. And she would need money, too.

"What's wrong," she asked.

He had been so relieved by what this conversation was not about, he had completely lost sight of the fact that what this conversation *was* about was leading him right back to the very crisis he had thought averted.

"Brad, what is it?"

"I was just . . . thinking."

"About the plane tickets? I was wondering about that. Can we afford it?"

"Oh, sure. We've got the money."

"Well, there's not much in checking. And I don't think there's much on that card I carry, either, because we put all this furniture on it. I really wish we hadn't done that, but . . ."

She went on. He didn't hear. He was looking out the picture window, into the sky. The blue, open sky.

And he was running. Running from a thing that wanted everything he had. That wanted to eat him, piece by piece. He had run from it for days that had become weeks, and months that had become years. And it never took a rest. Only minutes ago he thought he had thrown it off the trail. But it had been there still. The way it always was. Always in pursuit. Always gaining on him. He could never escape it.

And he was so very tired of trying.

So just stop.

". . . Anyway," she said, "you've got that other card. Is there enough on it to just get us there and back?"

Passing a hand over her soft cheek, he gazed down into her green, watery crystals. And even in their brooding sorrow he found a trace of it: That look. That look that told him who he was and blinded him to all the world but her.

He smiled. "You could use that card," he said, "or we could use money from our investments. But I've got something else." He reached into his back pocket and took it from his wallet.

She drew away. "Oh, Brad, a *third* credit card?"

"Yeah, but it's got a special low rate." Another lie—but a comforting one. "And also . . ." He reached into the wallet. "Here's three hundred dollars."

She looked uncertain.

"Go ahead," he said. "I want you to have it."

She took the card and the money, gripping both in one hand as she hugged him tightly.

"You take such good care of me." She was crying now.

"You need to see your mother."

"You don't even like my mother," she said, a raspy laugh gushing through her sniffles.

"I love you, though," he said, holding her. "Forever."

Chapter 29

Killing Time

Sally slept little the night before. Eamon had never been on a plane, and the prospect of transporting both him and his profusion of medical supplies from Wichita, through a stop in Denver, and on to LAX had her on edge.

Anticipating a hassle, she packed the child's provisions on the assumption that, at some point, someone with a badge would be unpacking them. She put all the meds in a backpack and, with few exceptions, sealed them according to function—antibiotics, bronchodilators, corticosteroids, pancreatic enzymes, nasal sprays—in separately labeled zip-lock bags. One drug that had to be handled differently was a nebulized medication Eamon took only in the morning—a mucus thinner—that required refrigeration. On car trips, she stored it in a small ice chest, but for the purpose of air travel, it would have to chill in an insulated lunch box. No doubt, she thought, the airport cowboys would be just dying to open that one.

But she thought they would be just as interested, if not more so, in the other carry-on—a case containing the therapy vest and its hefty compressor. That bag would also hold the nebulizer gear, the pulse oximeter, and a peak flow meter, all of which, to the poorly trained, might seem like the tools of a suicide bomber.

She had done her best to head off such difficulties, speaking with the airline on Saturday about the boy's medical needs. Given the situation, they had said, there should be no more than a slight delay, but had added that a letter from Eamon's pediatrician, explaining why the child required a traveling pharmacy, might be nice. The doctor had willingly obliged. Even so, she was reconciled to the idea that the TSA screening would be an ordeal.

Then again, that fairly described her expectations for the entire trip—from contending with Eva, to making small talk, day after day, with a shriveled, cirrhotic woman in something other than her right mind. And in a hospital, no less—her favorite place.

The thought of it made her nauseous. She felt for her mother. She was sorry for her. But just the same, she did not want to go. And what good was it really going to do Eamon? Frankly, she did not care if he saw his grandmother again. Better, perhaps, if he didn't.

But as unpleasant as the next week was bound to be, what bothered her most was that this was just not a good time to be away. There was something going on with Brad. She had noticed it since Friday—and, to a lesser degree, for some time before. He had always been the brooding type, deep in thoughts he did not easily share. But this was different. Worse than she had ever seen him. He seemed half dead. Staring off into space and, at times, all but unresponsive. It was not another woman. She was sure of that. And it couldn't be his job; he had those people at the firm eating out of his hand.

Maybe it was money. She knew that between what he earned and what they spent, things were tight. But he had said there was plenty set aside, and he had never lied to her.

That she knew of.

Something, though, was tearing away at him. Something bad.

———

The flight left late afternoon. Brad drove them to the airport. At the ticket counter, Sally checked the suitcase of clothes and toiletries she had packed for herself and Eamon. It was small enough to carry on, but handling a third bag was not an option. Not while keeping track of a six-year-old.

And, fueled by the anticipation of his first plane ride, the boy was in a lively mood. They were moving toward the security checkpoint as he charged ahead, Sally calling after him.

"Eamon! Eamon! Get back here!" Lugging the backpack, she caught and harnessed him by the shoulders. "You have to stay with me," she said between heavy breaths. "Right beside me. All the time. I mean it."

The boy was bouncing like a pogo stick as Brad came up with the other bag.

"I really don't want to do this," she said to him.

He looked at her as if he hadn't heard.

She glanced toward the checkpoint. "I wish you could go with us to the gate."

"Rules are rules," he said.

Eamon tried to dart away. Sally grabbed him.

"I'll call you when we get to Eva's," she said, "and maybe Denver."

"All right."

"Are you working today?"

"I don't think so."

He hadn't worked all weekend. He hadn't done anything.

With Eamon's attention elsewhere, she mouthed the words *Are you okay?*

He nodded.

Clearly, he wasn't. She reached for his hand.

"Dad?" Eamon piped up.

"Yeah?"

"Will you take care of my town?"

"What town?"

"The one in my sandbox."

"Oh . . . sure."

That reminded her. "My God, the yard! I forgot to mow."

"I'll take care of it," Brad said.

"Well, if you can. I'd hate for us to have to pay those people again."

His outburst hit her like a jolt of electricity.

"Dammit, Sally! Stop thinking about the money!"

"Sorry." She felt herself trembling.

Shaking his head, he smiled, weak and apologetic. "So am I."

———

He had, at first, considered just lighting a match. But the problem with a fire was that a good investigator could tell right away if it was arson. He did not want another crime on the list. Also, he had not checked his home-owners policy, but he seriously doubted that Sally could collect anything if the damage was caused by the intentional act of one with whom she jointly owned the house. He hated to think she might lose the equity they had put into the place, not to mention the value of the contents.

But a gas explosion, he thought, was more likely to be seen as an accident. And the house had a gas range. It seemed altogether plausible that a person might inadvertently bump one of the stovetop dials, triggering the gas to a burner, and some time later—whoops—flick a light switch. The amount of methane it would take to level the house, he had no idea. But total destruction was not required. In fact, property damage wasn't necessary at all. He did, however, need some element of tragic mishap. Simply starting his car and sitting in the garage was not going to cut it.

He did not want people thinking he had done it deliberately. It wouldn't matter on the life insurance. He was well past the two-year suicide exclusion. But he just did not want the stigma of it. He wanted something dignified, as a man should have. A fond memory. *Loving Husband and Father.* It had worked for Ezra Billups.

He wondered if they would check his email. If they did, that would mean they suspected something more than an accident, and then they would find his exchange with Ron, which would cook that asshole's goose. He liked the idea of that. But there was a greater downside, because then everyone, including Sally, would learn what Ron knew. He couldn't take that chance. The emails would have to go.

He turned one of the dials on the stove past the point where the electric starter would light the burner. There was a faint seeping noise. He thought there might be some sort of safety shutoff, but there didn't seem to be. Maybe it was broken. Or maybe Mike Renner had just bought a cheap stove.

Wanting to move things along, he turned all four dials to high. The sound of flowing gas became distinctly noticeable. The smell filled the kitchen.

At the kitchen island, he turned on his laptop, accessed his firm email account, found his exchange with Ron, and deleted it. That hurt. The proof was gone. The disgusting creature that had wrecked his life would now go on merrily with his own.

Unless, of course, there was a God. But he had never been one to think much about that.

He told himself to just forget it. Forget it the way he had forgotten so much else.

He wanted no interruptions. He turned off his cell phone and, for a time, sat quietly at the island, waiting, listening to the gas stream from the unlit burners. Gradually, though, he began to discern a bit of a headache, and it occurred to him that if he stayed here much longer, he might be sick to his stomach. Might even pass out before he could get the job done properly. And where would that lead? Death by asphyxiation. That certainly wouldn't do. It would give the wrong impression.

It seemed advisable to just go away for a while—maybe an hour or so—and let things run their course. Let the place fill to capacity. Then, just a little spark . . .

So, how to kill an hour?

That was funny. He actually laughed.

He was feeling light-headed. He went into the garage and breathed deeply. It was better there. But stuffy. What he needed, he thought, was a drive. A long, leisurely drive.

But as he headed for his car, he noticed, in the far corner, the lawn-mower.

That would take about an hour.

And he had promised.

Chapter 30

The Usual Passerby

He did not hurry the job. In fact, he decided to catch all the clippings, which he knew would take considerably more time. He knew also that if he was going to do it right—the way Sally liked—he should trim as well. And it wouldn't do to stop with the back yard; he should cut the front and sides, too. In all, he thought, it would take closer to two hours than one. Maybe longer. He would probably not finish before dark. But it was another nice day, and he didn't mind the extra work.

He started in the back, and as he cut the initial strips around the perimeter his eyes wandered to the empty lots on either side. They were turning brown. The commons looked much the same. All around, the growing season was plainly over.

Over, that was, except within the lush circle that covered so much of his yard and surrounded the sandbox. The cottonwood retained its leafy-green dressing even as the pear trees to the west stood nearly bare. There had to be a reason for it. But he would never know.

His thoughts turned elsewhere, and it occurred to him that people might well appreciate this final act for something other than what it was. Why, they would ask, had he gone to the trouble of mowing—not to mention all that bagging and clipping—if he had been planning something desperate? Such behavior was hardly that of a man bent on a violent end.

Yes, he thought, as impulsive as this had been, it would turn out to be an excellent way of covering for himself.

But he realized it could be even better. What he needed was a witness. Someone just happening by who could later swear to the regularity of his behavior: *No, I didn't notice anything strange about him. We talked awhile. He seemed okay.*

Surely, he thought, on this fine afternoon, sooner or later, somebody would show up.

Somebody did.

———————

Within an hour, two yard bags brimming with grass lay against the fence near the side gate, and Brad was dragging a third toward the others when, from the corner of his eye, he saw a familiar figure emerge from the cedars of the commons.

"I see you're still hard at it," came the chipper greeting.

This was not at all what he had hoped for. A brief, mindless, upbeat exchange—that was what he had wanted. This would not be such a conversation.

You want me to talk to him?

Didn't I say that?

He left the grass bag and went to the commons gate, where the old man waited in a sky-blue baseball cap emblazoned with a silver USAF, his hands in the pockets of his camouflage jacket.

"Hi, Paul. What are you up to?"

Irvin flashed his characteristic smile. "Oh, about five-seven."

"Just out for a walk?"

"Yeah, that's what I do. I haven't seen much of you lately. Been busy?"

"Very."

"See your wife out quite a bit, though. And your son."

"So I've heard."

The remark—and its tone—clearly caught the old man off guard. His smile began to dissipate.

"Paul, look, we've talked a couple of times, but I don't know you very well. And you don't know me. But I need to speak to you candidly about something. And I don't mean to seem like a jerk . . ."

The smile was gone. "Go ahead."

Brad told himself to stop dancing around it.

"I just want to know," he said, "what's the attraction?"

"The attraction? What do you mean?"

"I'm talking about why you're here, Paul. About why you're *always* here. Again, I don't mean to be a jerk, but I'd like to know what's going on."

Irvin pushed his hat up and looked toward his feet. "Now, Brad, I'm not always here. I go different places."

"But you always come back. You stand right here. Or back in the trees. Constantly. And you look at my house. Or my yard. Or . . . something."

Brad felt himself heating up. That was not how he wanted to play this. Appearing overly disturbed could raise suspicions after the fact. (He could hear the old man now: *Yeah, somethin' was definitely wrong. I'd never seen him like that before.*)

He tried to calm himself.

"Anyway, Paul, I think it's a fair question. What's so interesting back here?"

Irvin crossed his arms. "You wouldn't understand."

"Try me."

The old man glanced one way, then the other, rolling his tongue along the inside of his mouth.

"Well, okay," he said. He stalled for another moment, kicking the toe of his hiking boot against the ground. "We've talked about how the grass grows in your yard. And you've seen it for yourself. Do you think it's normal?"

"Probably not. But grass varies from yard to yard."

"But have you ever seen another yard that grows like yours?"

"I really haven't paid much attention. I'm sure there are some."

"Well, let me tell you, there *aren't*. This yard is one of a kind. I've been to every damn state in the Union and half the countries in the world, and I've never seen grass like this."

"And that's why you hang around? To watch my grass grow?"

"Not just the grass," Irvin said. "I assume you've noticed your tree? The one in the sandbox?"

Brad took a glimpse at the cottonwood. "Yeah."

"Have you ever seen a tree grow like that?"

"To be honest, I haven't. But I don't understand how that or the grass, either one, could bring you by here ten times a day. Are you some kind of amateur botanist?"

The old man replaced his hands in his jacket pockets and looked at the ground.

"And please don't tell me about watching the planes," Brad said, gesturing with a nod to the empty sky.

For another moment, Irvin kept his eyes down, sadly shaking his head—then, more resolute, looked at Brad.

"Okay, let's talk about somethin' else," he said. "And I know this question may seem a little crazy, but have you ever heard a peculiar sound in this yard?"

"What kind of sound?"

"It's like a soft hum. Most of the time it's just below all the usual noise, sort of hidin'. But when it's nice and calm, with nothin' to drown it out, well, all at once, there it is."

"I don't know what you're talking about," Brad said. He was ready to move on. The promise had been kept.

"You're sayin' you've never heard that sound?"

"Yes, Paul, I'm saying that."

"You mean you didn't hear it the very first day you were out here? I met you right here at this fence and *I* heard it. I hear it all the time."

"Paul, there are sounds all around."

"Not like *this* sound!" The old man pointed emphatically into the yard. "I can stand across the creek and not hear it. I can stand in front of your house and not hear it. I can even move back twenty or thirty feet from here and not hear it. But if I'm right here, by your fence, and the wind drops, I can *hear* it."

"Meaning?"

"Meanin' it's comin' from your yard. Or under it."

"And just what do you think is making this sound?"

"Hell if I know."

For a short time, neither of them said anything, Irvin catching his breath and Brad, more now than before, wanting to exit the conversation.

"Paul, I really don't want to seem rude, but I have things to do, and I would prefer that you not come by here any more."

Irvin sighed, gazing toward the setting sun. "I knew you wouldn't understand."

"Paul, there's nothing *to* understand. I've got a yard and a tree that are a little overactive, and sometimes you hear noises. Big deal."

"So you've never *seen* anything either?"

"No."

"Nothin' out of the ordinary? Nothin' at all?"

"You mean like a ghost light?" That, Brad knew, had not been necessary. The old man winced, gritting his teeth.

"Sounds like you've been talkin' to my friend Mr. Renner," he said. "And I guess now you're gonna start actin' like 'im."

"Paul, that's not my intent."

"So, what did he tell you about me? And by the way, was that before or after you were too scared to give me the codes to your locks?" He grabbed the padlock and pulled it, the latch of the gate banging against the fence, metal on metal. "Yeah, I suppose that'll keep me out," he said, stomping into the cedars.

Chapter 31

The Garden of Eva

They landed in L.A. too late to make visiting hours at the hospital. The flight from Denver had been weather-delayed.

Eva was in a tiff as she met Sally in baggage claim. "You ought to have your head examined, flying through Denver this time of year."

"Nice to see you, too," Sally said.

Eva's long, once-dark hair sat atop her head in a drooping, salt-and-pepper updo, strands of the formless coif falling in her face and under the collar of her baggy blouse. A well-worn pair of spandex Capris covered her lumpy hips.

She had brought her two youngest. Twelve-year-old Laurel led Eamon by the hand as Derrick, an oversized eighth grader, helped with the luggage.

Derrick sneezed as he slid into the back of Eva's battered Camry.

"Do you have a cold, Derrick?" Sally asked from the front passenger seat.

"No, ma'am," Derrick said.

Eamon sat next to him, within range of whatever germs he might be spewing.

"Is anyone at your house sick?" Sally asked Eva.

Eva seemed annoyed at the inquiry. "Well, I'm not. And they're not," she said, gesturing with her head toward the back seat. "And Tina's moved out."

Tina, Eamon's favorite, had graduated high school two years previous. There had long been friction between her and her mother, but Sally thought the girl's leaving probably had just as much to do with having to share one of Eva's three bedrooms with adolescent Laurel.

Eva cranked the ignition as Derrick sneezed again.

"Are you sure you're feeling okay, Derrick?" Sally said.

"Yes, ma'am, I'm fine. I think it's the air freshener."

What he referred to hung from the rearview mirror in the shape of a crucifix.

"Do you think that smells good?" Sally asked her sister.

"I certainly do. Don't you?"

"Heavenly."

———

Hawthorne wasn't the worst city in Los Angeles County, but with relatively high crime and unemployment, neither was it the best. On the positive side, it was only minutes from LAX, and when Sally and Brad had lived in Santa Monica, it had been a short drive for Tina—when Eva had let her use the car—to come up and babysit. But for Sally, it had no other appeal. It was the kind of place where she had grown up.

Eva had been there since her divorce. She had a mobile home in a trailer park that had its share of both decent and run-down units. She had one of the nicer ones. Their mother, however, who lived in the same facility, did not. Margie had an old, cramped aluminum travel trailer in the slummiest quarter of the park. The place was terminally filthy. Sally hoped not to lay eyes on it.

In the headlights, Sally spotted Eva's mailbox—still marked Rutledge, although in the last couple of years she had gone back to using her maiden name.

They passed the mailbox, not slowing down.

"Where are you going?" Sally asked.

"To Mom's."

"Why?"

"Because that's where you're staying."

"What?"

"We talked about this."

"The hell we did!"

Eva looked over, piously alarmed. "Sally . . ." She glanced toward the back seat. "Your language."

Screw you, Sally thought. Eamon was asleep anyway.

"I did not," she rephrased, clipping her words, "agree to stay at Mom's."

"You most certainly did."

"It was never even mentioned. And do you honestly think I would let Eamon spend the night there?"

"Eamon will stay with me," Eva said. "He can have Derrick's bed. Derrick can sleep on the couch."

"And I can take Tina's bed."

"She took it with her."

"Then I'll sleep on the floor."

"No, because someone needs to stay down here."

"Why?"

"So people know someone's home. Otherwise, they'll just help themselves."

"Eva, there's nothing to take."

"They're Mother's things."

"So I'm the security guard? Forget it."

"Well, I'm just asking you to take your turn," Eva said. "I stayed last night."

No, you didn't, Sally thought. She felt herself about to scream as Eva brought the car to a stop at the street's dead end. Beside the road sat the trailer, its siding peeling away.

"Here you go," Eva said.

"I'm not going anywhere."

Eva narrowed her eyes, drumming her fingers on the steering wheel.

"Just take us to a motel," Sally said. "I've got money."

Eva drummed another chorus as Sally looked back at Eamon, his unconscious head cocked like a crash victim. His day was done.

"He can skip his meds tonight," she said, opening the door. "And tomorrow we're staying somewhere else."

———————

She had called his cell when they arrived in Denver. The call had gone straight to voicemail, so she had tried the house phone. Later, still in Denver, she had again tried both phones. Twice. And she had tried again from LAX.

She had left a message with every call. Surely he had checked one or the other of the phones. So why hadn't he called? And even if he hadn't gotten *any* of her messages, *why hadn't he called?*

Something was definitely wrong. But what to do? It was a quarter of eleven. That made it 12:45 in Wichita. Too late to try again tonight. And it was useless to worry—though, sitting in the stench of her mother's trailer, that was just what she did.

In time, however, one worry was replaced by another: Eamon. It left her restless, being away from him for the night. She had done it only once before. The house-hunting trip to Wichita. Tina had watched him then, in Santa Monica. It was better this time, she told herself. Tonight, he was just down the street. But it was not really the distance; it was the separation. Something about it felt like desertion. A sample of how it might have felt for his mother before. The one who had given him up.

Sally had always wondered if she—whoever she was—had known. If she had learned of his illness and just decided to let someone else deal with it. It probably hadn't been like that. But if it had, then so be it. It wasn't like being lied to by some used car salesman. She refused to think of it that way. She left no room for regrets.

And yet, at times, they found room. She had wanted a child. Her own child. A piece of herself. But that could never be. So, she had gotten the next best thing.

The next best thing.

She was ashamed of herself for thinking like that. For thinking, for even a moment, that she did not have precisely what she had wanted. Yet think it, she did. She could not help it. But that didn't mean she wanted something different from what she had *now*. She would not let herself even consider that notion. Because that would be like trying to wish him away, as if he had never existed. No real mother would ever do such a thing.

Some two hundred yards from where he slept, she could hear, in her mind, his every breath. The smooth flow of air, in and out. He would be fine, she told herself. Eva could handle things. She had sat with him a few times. She knew the danger signs. If things got rough, she would call.

But God, what a bitch.

Eva had a mean streak, but it had never been like this. Exiling her to this hellhole. It was just more proof of what Sally had, over the years, come to understand: Her sister did not like her. Eight years older and adjusted to her status as the only child, she had not welcomed a sibling. In her mind, a competitor. And as the years had passed, displays of envy, though usually subtle, had not been infrequent. It had gotten worse, though, after Bill had left her. They had separated just before Brad had come along. Brad, with his good looks, his charm, his important job. It tortured Eva that her sister could have such a thing, and she could not.

But if only for one night, Eva had her right where she wanted her. Right smack in one of the grimiest dumps on the West Coast.

Still, there was one possible advantage—and only one—to staying here. And after the long day and being nerve-racked over Brad, the prospect of it, as awful and neglectful as it made her feel, had been enough for her to let Eva have her way.

She opened the rusty mini-fridge to find a soggy, half-eaten sub from a convenience store, four eggs, a crusty jar of expired mayonnaise, a similar jar of grape jelly, a large open can of Hawaiian Punch, and a half-full liter of tonic water.

And mold. Lots of mold.

She removed the tonic and began a search below the sink and through the drawers and cabinets in the kitchenette, where she ran across an amalgam of dust balls and dead bugs, a collection of mismatched dishes and silverware, and several cartons of cigarettes—but not what she hoped to find.

Eva had undoubtedly run a sweep of the place. She was always doing that. But her imagination was rather limited.

Along one wall was a short built-in sofa bed. Bleeding yellow foam from its torn cushions, it had been Margie's seat of choice. Very likely, Sally thought, the old woman had kept something there. But she looked under the cushions and even pulled out the bed, only to reveal more bug carcasses and globs of multi-colored hair from a Calico cat that had—the last she knew—run off months ago.

She looked through the surrounding storage cabinets and then in the bathroom—but only briefly; the smell forced her out.

She moved on to the bedroom area. On the bed, the rumpled mass of unmade sheets might have been clean a month ago. Or a year. Their questionable stains offered no clue as to which. But nothing lay beneath.

She was about to look under the bed when, merely in the interest of being thorough, she raised the mattress. And there, on the box springs, tucked in beside two spent cigarette butts, lay an almost full pint of gin.

The tonic was flat, and there was, of course, no lime. But she found enough ice in the freezer to call the thing a cocktail. She mixed it in a dubiously washed Flintstones glass from the cupboard. Years ago, she had downed her share of milk and soda from that glass. Incredible, she thought, that it was still around. Her mother had pretty much lost everything else.

She sat on the sofa bed and drank. Close by, on a metal tray, was a dusty, decrepit television. But her mother had never had cable, and she thought that what might be tuned in via the rabbit ears would not be worth straining her eyes over.

From a short distance away, she heard the sound of squealing tires and, from the same direction, a man's voice. An angry one.

"You piece of shit!"

There were planes, too. Los Angeles Air Force Base was just down the road. Nearer, even, than LAX. The constant air traffic was reminiscent of home.

Home. Yeah. All those miles away. That was home now.

And why hadn't he called?

She checked her cell phone for the time. In Wichita, it was just past one. No, definitely too late. She would have to wait for morning.

She finished the drink and fixed another, returning to the sofa and wondering if tonight—even after the exhausting day—she would have any rest. She did not think so.

She heard a noise as if something (the Calico?) was scratching at the outside of the trailer. And the angry guy was yelling again. There were other voices, too. Growing closer from the lot next door. Men talking in Spanish. Laughing. Cavalier voices flush with alcohol or something stronger.

She contemplated Fred and Wilma on the side of the glass and took a long drink.

She held the phone tightly. It was only getting later.

And the voices were coming closer.

She sat motionless with her arms crossed, the phone against her chest as she heard the raucous conversation approach and pass within several feet of the trailer. The men lingered for a moment and went on.

She looked again at the phone.

Screw it.

She hit speed dial.

There were four rings, then the disheartening sound of her own voice.

"Hi, you've reached the Manfords. At the tone, please leave a message."

PART FIVE

THE
LAST DAYS
OF
BRAD
MANFORD

Chapter 32

Masquerade Obscura

"Mr. Manford," the doctor had said, "a question, if I may."
Brad sat with his face in his hands. Outside, the storm, short-lived
in its fury, was slacking.

"This discovery you made in the cemetery, what was your wife's
reaction?"

Brad looked up. He took a long breath. "She didn't know about it. I
told her my parents were buried on up the path, but that I had changed my
mind about going there. So, we turned back."

"Have you ever spoken with her about the possibility that your parents, as you remember them, never existed?"

"No. She'd think I'm crazy."

"Do *you* think you're crazy?"

"I think I have to be."

Offering no hint of his own opinion, Dr. Mahindra crossed one arm
in front of himself, propping upon it the elbow of the other and resting his
chin on his hand.

"Let's talk, if you please, about memories of things beyond this town
in Vermont. For instance, do you recall leaving there to live elsewhere?"

"I remember going to college."

"Where?"

"Dartmouth."

"For how long?"

"Four years."

"And did you, in fact, attend Dartmouth for four years?"

Brad drew in a shallow breath, exhaling audibly, his shirt dampening with sweat.

"Doctor," he said, "do you agree that whatever we say here is confidential?"

"Certainly. Absolutely."

"No one else will ever know?"

"No one will know."

"I just want to be sure, because I may be about to tell you some things that could get me in a lot of trouble."

The doctor leaned forward, hands on his knees. "You have nothing to fear. Please proceed."

In a way that might have suggested relief under other circumstances, Brad fell back in his chair, tilting his eyes to a point high on the room's far wall.

"When we got back from Boston, I spent a couple of weeks trying to make sense of it. Of course, I couldn't. But I knew one thing: I wasn't who I thought I was. My childhood, my teen years, they were all lies. And I began to wonder what other memories weren't real. I mean, how far did this thing go?

"That's when I hit on an idea. I would have myself investigated. You know, like you would have someone checked out. Someone you didn't trust. So, I hired a private investigator. He wasn't anyone my firm had ever used. I made sure of that." Brad laughed to himself. "You should have seen his face when I told him what I wanted him to do."

"And what exactly was that?"

"To look everywhere, under every rock. To take nothing for granted." He shifted to the front of the chair, bending toward the doctor. "I had him start with Dartmouth. I gave him a list of people I remembered. People I knew. Classmates. Professors. Everyone I could think of. I told him to track them down. To find out who remembered Brad Manford. And do you know what? *Nobody did.* He talked to eight people. None of them had ever heard of me. Then he talked to five or six people I remembered from law school. Same thing."

The doctor flexed one side of his mouth in a half frown, seeming, suddenly, the skeptic.

"But just a moment," he said. "You're saying these are real people. Not people, if you will excuse me, as you remember your supposed parents, but *real people*. And they didn't remember you. But what does that prove? The fact is, *you* remembered *them*. So you must have known them in some capacity. And how would that be possible if you had not attended school with them?"

"But all those people, they wouldn't just forget me."

"Can you be so sure? Do you remember these persons as close friends?"

"Well, not really."

"Do you remember having *any* close friends in college?"

"I really don't. But are you saying I went through four years at Dartmouth and three more at Franklin Pierce Law Center without making the slightest impression on anyone? That I drifted through seven years of college like some kind of ghost? Do I seem like that kind of person to you?"

"Quite frankly, no, but . . ."

"Look, you think it's no big deal that I remember people—real people—who don't remember me. But I also remember a yellow, two-story house with blue trim in North Frederick, Vermont. I remember it to the last detail. And that's real, too. But my memories of it are not."

Mahindra nodded, conceding, for the time being, the logic of it.

"And this investigator," Brad went on, "he found no record that I had ever lived in any of the apartments or student housing that I remember. He found no record that I had ever held a Vermont or New Hampshire driver's license. He couldn't even find a birth certificate for me. Not anywhere."

Through the tapping of gentle rain, the doctor sat deep in thought, pulling at his lips as if hoping to extract something of value. Shortly came an idea.

"You mentioned housing," he said. "You must remember, at some point, having a roommate?"

"No."

"A girlfriend?"

Brad nearly came out of his chair.

"No! Can't you understand? *I wasn't there.* If I had been, someone would have remembered me. And there would be a photograph. A picture in the yearbook. *Something.* But there are no pictures of me during my supposed college years. Just as there are no pictures of me before that. And I have no diplomas. I've looked everywhere. I don't have one. And if I didn't go to college and law school, then . . ."

He stopped himself.

"Then what?"

At the edge of the chair, his knees splayed out, Brad let his head drop. He spoke toward the floor.

"If I didn't go to college and law school, then I don't legally have a license to practice law."

"Do you believe that to be the case?"

"I'm certain of it."

For a few seconds, Mahindra tapped his pen on his notepad, formulating his next line of thought.

"Mr. Manford," he said, "legal or not, I assume you *have* a law license."

"Yes."

"And isn't it true that to be a licensed attorney in this state, one must take and pass a rather lengthy and difficult examination?"

"Yes."

"And did you take and pass that examination?"

"There's a record that says I did."

"Do you remember it?"

Brad looked at the doctor. "I'm not sure."

"Why aren't you sure?"

"Because my memory of it, if I can call it that, is so incredibly vague. It's almost like somebody just told me what happened, like I wasn't really there. Or like, I don't know, like it's someone *else's* memory, if that makes any sense."

"But Mr. Manford, that memory, however limited it may be, is in *your* mind."

"I know, but . . ."

"So the fact is, you have at least some recollection of taking that test. And according to you, there is documented evidence that you *did* take it. And that you passed it. And that being the case, how do you believe that you were possibly able to pass such an arduous examination covering diverse legal principles without ever setting foot in a law school?"

"Do you think I haven't asked myself the same question?"

"Well, perhaps you got lucky," Mahindra said, tongue-in-cheek. "Miraculously lucky. But that aside, in order to even sit for that examination, weren't you first required to present verification of the proper educational background?"

Believing his point made, the doctor, pen and pad in his lap, calmly awaited a response.

"College transcripts," Brad answered with a gloomy grin.

"Correct. No doubt, the California bar examiners received something along those lines, true?"

"Yes," Brad said, "they did. And I have seen those transcripts. One from Dartmouth. One from Franklin Pierce. They both look very official. But they aren't. They're fabrications. It's obvious."

Mahindra closed his eyes, shaking his head in frustration. "I don't understand."

"Then I'll try to explain. And let me emphasize the word *try*." Brad stared into Mahindra's thick glasses. "Doctor, do you know anything about social security numbers?"

"I know a person in this country can't do much without one."

"But do you know anything about what the numbers mean? The nine numbers that make up a social security number?"

"I'm afraid I do not."

"Well, I learned something very interesting about that from this investigator. He told me that the first three numbers are a code for the state where the social security number was issued, and the next two numbers contain a code that tells you *when* the number was issued."

Mahindra cut in. "Mr. Manford, a thought crosses my mind. Do you have a social security card? Because if you do, it could be very helpful in finding out . . ."

"Oh, I have one," Brad said. "I gave the number to the investigator. And it turns out, it's a valid number. It's *my* number, issued to Bradley Manford."

"That's the key, then! You can use that number to find out where you've been, and what you've . . ."

Brad shook him off. "I've tried that. Or rather, the investigator did. But the information he was able to obtain was somewhat incomplete. Because, you see, he found that the number was not issued in Vermont, the state where I was supposedly born. It was issued right here in California."

"Really?"

"Yes. And it was issued only five years ago. The same year I *supposedly* took the bar exam."

Mahindra's head moved backwards. "A replacement," he proposed. "You must have required a new number. Your identity was stolen."

"No. That social security number is the only one ever held by anyone answering my description. And even stranger, it was apparently issued without any sort of formal request. There is no application on file."

The doctor absorbed this with some difficulty. He adjusted his glasses and scratched his head.

"Strange, indeed," he said. "But how does any of that relate to the forgery of your college transcripts?"

Brad spoke slowly, expressionless. The last of the lesson.

"Every college transcript contains certain information that identifies the student—either a student ID number or a social security number. My transcripts bear my social security number. But it is the number I obtained five years ago, *after* I had supposedly graduated from the schools issuing the transcripts."

Mahindra glanced about his office, seeming disoriented. He started to speak.

"How . . ." A false start. "But . . ." Another one.

For some time, the doctor sat in quiet contemplation. The storm was over, and the only sound was of water dripping on the window ledges.

Chapter 33

El Monstruo

He had a theory. He had tried to explain it.

The whole thing had been intended as an elaborate deception. A collection of fabrications mixed with just enough truth to create—for reasons unknown—a false persona above suspicion.

He had stories about the town where he claimed to have grown up—a real town, if anyone had the inclination to look on a map. But a town very small and far away. A place so obscure that the tales he told about it would never be scrutinized.

He had stories, too, about people he claimed to have known in other places. Real people who others might know, whose names he could drop. And if he should run into them, so what? They wouldn't remember him, but they might pretend to. Either way, though, it didn't matter, because no one was going to seriously question who he was. He had learned his lies to perfection.

It was all so believable. So believable, in fact, that at some point, he himself had started believing it. Maybe just a little at first. But then, something had happened. Something that had caused his belief to fully and finally trump reality.

And if you are correct, the doctor had said, then what of your former self?

That's what I'm trying to find out.

In order to return to another life?

No. Never. I want what I have. My wife. My son.

Mahindra had smiled.

And quite rightly. Ah, Mr. Manford, now listen. You may believe you have lapsed into some dissociative state. Become another person. But such a malady is exceedingly rare, and its victims do not suddenly assume well-paid professional identities for themselves. They wander about confused. They know neither who they were, nor who they are. They do not magically receive social security numbers and high-level college degrees. And they most certainly do not make such arrangements for themselves in advance of switching personalities.

You don't believe me.

I would merely urge you to consider another possibility. Consider, Mr. Manford, for a moment—just consider—that you have always been precisely who you believe you now are, and that your memories of growing up and going to college are, in fact, real. And that the other things—the things you have related about your trip to Vermont, and this investigator and everything he has supposedly told you—are merely, shall we say, delusions. Fantasies much like the disagreeable dreams and thoughts you described earlier.

The doctor had looked at his watch.

It is rather late, he had said.

A fantasy? The old man at the house? The man at the inn? The cemetery?

Bullshit.

And Ron Delvechio? That bastard was damn sure no fantasy. But what use had there been in prolonging things with a show of indignation? Or, for that matter, in seeking out another therapist?

In a seedy part of town, he sat in his car in a dark parking lot, his fingers sliding over the wrinkled envelope, the single word in its top left corner barely visible—but burned in his mind.

MEXICALI.

He pulled out the folded paper. In his muddled thinking, he had almost forgotten about this loose end. What a disaster that would have been. He'd had every intention of ripping it up in that Chicago hotel room. He had promised himself then that he would never look at it again. But there had been another time. And another.

And now, tonight.

As always, it was shouting at him.

Se Busca!

Recompensa!

US $50,000!

He examined the sketch in the pale illumination of a faraway streetlight, looking, as he always did, for something inconsistent. Something by which he could convince himself that the image was not what it seemed.

Of course, a drawing was hardly proof of anything. No better than a cartoon.

Yet he could not deny it.

It was his chin.

His cheeks.

His nose.

His eyes.

Ron may have believed it, too. But for a mere fifty grand, it just wasn't worth chancing a call to Mexico. Because to Ron, this was the proverbial gift that kept giving.

The Mexicans had so little evidence. Nothing, really, but this poster. This mysterious face. And to turn in some gringo and possibly be told he could not be connected to the crimes, well, that might put an end to the gravy train. But the way it was now, with Ron taking a few thousand every so often, it was like a credit card without a limit. A means by which he could ultimately gain far more than the bounty offered.

But then, Ron knew about other things. He knew about obtaining a law license under false pretenses. Fraudulent acquisition of college degrees. Fraudulent acquisition of a social security card. And fraud in connection with every other representation ever made by the person claiming to be Brad Manford.

There was even fraud in the adoption of a certain child. Ron had his fingers deep in that one, too, but it was something neither of them talked about. Brad had just been so anxious to give Sally what she wanted. What she could not have otherwise.

She had never known.

He looked hard for what he told himself was the last time. He could not stand the sight of it. He wadded it up and held it tight in his hand.

The clock on the dash read nearly three a.m.—well past time for getting this over with. But he had taken that long drive, after all. And one thing had led to another. He had no sooner left the neighborhood before his thoughts had turned to food. How he could possibly have had such a thing on his mind, he had no idea, but once he did, a last meal had seemed obligatory. On the other hand, with less than five dollars in his pocket, there had been no opportunity for a sumptuous final indulgence. He had pulled into a Taco Bell.

After, he had driven north on I-135, out of the city some fifteen miles before jogging west and heading back south on Highway 81, which, as he hit the city limits, became North Broadway.

It was not a choice part of town. He had passed crummy-looking buildings, a dusty jumble of railroad tracks and cars, the graffitied skeleton of a closed and moldering pet food plant, and all along the way a series of darkly lit side streets and alleyways, each, it seemed, holding the promise of some ill-fated encounter.

He had continued on, through the heart of downtown, with its mostly low and mid-rise buildings. Beyond were dozens of used car dealerships and a succession of dumpy motels, hole-in-the-wall bars, and pawnshops. Some five miles south of downtown, just short of 47th Street, he had turned around at a strip mall and gone back north up Broadway, occupying himself by counting car lots. By the time he had again reached the business district, the total was forty-eight.

Perhaps, he had thought, he would go back and count the motels, too. But he had known what that was about. He was just putting it off. Stalling for time. But what of it? He was calling the shots. And if he wanted to stall, he would stall.

And so, he had. He had stalled his way all over south Wichita. And now he sat here, behind a church, facing a side street with his lights off and the car idling. The night was cold. Just below freezing. He'd had the heat on high, though, for some time. He was hot and low on gas.

He turned off the car and released his hold on the crumpled poster, smoothing it out for another viewing. The last time, he told himself.

Se Busca! Se Busca! Se Busca!

It never stopped shouting.

Yes, this was the last time. This was it. And now he would get rid of the damned thing once and for all. But where? One did not just casually dispose of such an item.

There was a large dumpster sitting in the shadow of the church, thirty paces away. That would work, he thought. Reduce the thing to a jigsaw puzzle and let it mingle with the refuse.

He got out of the car, tearing the paper as he walked. By the time he reached the dumpster he had turned one piece into sixteen. But they all needed tearing once, maybe twice, more. He was working on that when headlights bounced into the parking lot. There was the sound of an engine revving and tires grinding on asphalt as the vehicle swerved toward him.

Red and blue lights whirled. He was caught in a spotlight.

"Stay right there!" said a voice from a speaker.

He froze for a moment, then gave the papers another tear.

"Do not move!"

The cop got out of his vehicle. He was a hulking, broad-shouldered man with a shaved head, walking tall and tough.

"Good evening, sir," he said, approaching, his features hidden behind the beam of a flashlight. "May I see some identification?"

Brad quivered, his foggy breath clouding the beam of light. "I don't have any."

"What's your name?"

"Skip Sellers."

"And what are you doing out tonight, Mr. Sellers?"

"Nothing much."

"Is that your vehicle over there?"

"No."

The officer shone his light on Brad's right hand. "What are you holding there, sir?"

"Just some paper."

"May I see it?"

Brad tightened his grip and put the hand in the pocket of his jacket. "No."

Wasting no time, the cop gave Brad a push. "All right, turn around, spread your legs, and place your hands above your head, fingers together. Right now!"

Pivoting, Brad left the shreds of paper in his pocket and started to comply. In the same moment, the officer glanced down to pull a handheld radio from his belt. It was the smallest of openings.

Brad took it.

All in one motion, he spun back around and brought a forearm crashing into the man's thick neck, driving it down between head and shoulder, into the throat, as hard as he could.

The blow took the man to his knees.

"Oh . . . Jes . . ."

In the next instant, a flat-footed kick to the face. It caught the cop squarely in the mouth and nose and sent him over backwards, his nasal bone shattered, broken teeth dribbling over the asphalt.

The big man moaned as blood gushed and dripped. He writhed in its puddles. It clouded his eyes.

Brad, about to bolt, saw the man groping at his waist, fingers searching for his service revolver. He sent a foot hard to the kidneys, and another to the ribs. With the latter came a dull, cracking sound, and a high-pitched, helpless cry.

Seconds later, the man lay silent, seeming as lifeless as the bloodied pavement.

"I'm sorry," Brad said. "I really am."

But sprinting to his car, he was thinking something quite different.

———————

For three blocks he did sixty in a forty. He ran every light. He shouted and pounded the steering wheel.

He was in awe of himself. He had taken down a man almost twice his size. And it had been so effortless. So instinctive.

And he had not thought once about the injuries he was causing. Or the pain. He had felt no more for the victim than if he had been squashing a bug.

And if he didn't slow down, he thought, he would soon be attracting more of them.

He let off the accelerator and pressed the brakes, bringing the car to an innocent speed. Minutes later, he took the on-ramp to US 54, heading east.

Heading home.

And by then, depressingly, the excitement was over. He was again the man he knew. The one he could no longer live with.

Clearly, it need not have come to this. If only he had settled for passing his days in ignorance. But he had been so desperate to know things. His craving for the truth had made him reckless. So much that hiring Ron Delvechio had actually seemed like a good idea. But of the zillion P.I.'s in L.A., he had managed to pick the least scrupulous. He had not even asked for a reference.

The meeting had occurred only days after his visit to Mahindra. Ron had pulled the paper from his desk drawer, withholding it theatrically as he set the stage.

Still looking hard for clues, partner. Been looking under every rock, just like you said. But you know, it's not cheap.

I'll pay you. Just tell me what you've got.

Oh, I'll get to that in a minute. But first let me tell you a little story about some things that happened a while back, down in Mexico.

He felt queasy, just as he had that day in Ron's office. He lowered his driver's window partway, letting in a blast of cold air.

It went on for months. The most depraved and senseless shit in the history of Mexico—and let me tell you, that's saying something. The Federales were all over it, but they couldn't catch this psycho. The locals were scared out of their fucking minds. Thought he must be some kind of demon. Started calling him the Mexicali Monster.

He was feeling worse. He thought about pulling over.

So, what does this have to do with me?

Where were you six years ago?

That's just it. I don't know.

I do.

Brad reached into his pocket and grabbed one of the torn bits of paper. He held it up, momentarily pulling his eyes from the road to examine it. By way of passing streetlights he could, intermittently, see well enough to read. But the scrap held nothing legible. Not even a decipherable image. A mere splotch of black on white.

He let it fly out the window, into the night, then went back into his pocket and pulled out another and another, converting piece after piece to haphazard road litter.

Take a good look, Manford. Take a real good look. See the resemblance? It's you, pal!

Ron had laughed. A mocking, pitiless laugh that would become all too familiar. Before that laugh had stopped, Brad had thrown up in a bathroom down the hall.

And now, directing the car from the middle lane of traffic, he stopped, flung open the door, and did the same on the shoulder of US 54.

As he caught his breath, he let go the last of it. A semi whizzed by, the pieces sucked into its slipstream. Gone forever.

But he heard their message, still.

Se Busca!

Recompensa!

EL MONSTRUO DE MEXICALI!

Chapter 34

Air Supply

He half expected the place to be gone. He had been away over nine hours. In that time, he thought, even the tiniest spark would surely have done it.

But as he grew nearer, he saw no glow in the distance. No fire trucks. No news vans.

The house stood as it always had.

Waiting.

The car's headlights shone on the garage door as he pulled into the drive. Without thinking he pushed the remote opener—then prepared for the worst; with a houseful of flammable gas, he knew it was precisely the thing he should not have done.

Yet, without incident, the door went up.

The garage held only a suggestion of it. But as he entered the house, the odor was overpowering. He reminded himself not to turn on any lights. Not yet. Ultimately, he would. But first he would turn off the stove burners and change into his bedclothes. He had decided that would be the best way, the most convincing way, to make it look like an accident. Like there had been a gas leak and, awakening to the smell, he had simply gone to investigate.

In the kitchen, the hissing from the stove confirmed that the burners were still pumping out their lighter-than-air product. But in his absence, there had nevertheless been a change: In the otherwise pitch black, a small red "5" flashed on the answering machine.

It made no sense. The ringing of a phone—the mere electrical activation of the sound—should have sent this place up in a mushroom cloud.

He could not imagine why it hadn't.

He felt his way over to where the phone sat on the built-in desk. For a while he stood motionless, a hand beside the machine. It was her. It had to be. And just to hear her voice, one last time . . .

But he knew if he turned on a light, things would go boom. And how would hitting playback be any different?

He pulled out the chair at the desk and sat staring at the blinking number. Five calls. He tried to imagine each of them. It was all he had left of her. Just make-believe.

And, of course, memories.

He wanted to think of them all, from first to last. But he could not get past the beginning. That story she had told Charley Miller. His memory of it was so very different than that of things before. Different, certainly, than his artificial recollections. But different, too, than his blurred memories of real, but earlier, events—the dim, detached impressions of someone, it seemed, merely claiming to be Brad Manford.

But in time, less and less a pretender.

Then, that day. In a building. A glass atrium. Warm in the morning sun. The sound of his heels on marble. Pushing a button. Hearing an elevator ding. Stepping into the car.

And, with a growing clarity of mind, going up. And floor by floor, the last remnants of another life, another existence, falling away. Pieces no longer wanted or needed. Rising ever closer to the end of something. The birth of something else.

The car stopping.

And with the parting of the doors, a crowd in a bustle. People talking. Shutters clicking. And the collection of everything—lights, eyes, cameras—converging on a white couch.

And on the couch, a woman. An angel in tight pants. Bikini top. Stiletto heels. On hands and knees. Lean, bare back arched and denim-covered hips jutting round and firm.

And above the clamor, a voice loud and distinct: *Gimme that look, sweet Sally. C'mon, babe, you know that look.*

But with the sound of the elevator, she had turned her gaze. And in that instant—that split second—the one he had been vanished completely.

She had given him that look.

How long had he been sitting here? Had he been sleeping?

He glanced around in the dark, his head heavy and throbbing. The number on the answering machine had become but a clouded dot. From the stove, the hissing continued, but a room that had once reeked like a bucket of rotting eggs now seemed quite tolerable.

He pushed back in the chair to stand and suddenly—oh, what was this?—he was tipping over. He caught himself, but there was a dizziness far worse than anything he had felt when he had first spun those burner dials so many hours ago.

Then, an increasing need for air. At once, he was panting, unable to draw much in. He groped for the kitchen island. Finding it, he steadied himself and came to the alarming realization that he did not have much time.

In a sluggish panic he moved along the island toward the stove. Get the burners off, he thought. Get them off, then get upstairs. Change clothes. Pull down the bed covers. Make it look good. You can flip a switch in the hall. It'll be thicker there, anyway. More concentrated.

If that was possible.

He was feeling a separation from the room. A floating sensation. He wanted to sit down again. Or lie down.

But he knew what would follow. No, he had to get upstairs. And he had to hurry.

Gasping, he fled the kitchen and fell over a chair in the dining room. The chair fell with him. Fumbling about, his hands found it lying on its side. He braced against the edge of the seat and pushed himself up, stumbling in the direction of the staircase until running smack into its big square newel post. The impact took him in the chest and stomach, knocking out of him what little wind he had.

Bent double, he tried catching his breath, but it was useless. By the second, a kind of unseen grip—something like the squeeze of a killer snake—wrapped him tighter and tighter.

Halfway up the staircase his lungs turned white-hot, screaming for a puff of anything breathable. He staggered and fell back, grabbing the railing to save himself. His legs wobbling, he dropped to his knees. On all fours, he resumed his ascent, first wheezing, then groaning, then howling until, at the top, there was nothing. No voice. No means of moving anything in or out.

In the upstairs hall he began to resign himself. The master bedroom was still far. Too far. He crawled like a worm. His mind shutting down. Lights flickered and burst before his eyes.

He clawed at the carpet, dragging himself by inches. A moment later, all but stopped, his limp hands flopped vainly about, one thrashing the floor, the other banging the wall.

Or not the wall?

The sound was that of a door. A closed door.

With what little he had left, he raised himself on one elbow, a hand flailing for the knob, fingers brushing over it. Then, in a last effort, taking hold. Twisting. Pushing.

The door stuck a bit as it opened, its bottom swishing flush against the carpet. He dumped himself through the threshold, parts of him—a shoulder, his head, a hand—finding the door's far side. Falling against it. Slamming it shut.

He could breathe again.

Chapter 35

Sanctum Sanctorum

He lay sprawled, face down, his lungs heaving in desperate reflex as he felt himself moving back from the brink. But as he went on gasping and choking, his arms and legs still all but unworkable, he began to understand that the air here was only slightly better than in the hall. And what little oxygen there was, he was using fast.

Groping in the dark, he again found the door and, from that point of reference, writhed about until he had turned himself the opposite way; then, on knees and elbows, drove himself forward, his head dragging the carpet like a ball on a chain. With the struggle, his breathing grew yet more frenzied and he heard a sound almost like a man crying as he bumped drunkenly into the corner of something solid and wooden, and then, veering away, bumped something else. A wall, perhaps.

But ahead, filtered through the half-open slits of a louvered blind, came faint strains of light, and with his chest afire, he flung himself into the scattered glow, his head lagging and his hands scratching up a wall until his fingers found, at last, a window sill.

Standing on his knees, he thrust his shaking hands under the blind, pushing with everything he had at the bottom pane of the single-hung window. The thing refused to yield. It was latched. But where? In the shadowy dark, in his pain and panic, he couldn't figure it out.

But with a fist—and a force as great as he had used to fell a man an hour before—he solved the problem.

From behind the metal blind came a shattering, and the sound of glass falling in shards against the storm screen and window ledge. And then, pouring through the jostling louvers, like a wave of ice water in a desert, a surge of night air washed over him. He took it in gulps, ravenous for every breath, feeling it cool the flood of sweat on his face and neck. Feeling his pulse run fast and shallow, and then, as relief came, slower and stronger, his head pounding with every beat.

He was healing. He gave himself a few moments longer before feeling to his right for the chair he knew was there. With both hands on the seat, he pushed himself up and onto it.

He tugged the lift chord to raise the blind, bringing in more air. He noticed then, over his shoulder, a full moon on the rise, and in its soft light he fell back and shut his eyes, bathing in the cold November breeze.

He had come so close, he thought. So very, very close. But as his mind replayed the chaos of events, he was struck with a realization of the utterly ridiculous: He could have simply opened a door downstairs. Walked outside. Caught his breath.

And there was another oversight: Those burners he was going to turn off? They were still spewing gas.

Clearly, he had not been thinking straight. A product, no doubt, of the oxygen deficit.

But then, his thinking had been bad for a long time. It had started with the idea of moving to a place for reasons he could not explain and buying a house he could not afford. And it had continued with the purchase of items such as this very expensive desk he sat behind. Two months ago he had bought it new, and since, it had sat, like the rest of this room, unused.

A waste, he thought. All of it.

He opened his eyes, and in the pale light could just make out the print of Dali's work on the far wall, its blue, shadowed clocks wilting like cheese under heat. And on the wall to his left, in two ascending rows, hung his Big Sur photos of Sally and Eamon, the glare of moonlight obscuring a part of each picture. Yet, with some effort, he could imagine what he could not see.

The boy was in every frame, looking sick and frail. He was so different now. Bigger, broader, rosy-cheeked. Not perfectly healthy. But a child, nonetheless, very unlike the one depicted here.

And in the nearest picture, the child in her arms, her eyes met the camera. Green gems calling like a siren. There were no other eyes like that.

Gimme that look . . .

That look, that in so many ways seemed like an answer to his every question.

And the lips. The scent. The curve of her back and hips.

His fingers moved impulsively, as if to hold something, to caress it. He could feel her flesh in his hands, her warm breath in his ear.

Hey, boy.

Turning his head, he almost called her name.

Dali's clocks stopped him. There, on the wall, they served notice of reality. Or some version of it.

The Persistence of Memory.

But what, really, did that mean? Memories, after all, were of two kinds. The memories of a woman—of her eyes, of her touch, of many touches—those were of one type: The undying reflections of things past. *True* memories.

There were also, however, memories not so true—yet just as persistent. Memories that were, in fact, not memories at all, but mere imitations. Years upon years of pseudo-recollections no more genuine than a Hollywood film. Thoughts woven into an elaborate, fictional backstory that masqueraded as the history of the one calling himself Brad Manford.

MIS MUNDOS.

Those simple words, embedded by a finger into the room's other so-called piece of art, were as enigmatic as Dali's title. And the symbols below—those circles—far more mysterious. Yet he—or perhaps more accurately, someone claiming to be him—had put them there. Most certainly, they meant something. A cryptic message from his former self. But its import was lost. That memory had not endured. It had gone the way of so many others. Into nothingness.

He thought, as he had so often, about those lost years. Of all that had been forgotten and nearly forgotten. Of acts immoral and hideous. Of another man with other motives. A base creature. A thing he could only hate. But for the first time, here in this place he had made for himself, in this sanctuary, he was beginning to understand that such thoughts were inherently pointless. They always had been. Because all that mattered—all that would ever matter—was right now. Who he was in this moment. And having those things that a man should have. And keeping them.

Keeping them.

In the now cold and airy room, he felt his mind clearing, a resolve building. It was time, he thought, to turn the burners the other direction. To reverse this madness and put things as they should be. As they were meant to be.

He stood, and as he did, the room darkened. The moon, it seemed, had been masked by a rolling cloud.

But he turned and saw only black sky and twinkling stars. There was no moon. There never had been.

He looked down into the back yard. Something was moving. A light sailing atop the grass.

———————

In the first light of morning, birds chirping, he sat on the top step of the deck stairs, waiting with tired, swollen eyes as Paul Irvin emerged from the commons.

Abruptly aware of Brad's presence, the old man came to a hard stop.

"Paul."

Irvin did not answer.

"Forty-eight, twenty-nine, seven."

"What's that?"

"That's how you get through the gate. Want some coffee?"

Chapter 36

Coffee Talk

Irvin came up the deck stairs to the open door, hesitating at the threshold. In the kitchen, Brad was scooping Folgers into the Mr. Coffee.

"Come in, Paul. Have a seat."

The old man entered, looking warily about as he removed his cap and half unzipped his jacket.

He raised his nose in the air. "Smells like gas."

"It's from the stove," Brad said. "One of the knobs got turned by accident. I've got the windows open."

Leaving the door ajar, Irvin sat on a stool at the kitchen island. "Lucky you're still around," he said, his breath showing in the cold room. "It doesn't take much of that stuff to send a guy on his heavenly ride."

"Really?"

"Yeah, in fact, as little as a five percent concentration'll do it—along with, of course, a spark of some kind. But then again, that five percent can take a while to build up, dependin' on the configuration of the space and all."

"I guess asphyxiation's possible, too," Brad said, filling the carafe from the sink.

"It is. But what most people don't understand is that if you're suffocatin' from natural gas, you're already way past the point where it'll explode."

Brad stopped short of pouring the water into the coffeemaker. "What do you mean?"

"Well, like with anything flammable, natural gas needs oxygen to burn. And you can reach a point where there's so much gas and so little oxygen that the gas won't ignite. But even then, there won't be enough gas to asphyxiate a person. That takes a whole lot more."

Brad put the carafe down. "So you're saying that the more gas you have, the less likely it is to blow up?"

"In a way."

"And if there's so much gas that you're suffocating, it *can't* blow up?"

"Oh, definitely not."

"You're sure about that?"

Seeming more at ease, Irvin chuckled. "Brad, I didn't graduate from the Air Force Academy for nothin'."

Embarrassed, Brad poured in the water, thinking that in Irvin's tutorial quite probably lay the explanation for why none of those phone calls had leveled the house.

He looked over at the answering machine, its red "5" still shining, its messages, amid the confusion of other events, still unheard.

He turned on the coffeemaker.

"You know, Paul," he said, "I owe you an apology for the way I acted yesterday."

Irvin waved a hand. "Naw, skip it."

"No, really."

"Let's just chalk it up to a misunderstandin'."

"Yeah, well, to be perfectly honest, that's exactly what it was." Brad gave the old man an insightful look. "You tried to tell me, and I wouldn't listen, but a few hours ago . . ."

Irvin's eyes came alight. *"You saw somethin'."*

"I did."

"What?"

"A light. It was just . . . floating."

A smile swelled the old man's face. "Like a *ball* of light?"

"Yeah."

"About the size of a grapefruit?"

"Maybe. I wasn't that close. I saw it from an upstairs window and ran down to get a better look. By that time, it was gone."

Irvin slapped the granite counter like a man whose horse had come in.

"By God, I thought I'd never see the day!" He laughed, slapping the counter again. "Some crazy old fool, huh?"

"If you're crazy, we both are."

"Oh, but we're not. We're just fine, you and me." Crossing his arms,

Irvin sat back with a wide grin, vindicated.

"Paul, I'm sorry I doubted you."

"That's all right," the old man said, his smile waxing.

"So what do you think it is?"

The elation waned. "Brad, I don't want you to go back to thinkin' I'm some kind of mental case. I really don't. But I've been watchin' this thing for three years, and bein' a military guy, it strikes me that it may be some kind of probe or surveillance device. Or maybe—and I know this sounds even more bizarre—maybe some sort of intelligent life form."

Brad nodded impassively. "How often do you see it?"

"There's no regularity. Sometimes it'll show up every night, and sometimes once a week. Sometimes, too, it's there in the evenin' or early mornin'. I've even seen it a number of times in broad daylight. But since you moved in, it's been there a lot. More than before, I'd say."

"You know," Brad said, "I think my wife may have seen it. But only once. And I've never seen it till this morning. If it's there so much, why haven't we noticed?"

"'Cause you're not lookin' for it. You're not payin' attention. Lord knows how many things happen in this world, right in front of us, and we don't even bother to look up."

Brad looked over at the Mr. Coffee, watching the carafe fill, thinking.

"But what does this thing *do?* Just drift around?"

"Oh, hell no. I've seen it dart and dash faster'n a jet plane. I've seen it fly right off into the sky and out of sight. It always comes back, though."

"To my yard, you mean?"

"'Fraid so." Irvin laughed, childlike.

Brad glanced out the open door into the back yard. It was almost sunrise. "So where is it now?"

"Underground, maybe. It always comes and goes from around that sandbox. Comes right out of the ground and goes back the same way, like a pilot comin' back to base. And you know, time and again I've tried to get a picture of it. But I've never been able to. It's like there's somethin' about it that makes it impossible to photograph. Like it's not altogether in this world."

Brad rechecked the coffee and took two cups from the cabinet. "So that's why you come around here? To look for that light?"

"That's one reason," Irvin said. "But there's more. There's that hummin' sound I mentioned yesterday. You told me you hadn't heard it, but . . ."

"Actually, I have."

"I *thought* you were fibbin' about that." Irvin shook a scolding finger. "And then there's that cottonwood. The one in the sandbox. How tall do you think that tree is?"

"Not that long ago I measured it. It was almost seventeen feet. But I'd guess now it's more like twenty."

"And bein' that size, how old do you think it is?"

Brad shrugged. "I don't know, but as you gathered yesterday, I talked to Michael Renner." He waited for a reaction; there was none. "He said he didn't know anything about that tree, and if that's true, it can't have been there even than a year."

"It hasn't," Irvin said. "That tree sprouted from a seed late last May."

Brad did the math. *"Six months?"*

"Six months," Irvin said, straight-faced.

"Paul, that's not possible."

"It's true. I swear."

Brad looked out at the tree, still with its leaves—its mostly green leaves—even as others had been stripped bare.

"I don't understand what could cause a tree to grow like that," he said.

"I don't either. But whatever it is, it's the same thing that makes your yard grow the way it does. And that makes that sound. And that light."

The Mr. Coffee gurgled. The carafe was full.

Irvin shifted his eyes with a kind of paranoia.

"Say," he said, lowering his voice, "if you've got time, I'll show you somethin' else pretty amazin'."

"Where?"

"It's in the commons, down through the trees."

Chapter 37

Limbo

At 7:20 Wichita time, she tried again. She would catch him, she thought, before he left for work. She tried the house first, then his cell.

She waited three minutes and tried again.

And three minutes later, tried again.

Get it through your head. The man is not going to answer.

Or perhaps, she speculated, for any of a variety of reasons—reasons she did not care to think about—he simply couldn't.

It was too early to go to Eva's. She waited another hour on the sofa, sitting, as she had through the night, with her head back, her eyes closed. But there was no rest. She could think only of Brad. And she had such a pain behind her left eye.

Pushing herself off the sofa, her foot knocked against the pint of gin— or rather, the container that remained. Somewhere in the night she had finished it. The empty tonic bottle lay on the floor beside it.

She picked up both bottles and considered the situation. Eva might have been aware of the tonic, and it would be best to give the impression that nothing had changed. She half filled the bottle with water and put it back in the refrigerator. The gin bottle found the weeds behind the trailer.

It was getting light. Starting down the road, she felt sick to her stomach. She'd eaten nothing since Denver International and her head seemed larger than the rest of her.

She felt even worse knowing where she was headed.

Disheveled and absent makeup, Eva answered the door in her bathrobe.

"How did you sleep?"

"I didn't," Sally snipped.

Avoiding her sister's glare, Eva toddled off in the direction of her bedroom. "Have some breakfast," she said over her shoulder. The offer apparently involved a box of Cheerios sitting on the kitchen table.

In the adjacent family room, a pillow and rumpled blanket lay on the couch, and from the bathroom at the trailer's far end came the sound of running water—signs Derrick had risen and made for the shower. Sally went the same way, passing Laurel's room and cracking the door to Derrick's to peek in on Eamon, who was sleeping soundly.

She gently shut the door and pulled the phone from her jeans pocket. *What good would it do?*

Then, an idea: *the office.* By now, the firm was open for business.

The receptionist answered with a joyful greeting. Sally asked for Brad.

"I'm sorry, Mr. Manford isn't in yet. Would you like his voicemail?"

"No, thank you." Another idea: "What about Hugh Miller? Is he there?"

"No, but I expect him any time."

"I'd like his voicemail, please."

Sally was finishing the message as she heard Eva calling from the other end of the trailer.

"Sally, dear? May I speak with you?"

Sally came into the family area far enough to see Eva at the door of her bedroom, still in her robe, but having applied mascara and rosy lipstick.

"I'd like to say something in private," Eva said.

As if anyone else is listening, Sally thought, trudging along.

Eva waited for Sally to enter, then closed the door, clasping her hands to her bosom.

"Sally, I want you to know something. I prayed about this last night, and the Lord has led me to understand that I mistreated you. I should not have made you stay at Mother's. Will you accept my apology?"

Sally massaged her throbbing eye. "Sure."

"And there will be no motel for you and Eamon—at least, not until they release Mother from the hospital. She will have to come here, you know."

"I know."

"But until then, I want you here with me. And I swear I will never act so badly toward you again."

Such things had been said before.

"That's okay. Just forget it."

Eva wasn't done. "It's just that it's been so hard! You moving half the country away, and Mother getting worse, and now she's . . ."

"She's dying," Sally said.

"Yes." Eva's large chin began to quiver.

Sally looked everywhere but straight ahead. "I need to get Eamon up for his treatment."

"You know, Sally," Eva blubbered, "I hate to say this, but you don't seem very concerned about our mother."

"I'm concerned."

"Well, you certainly don't seem that way."

"Eva, I've got things on my mind."

"And I have things on *my* mind."

Sally turned away. "Good for you."

She opened the door and walked out, staring at her phone.

Chapter 38

Rock of Ages

The sun was breaking the horizon as the old man led the way through the fence gate and into the commons. Following the well-worn trail into the stand of cedars, they were almost instantly out of sight of the house. The path wound around several evergreens before becoming slightly wider on a downslope strewn with cottonwoods and Osage orange, all nakedly poised for winter, their fallen leaves crunching underfoot and hiding hedge apples rotting beneath.

"You ever been down here?" Irvin asked.

"Can't say I have," Brad said.

"Well, it's a peaceful spot. I started spendin' time here when my wife got sick. And I'd go up and walk along where your house is, too. They were just places to get away, at first. But then I started noticin' things like the light, and that sound, and, well, I'm gonna show you what else."

The slope was short but steep, and Brad could see, at its bottom, a slender, meandering stream of dark water. The trail, still visible in the dust and scattered leaves, stretched on to the creek's bank, where a massive, reddish chunk of stone lay embedded in the channel, forming a natural bridge.

There, Irvin stopped.

"That's a heck of a big rock," Brad said.

"It is," Irvin allowed, seeming studiously amused.

Brad looked across the stream.

"That's my place," Irvin said, pointing. "You can see it there, through the trees."

There was a gradual upslope leading to the old man's house. Near the top, yellow sunrays sliced here and there through barren branches.

"Are we going on?" Brad asked.

"No, we've arrived."

Feeling more of a chill than he had expected, Brad zipped his jacket to the neckline. He glanced around. "You wanted me to see something."

"And you have."

"What?" It took a moment to sink in. "The rock?"

Irvin nodded. "What do you notice about it?"

"Well, like I said, it's big."

"What else?"

"It's kind of red. Maybe even a little pink."

"Do you know what kind of rock this is?"

Brad shook his head. "I don't know much about rocks."

"This is what they call Sioux Quartzite," Irvin said. "It's a very hard, metamorphic rock that was formed over a billion years ago. It occurs naturally in South Dakota and Minnesota and Iowa, and a tiny bit in Nebraska. It's not indigenous to Kansas, but that's not to say we don't find it here."

"Yeah, like *right* here," Brad quipped.

Irvin smiled politely. "Have you ever heard of the term 'glacial erratic'?"

"Doesn't that mean a rock that's been moved by a glacier?"

"Yeah, that's basically it. In this case you've got glaciers that came down from the north something like six hundred thousand years ago, and as they crept along, they picked up rocks in one place and left them in another. Some of those rocks were Sioux Quartzite. But a geologist will tell you—and I talked to one over at Wichita State—that those glaciers only came as far south as northeast Kansas. And if you want to find Sioux Quartzite in Kansas, that's where you go. A hundred miles or so northeast of here, you'll find rocks like this all over the place. But you see, that's where it stops. The glaciers never came down this far."

"So neither did the rocks," Brad concluded.

"That's right."

"Except for this one."

"Sure enough," Irvin said. "So, how did it get here?"

Brad deduced the obvious. "Someone put it here."

"No question about it. But tell me this: Who was it?"

"I have no idea."

"Then how about *when?* When was it brought here?"

"No clue."

"Then just tell me what method was used to move it."

Shivering, Brad shoved his hands deep in his jacket pockets and shrugged his shoulders. "Paul, I can't."

"Neither can I. But the fact is, this rock is now, at the very least, a hundred miles from where it should be, and it didn't get here on its own." Irvin looked at the stone. "How much do you think this thing weighs?"

"Gosh, I'm not very good at estimates. I don't know. Five tons, maybe?"

"Could be," Irvin said. "But I rather doubt that the developers of this housing community hauled a five-ton rock a hundred miles and dropped it in this creek for ornamental purposes. Don't you?"

"No, I'm sure they didn't."

"And if someone had wanted a bridge across this creek, they'd have just built one, right?"

"Right."

"So logically, this thing was here before any of the houses that are out here now, agreed?"

"Yeah, I suppose so."

Irvin stepped onto the stone, pacing its length.

"You know, Brad, before this development was here—either the houses on my side of the creek or yours—this was nothin' but farm and ranchland. And it'd been that way since white people settled here a hundred and fifty years ago. Before that, the Wichita Indians lived here—the same people that were here in the sixteenth century when Coronado came through lookin' for the so-called cities of gold. You've heard of Coronado, I guess?"

"Spanish guy," Brad answered.

"A *conquistador*," Irvin said.

"I heard he didn't find anything."

"No gold, anyway. Or, for that matter, anything like a city. But as I said, there were people here. And they had been here a very long time. A few miles from here, they've found evidence of villages that date back as far as three thousand B.C. And arrowheads found around here have been dated more than twice that old.

"But Brad, the thing is, all of those people were just what we call hunters and gatherers. They were nomads with primitive technology. They lived hand to mouth. They had no concept of the wheel. They didn't even have horses, because at that time there weren't any in North America." He tapped the rock with his foot. "Do those sound like the kind of folks who would or *could* move somethin' like this a hundred miles?"

Brad was bouncing on his toes to stay warm.

"I see your point," he said. "*Someone* moved it, though."

"Someone did. But don't you see? It was someone not in the history books. Someone who was here long before anyone the archeologists have found."

"Like who?"

"A civilization that, if discovered, would probably redefine everything we know about human history," Irvin replied solemnly.

Well, Sally had always said he was crazy. And now it appeared she had been dead on.

Brad searched for a tactful response. "But Paul, do you honestly think . . ."

"I do."

"But . . ." Irvin was staring at him. "Look, Paul, this rock is definitely unusual, and we don't know how it got here, but that doesn't necessarily prove that we're standing on the ruins of Atlantis."

"I didn't say anything about Atlantis," the old man snapped.

"No, Paul, but I'm just saying, that's the sort of connection you're trying to make. You're saying this rock is evidence of some great and unknown ancient culture."

"You're damn right I am."

The old man was getting worked up.

"But Paul . . ."

"You think I'm nuts, don't you!"

Really worked up.

"I'm not saying that."

"You don't have to."

"Paul, come on."

"You're just like goddamn Renner."

"No, I'm not."

"You are!"

"I'm not."

"The hell you're not!"

"All right, maybe I am!" Brad said, losing patience. "And this is just a rock!"

Cold and tired, he turned to go back up the slope.

"It's *not* just a rock!" With nimble, manic steps, the old man moved around Brad's flank, cutting off his retreat. "It's just like I said up at your house! You're not lookin'! You're not payin' attention!"

The old man blocking his way, Brad threw up his hands. "Attention to *what?*"

Their eyes met. Scrunching his face in a grimace, Irvin looked away and, for a short time, stood silent, catching his breath. Composing himself.

He looked again at Brad. "I'm sorry. I didn't mean to act like that."

"Neither did I," Brad said. "But Paul, you seem a little—should I say?—*touchy* about all this."

"I know, dammit. And like I say, I'm sorry." The old man shuffled his feet and seemed as if throwing something might make him feel better. "But Brad, if you'd just look at that rock one more time. Just look. Please."

What could it hurt, Brad thought, to appease the old fool for a few more frigid minutes? He nodded and moved back toward the stone.

Irvin flashed an appreciative smile.

"Okay, now," he said, "I know it's big and sort of red, but what else do you see? What about its shape?"

Brad made a show of examining the slab. "Well, the far end is pretty wide, but then it tapers down and comes to a point."

"Right. And *look* at the point. Any question in your mind that somebody intentionally shaved it that way with a blade or machine or device of some kind?"

"To be honest, Paul, I don't know. I guess it's possible."

"All right, but let's *assume* that's what happened. And let's further assume that this stone was placed here for a purpose. A specific purpose. And if it was, then what is this stone doin' here? What purpose is it servin'?"

Brad took another glance at the rock. "Could be it's pointing at something."

"Could be," Irvin said, with contained excitement. "And if it is, what is it pointin' *at?*"

Brad ran his eyes from the tip of the stone up through the trees to where the cedars obstructed the view of his property.

"Any number of things, I suppose," he said. "My yard, maybe?"

"Not *just* your yard." Irvin came a step closer. "Brad, what do you think you would run into if you could walk a straight line from the point of this rock up into your back yard?"

Brad ran his eyes up the slope again. "My cottonwood tree?"

"That's right!" Irvin bubbled. "That's it! You're gettin' it!"

Brad was not so certain. He looked up the slope a moment longer.

"Paul, I don't mean to sound condescending. Really, I don't. And you were right about the light in my yard, and my tree, and the way the grass grows. But to me, what you're saying here sounds pretty far-fetched."

With a long breath and closed eyes, the old man shook his head, now more disappointed than offended.

"I guess I'm just looking for another explanation for all of this," Brad said. "Something . . . I don't know how to say this . . . that's not quite so, you know, out there."

His head down, his fire faded, Irvin slogged past Brad, across the stone and to the other side of the creek, seemingly ready to move on home.

"There was a time I felt the same way," he said, lingering on the far bank. "But I decided to keep lookin' for the truth, whatever it might be."

"And did you find anything?"

"Yeah, as a matter of fact, I did." The old man smiled despairingly. "More than Coronado, anyway."

He kicked at the rock.

"You're gonna have to take my word for this, but not long before the Renners broke ground on that house of yours, I found some smaller pieces of rock like this up in what's now your back yard, right where Renner built that sandbox. They weren't easy to see. The place was all grown over with weeds and bushes. Growin' in the same way the tree and the grass does now. And like I say, they were smaller pieces, like a rock the size of this one here had been smashed into who knows how many chunks and bits. Most of 'em were half buried. But they were there, right on that spot."

"What happened to them?"

"Got hauled away when the builder came in. I didn't keep any of 'em. Should have. Anyway, it was clear to me that this rock here was pointin' up to where those broken pieces were, and I got to thinkin' that if there were two such rocks, and one was pointin' toward the other, there might be more of 'em out there somewhere. You know what I'm sayin'? A kind of line of markers all leadin' to a special place? So, I set out to see if I could find another of these things. And do you know what?"

"You found one?"

"I did. It's about three miles north of here," Irvin said. "I spent months lookin' around and never found anything. Then one day I was drivin' through a neighborhood up there, mindin' my own business, and boom, there it was, sittin' in somebody's back yard. They were usin' it for a kind of decorative piece, growin' flowers around it. Obviously had no idea what they had. And it's still there. It's a good deal smaller than this one. Just a busted off part of what was probably once a stone the same size as here."

"Does it have a point like this?"

"Not anymore. But there's no doubt what it is—or was. I mean, it has the same ..." His voice trailed off.

"The same what?"

Irvin appeared as if he had let slip something he thought better left unspoken.

"I don't know if I should go into it," he said. "The geologist I talked to—he wasn't too keen on my theories either. I don't think he even believed this rock was really here. He wouldn't come out here. Just looked at some pictures I took and said it was on account of the way the rock had weathered. And I guess you could think that."

"I'm sorry, Paul. I don't know what you're getting at."

"Well, all right then. What the heck. Come here and take a look. You probably won't see anything."

Brad stepped to the center of the rock. "What am I supposed to be looking for?"

Irvin didn't answer.

Brad scanned the rock back and forth, then bent from the waist, looking closer. "Paul, I don't ..."

But then, nearly scoured away, all but undetectable ...

He cocked his head, changing his angle of view, and, keeping his focal point, moved himself a quarter turn.

Slowly—almost reverently—he lowered himself to one knee. Then to all fours.

He swept his hands over the stone, brushing away dirt and bits of leaves. But having cleaned its surface, he continued. Scrubbing. Scraping. No longer working to expose something, but, it seemed, to rub it out. His hands moved ever faster, gathering intensity until, frantic, he raked the stone in violent loops, his palms and fingers losing skin on the hard, rough surface.

The old man spoke in a panic: "Brad, what it is?"

Brad did not seem to hear.

"Brad? *Brad!*"

Abruptly, he stopped. Locked in a stupor. Eyes wide, but seeing only one thing.

And then, with a single finger oozing blood—hanging for a moment in mid-air before it steadily, and with purpose, descended—he traced, in crimson, a gentle curve, its shape following the line of a shallow, almost imperceptible trough to the completion of a perfect circle.

And within that circle, yet another.

He lifted the finger, blood dripping on the rock.

"Mis mundos," he whispered, his lips barely moving.

"Brad, goddammit, what's wrong?"

The next instant, he stood, the tip of the stone before him, his eyes marking a heading to a point unseen.

In clumsy, sleepwalking strides, he started up the hill.

The old man called after him.

By then, he was running.

Chapter 39

Breaking Ground

Off the trail, he charged up the raw slope, tearing through tangles of brush and ankle-deep leaves. Branches slapped his face. He skidded on lumps of hedge apples.

When he reached the cedars, the old man was still shouting.

He ran through the open gate, past the sandbox and cottonwood, up the deck stairs, through the kitchen and laundry room. On the landing of the garage steps he came to a sudden halt, panting as he had, only hours before, in the dark of a gas-filled house. Now, as then, there was a kind of separation from things. A strange mental drifting.

He flipped the light switch and saw his car, Sally's SUV, the lawn mower, a gasoline container, the weed whacker, electric hedge clippers, an extension cord . . . But why was he here? He had come for something. He *needed* something. What?

He couldn't remember.

He grabbed his head with both hands, his fingers holding clumps of hair as he staggered back to the kitchen, his thoughts coming in a rush too quick to process: The yard. The tree. The light. The stone. Sally. Eamon. MIS MUNDOS. Dali. Ron Delvechio. Crawling. Gasping for air.

Dying one vacuous breath at a time.

He stopped cold on that one: *Dying*. The gradual loss of life function. What was it but a progression of organ failures, the last being that of the brain? Gray matter shutting down for lack of oxygen?

He looked around the kitchen. Was he really here?

And suddenly—sadly—it made sense. He was here in mind only, and only in his mind had he entered the spare bedroom. In reality, his hand, seeking the doorknob, had missed its mark. And he was still there, in the upstairs hall, the last surviving neurons of his brain sparking and burning out. And the light in the yard, the old man in the kitchen, the stone and its fantastic symbol—even this sun-drenched morning—were all mere illusions of the end stage. Life's final, nonsensical visions. Clocks melting in the shadows.

He had done it, after all. Put an end to his horrible, suffering self. It was for the best, he thought. They wouldn't find him quite the way he'd wanted, but it was far too late for regrets.

Now, each moment could be his last.

He waited for it, bracing himself against the counter by the sink as a KC-135 came in low over the house. But with the windows still open, the unfiltered rumble of jet engines shook him just enough.

At once, he felt an awakening and found his gaze fixed on the back yard, his eyes trained on a child's sandbox and a cottonwood tree. A tree that seemed no less real now than ever.

His hands, too, seemed real, scraped of skin and stinging. He held them up, examining the cuts and drying blood. Blood drying just as surely as it now did on a hard red stone.

And the phone: It signaled additional messages in the time he and Irvin had been away. Three more to go with the other five.

This was no dying dream.

He hit playback.

"Hey, babe, we're in Denver. We're okay, but the plane's delayed. Some kind of storm over the Rockies. I tried your cell, too. I guess you're busy. Anyway, I'll call you when we get there. Or if you get a chance, call me. Love you."

That was real as well. That voice as warm as a kiss and a green-eyed glance.

"Sunday," said the machine in monotone, "five forty-six p.m. . . . Next message . . ."

"It's me. We're still in Denver. Can you believe this? We ate some dinner, though, and Eamon's doing okay. But if you would, please call me. Thanks. Bye."

So real, she might have been standing in the room.

"Sunday, six thirty-four p.m. . . . Next message . . ."

"Me again. And we're still sitting in this freaking airport! Brad, it's starting to look like they may cancel the flight. God, if that happens I don't know what we'll

do. Please call me as soon as you can. Please?"

"Sunday, six fifty-nine p.m. . . ."

Yes, it was real. All of it. Even the rock and its image. But clearly, he had jumped to an impossible conclusion. Irvin's geologist had been right: The slab had been marked by wind and water. Nature had etched its surface at random. And just as people see shapes in clouds or the Virgin Mary on a piece of toast, the mind of Brad Manford, seeking order from disorder, had wrongly assigned the stone's indiscriminate furrowing a common interpretation. To think otherwise was insane.

"Next message . . ."

"Well, we're finally in L.A. My lord, we sat in the Denver airport for over two hours and I don't know how long on that damn runway. Anyway, we made it. But call me. Please. Brad, I mean it."

"Sunday, eleven twenty-eight p.m. . . ."

But faultless circles? The mere product of arbitrary weathering? That, in itself, was preposterous. No, he had followed those faint contours just as they were. The stain of blood had left no mistake. And calling it impossible would not make it so.

"Next message . . ."

"Brad?" Her voice quavered. *"Why don't you pick up? I know it's late, but . . . Brad, if you're there, answer the phone. Brad, I'm begging you. . . . Brad?"*

"Monday, one nineteen a.m. . . ."

And neither was there any denying that, like an arrow poised to fire, that stone was pointing right here. At this place. At his tree.

His unfathomable cottonwood.

It was no accident.

"Next message . . ."

"Brad? . . . Brad! . . . Why don't you answer? . . . Brad!"

"Monday, seven twenty a.m. . . ."

Further questions were a waste of time. Fear and concern, too, were a waste. All thought was useless.

And he remembered then what he had wanted so badly only minutes ago: a shovel. Just a shovel.

Funny, he thought. He didn't even own one.

But Paul Irvin apparently did—a sturdy-looking, round-point, D-handle version—and he was bringing it through the back gate.

"Next message . . ."

"Brad! . . . Answer the damn phone!"

He walked out the back door as Irvin stopped at the sandbox. The old man unshouldered the shovel along with another tool—a short implement with an axe blade sprouting from one side of its head and a broad, curved chisel from the other.

"What's that?" Brad asked, coming down the deck stairs. "Some kind of fireman's hatchet?"

"It's called a mattock."

"You think I'll need it?"

"Definitely."

From the house, a heavy sigh. A sobbing plea. *"Brad . . . please . . . sweetheart . . ."*

"Monday, seven twenty-three a.m. . . ."

Irvin handed Brad a pair of worn leather work gloves.

"You'll need these, too," he said.

"Next message . . ."

"Brad! . . . Goddammit! . . . Goddammit, Brad!"

"Think you should do somethin' about that?" Irvin asked, gesturing toward the house.

Having donned the gloves, Brad rolled away one of the utility poles that bounded the sandbox and reached for the shovel.

"Later," he said.

"Monday, seven twenty-six a.m. . . ."

The shovel hit sand.

"End of messages."

Chapter 40

Bedside Manner

Sally stood beside the hospital bed as her mother, sunken and jaundiced, lay propped on a mound of pillows, bony arms wilted at her sides. From the room's other bed, hidden behind the separating curtain, came the sound of a woman snoring.

"Where's your little boy?" Margie asked.

Sally suspected she had forgotten the child's name.

"They won't let him up here, Mom. He's not old enough. Eva's with him, down in the waiting room."

"I thought Eva had to work."

"She took the morning off."

"To babysit your boy?"

"And drive us over here."

"Eva's such a good person."

Sally rolled her eyes. "Yeah, Eva's a dream."

The sarcasm went unnoticed as Margie tugged at the neck of her hospital gown, the white garment underscoring the purple hue of her venous cheeks.

"Oh," she said, "but I think they could let a woman's grandchild up here for a few minutes."

"Sorry, Mom, but that's the way it is. Anyway, he doesn't need the exposure."

"Exposure to what?"

"Germs."

"*Germs?* Why, this is a hospital. There aren't any germs here."

"Yeah, Mom, there are, and it hasn't been that long ago that he was in the hospital himself."

"Who was in the hospital?"

"Eamon."

Margie was taken aback. "He was?"

"For almost two weeks. Eva said she told you."

"She did? What did he have to go to the hospital for?"

"You remember. He has a chronic condition."

"A what?"

"He has cystic fibrosis."

"What's that?"

"It's the same thing he's always had. You know, he coughs and he can't breathe. And his stomach bothers him."

"He gets the shits?"

"Sometimes."

"I get the shits," Margie said. "I may have 'em any minute."

"I'll call the nurse."

"No, don't bother." Straining, Margie raised herself slightly, then, with a sigh of relief, settled back to the mattress. "I'm okay."

From behind the curtain, the woman in the other bed rustled about and cleared her throat, seeming awake, but, just as quickly, continued snoring.

"Anyway, Mom, you'll see Eamon when you get out of here in a couple of days."

"In a couple of days they'll let me out?"

"I think so."

Maybe sooner, Sally thought. They weren't going to have a charity case like this camping here any longer than necessary.

"Sally, would you send your father in?"

The man had been dead fifteen years.

"I will later," Sally said. "He's out having a cigarette."

"Well, I haven't seen him all morning. He doesn't pay any attention to me." The old woman frowned from one side of her mouth. "That's a man, for you."

"I guess so."

"Does yours treat you any better?"

"My man?" Sally managed a smile. "Yeah, Brad's wonderful."

"He is? Well, I don't know. He took you away from here. From me.

From your home. He didn't have to do that."

There were times when her mother was not totally gone. On certain subjects, she was almost lucid. This was one of them.

"We're happy, Mom."

"You don't look happy."

"Because he's far away."

"He wouldn't be if he hadn't gone off to God knows where. Why did he do that, Sally? Why did he take you off to live with farmers?"

"Mom, it's not like that. Wichita's a city. It's a lot bigger than Hawthorne."

"Well, it's not bigger than Los Angeles," Margie declared, as if ending the debate.

"But Mom, that's not really . . ."

"But *why*, Sally? Why did he drag you and little Ethan off like that?"

She thought back to the spiel Brad had given. "Look, Mom, it's a good place to live. A good place to raise a child. People are friendly. Things move a little slower there. And the cost of living . . ."

"Oh, hog shit! That's a load of it."

Yes, it was, Sally thought. Brad had known it, too.

Her mother had a look of concern. "What's wrong, little girl?"

"Nothing."

"I think you're crying."

"I'm not."

"You are," Margie said. There was no trace of confusion.

"I'm just happy to be here with you."

"I'm happy, too." Margie closed her eyes, seeming about to doze off. "And I sure hope he's all right."

"Who, Mom?"

"That man of yours."

Chapter 41

Entrenched

Hugh Miller double-checked the address on the big colonial at the end of the cul-de-sac. Alyssa had said what a nice place it was. She had not been kidding. Bradley, Hugh thought, was living awfully well for an associate attorney.

He parked in the drive and went to the front door, where several rings and knocks failed to produce an answer. Stepping down from the porch, he checked the front windows. Oddly, on this chilly day, they were open. He peered through the storm screen into the dining room to see a chair lying sideways on the wood floor. Nothing else, though, seemed amiss. Through the window he stated a greeting. There was no reply, but from the rear of the house—or perhaps the back yard—he heard the sound of a man's voice.

He crossed the driveway and walked along the side of the house toward a fence gate. Nearing the gate, the greater part of a large yard came into view, and his pace went from brisk to slow as he tried to make sense of the scene ahead: Brad, dressed in jeans and a windbreaker, stood knee-deep in a trench carved halfway around a small tree. Close by lay four sections of thick wooden poles, a shovel, and a freshly excavated pile of dirt and sand. Beside the pile, an older man in a camouflage jacket sat on the side of a metal-frame chaise longue, chattering away as Brad hacked at something with the axe blade of a mattock.

Unnoticed, Hugh jiggled the padlocked gate to attract attention.

Brad stopped hacking. The old man stopped talking. They both turned to look.

"Hey, Bradley," Hugh said.

"Hello, Hugh."

"Mind if I come in?"

"No," Brad said, sounding ambivalent. He called out the code for the lock.

Hugh stiffened as he crossed the yard with his hands in his pockets, his buttoned suit coat of little use against the biting breeze. Halting near the pile of dirt and sand, he was careful to keep his dress shoes in the grass.

"Well," he said, looking at Brad, then the other man, then back to Brad, "so what are you guys doing?"

Brad and Irvin exchanged looks.

"Landscaping," Brad said.

Pretending to understand, Hugh nodded and turned toward the man in the chair. "I'm Hugh Miller."

"Paul Irvin," the man said, rising.

"Nice to meet you." Hugh shook the man's hand. "Are you a landscaper?"

"No, just a neighbor."

"And an Air Force colonel," Brad noted.

"Is that so?"

"Retired," Irvin said.

"I see."

No one spoke as Hugh surveyed the poles and the dirt and the sand and the trench. He could see what Brad had been chopping at: Snarls of tree roots, dense and fibrous, poked out all along the walls of the ditch.

"Brad, I wonder if we could go inside for a minute," Hugh said.

"Are you cold?"

"No, it's just . . ." Hugh glanced at Irvin. "I need to talk to you."

"We can talk here."

"Yeah, but we need to discuss something that's a little sensitive."

"Lawyer stuff," Irvin said. "Hey, no problem. You fellas go ahead. It's almost lunchtime, anyway. I'm gonna go get somethin' to eat." He started toward the commons gate. "I'll bring you somethin', Brad," he yelled back.

Hugh waited until the old man had disappeared into the cedars. "Brad, what's going on here?"

"I told you, landscaping."

Leaning against the wind, Hugh frowned, stern and worried.

"Maybe so," he said, "but you do realize it's Monday?"

"Yeah."

"Brad, it's a work day. And at the law firm where you're employed, we're working on an acquisition worth millions. And you're the guy who's supposed to be drafting the purchase agreement. And we need it today."

"I know," Brad said. He turned away, tossing down the mattock and looking for the shovel.

"Because I've got to review it," Hugh said, "and Steve's got to review it, and the client's got to review it, and we've got to get it to the seller first thing next week. If we don't, the deal's not going to get done by the end of the year. And that absolutely has to happen. You know that."

Having found the shovel, Brad sliced into the floor of the trench.

"Brad, I mean it. This is serious stuff. It's serious for *all* of us."

Encountering resistance, Brad put his foot on the shovel, forcing it down further into the clay soil.

"And by that, I mean it's just as serious for Steve LeMark as it is for you and me," Hugh said. "And I'm sure I don't have to tell you that he's not the kind of guy who gives second chances to people who screw up major projects."

Brad slung a mass of dirt toward the pile, dusting Hugh's shoes.

"Brad, listen to me."

Brad looked up with a hard stare. "No, *you* listen. I'm going to finish this. Then I'll write your damned agreement. Got it?"

Hugh took a step back. "Brad?"

"What?"

"Are you all right?"

"I'm fine. I just want to get this done."

"Get what done?"

"I told you."

"Yeah, landscaping," Hugh said with some disgust.

Brad resumed digging as Hugh glanced around the yard, then at the house. As in the front, the windows in the back were open. And upstairs, one was suspiciously broken.

"Brad, your wife called me."

"She called me, too. Umpteen times."

"Have you talked to her?"

His head down, Brad was digging faster. "Not yet."

"Brad, she's worried sick. Don't you realize that?"

"Yeah."

"So call her."

"You call her."

"I intend to, to tell her you're still alive. But she'd rather talk to you."

"She will," Brad said, growling as the shovel struck a clump of roots, "in time."

Hugh stood fixed for another moment, hoping for something more as Brad traded the shovel for the mattock and began chopping with the axe head.

"Fine, then," Hugh said, exasperated. He started for the gate—then looked back. "Brad, that agreement. Today. Understand?"

Pounding roots in a fever, Brad did not seem to hear.

Chapter 42

Quid Pro Quo

"Problems at work?" Irvin asked.

"Not really," Brad said.

Legs dangling over the trench, they sat at its edge, eating the food Irvin had brought.

"Was that guy your boss?"

Brad chewed his Wendy's single. "I don't have a boss."

"Everybody's got a boss."

"I don't."

Irvin gazed into the trench. "Well, anyway, nice day for a picnic."

Brad stuffed a bundle of fries in his mouth. "It's fifty degrees," he said, the wind slapping his face.

"Could be worse. Shoot, I've seen plenty of days here this time of year with ice and snow. And the same down in Texas. Why, back when I was just a runt livin' in the Panhandle, we had the damnedest ice storm anybody ever saw. Down there, they still call it The Great Ice Storm. It hit just a day or two after Thanksgivin'. Three days solid of freezin' rain. Laid down a coat of ice half a foot thick. There was hardly a tree left standin'. And no phones, no power, nothin'."

"Wow," Brad said, less than animated.

"You ever been through anything like that?"

"Not that I recall."

"Truth is, I don't remember that storm. I was just a baby. But the old timers always talked about it. They used to talk about a blizzard, too, back

in the spring of 'thirty-eight. And that was worse than the ice storm. Way
worse."

"How?"

"You ever been in a blizzard?"

"Not that I recall," Brad said again, reaching for more fries.

"Well, the problem with an honest-to-God blizzard is that you can't
see five yards in any direction. Every which way is pure white, and you
don't know where you are. Oftentimes, a person just wanders around till
they freeze to death. That blizzard in 'thirty-eight went on for nigh half a
week, with heavy snow and wind blowin' seventy mile-an-hour. Ended up
killin' about a dozen people. Folks'd go out to tend livestock and just never
find their way back. Some of 'em died within steps of their houses. Never
knew how close they were."

Finished with his fries, Brad ate the last of his hamburger, washed
it down with a swig of Coke, and dropped into the trench. He resumed
digging as, slowly and with some stiffness, the old man stood and began
collecting the trash from the meal.

"Let me know if you need any help," Irvin said.

"I will."

"I'm old, and I've got a little arthritis, but I'm in good shape. I can still
work a shovel."

"I'm sure you can."

"I'm just sayin', why don't we share the load?"

Brad looked up at the old man.

"Sorry, Paul, but I'd rather not. This is my hole."

———————

Swinging the mattock several feet below ground level, Brad struck something that refused to yield. Scraping around the spot with the shovel, he
found a vertical root nearly as thick as the trunk of the tree above.

"Look at this," he said.

Irvin raised himself from his seat on the side of the chaise longue and
stood at the rim of the trench, squinting, his hiking boots level with Brad's
shoulders.

"Well, I'll be damned," he said. "That's a taproot."

"Should it be this big?"

"Hell no. In fact, it probably shouldn't be there at all. Generally speakin', cottonwoods don't have taproots."

"How far down do you think it goes?"

"Probably all the way to the water table."

"How far is that?"

"No tellin'. Could be another two feet. Could be ten."

"What happens if I hit the water table?"

Irvin laughed. "You'll be swimmin'."

"That'll suck."

"You know," Irvin said, "you're runnin' into some loose soil there. You go much deeper, it's gonna cave in."

With some impatience, Brad stuck the shovel firmly upright in the bottom of the trench. "So, what do you suggest?"

"Dig away from the outside of it, all around. Make it slope toward the tree."

Brad looked around the perimeter of the hole. "That'll take the rest of the day."

"And then some, I reckon." Irvin eyed the afternoon sky. Clouds were moving in. The temperature was dropping. "Like I said, I'd be happy to help."

Brad pulled the shovel from the ground, turning away from the old man.

"I just want to make myself useful," Irvin added.

"I could use some water."

The already gusting wind picked up further in the late afternoon. A storm appeared likely, but the darkened sky brought only a smattering of rain, the few drops coming in sideways. Afterward, though, the wind remained, repeatedly bowing the cottonwood to what surely seemed its snapping point. But again and again, the tree—its main root exposed and its peripheral system largely hacked away—withstood the strain.

Bent over against the gale, Irvin sat on the side of the long chair, watching for some time in uncharacteristic silence as, with abandon, Brad attacked the outer wall of the trench, angling it as the old man had advised. Moving yards of soil and severing sprinkler lines with indifference as the ditch, in the process, became a considerably larger expanse.

At last, the old man spoke: "You better take a break."

No response. Irvin thought, in the wind, he had not been heard.

"Brad," he said, louder, "I think you work a shovel harder than any man I ever saw."

Again, nothing.

Striking a lump of shale the size of a beach ball, Brad grabbed the mattock and, with its chisel, began a furious effort to unloose the rock from the ground. Even in the chilling wind, currents of perspiration tumbled from his head and neck, soaking the collar of his sweatshirt. Taking only a moment's break, he threw off his jacket before restarting the struggle.

Irvin watched as Brad fought the rock. He studied the youthful face, the way it flushed and twisted. A face painted with grit and rage and desperation, all swirled together. Almost fifty years ago and half a world away, he had seen that face everywhere.

What, he wondered, was it doing here?

"You know, Brad," he said, shouting over the wind, "yesterday, when we had that little disagreement, you said somethin' about us not knowin' each other that well."

Brad groaned. He was making no headway.

"And that's obviously true," Irvin went on. "We've only known each other a couple of months. And we haven't talked that much. But now, here we are, under what you might call unusual circumstances, and I'm curious."

"About what?"

"About you," Irvin said. "Aren't you curious about me?"

"No."

"Why not?"

Annoyed, Brad stopped and glared at the old man. "Because, Paul, I know enough about you as it is."

"Oh, really? What do you know?"

"I know you were born in Pampa, Texas, on February 8, 1940. I know you're supposedly related to the guy who was in command at the Alamo. I know you went to the Air Force Academy and graduated in 1962. I know you married a woman named Linda Harper in 1963. I know you did two tours in Vietnam. And I know that on July 12, 1968, you shot down three MiGs in five minutes and they gave you a big, fancy medal for it."

Somewhere during the recitation, Irvin had broken into a grin.

"Gee-mun-ee," he said, "you did your homework. Or at least, you tried."

"What's that supposed to mean?"

"It means you've got some of your facts wrong."

"Which ones?"

The grin had disappeared. "I'm not sure I should tell you." Irvin put his hands deep into the pockets of his jacket. "You see, it's a bit of a secret."

Brad shrugged. "We all have secrets."

"I'm sure we do." The old man sat up straight, stamping his feet to keep warm. "But some secrets are better than others." He gave Brad an affable look. "I'll tell you what. We'll make a deal. I'll tell you a secret if you'll tell me one."

"Then can we braid our hair and have a pillow fight?"

"No, I'm serious. I'll tell you somethin' I've never told a livin' soul."

Brad tossed the mattock aside and rested his hands on his hips.

"All right, go ahead," he said. "Tell me your secret. What is it?"

"July 12, 1968. I didn't shoot down any MiGs that day."

"When did you shoot down the MiGs?"

"That's my secret. I didn't shoot down any MiGs. Ever."

"But you said you did. And there were witnesses. Other pilots."

Irvin shook his head. "You're missin' the point. It was a lie, Brad. The whole thing. A lie."

"You lied?"

"I lied. The guys in my squad lied. My superior officer lied. Uncle Sam lied."

"Why?"

"Cover story," Irvin said. "Know what I mean?"

Brad uttered a short, perverse cackle. "Yeah, I think I do." He glanced down at the mass of shale, seeming deep in thought. "So, what were you hiding?"

"Huh-uh." Grinning again, Irvin shook his head. "That'd be another secret, and I've already told you one. Just suffice it to say that I was somewhere I shouldn't have been, doin' somethin' I shouldn't have been doin'."

"But why a story about shooting down three planes in five minutes?"

"It's not believable, is it?"

"I believed it."

"Yeah, but anybody who's ever flown a combat mission knows it's bull. 'Course, the point was to advertise that I was somewhere other than where I really was. But three MiGs? *Three?* In five minutes? In a *Thud?* If they'd have just said two, it'd have been a little more credible. I know two old Thud drivers who each got a couple of MiGs back in 'sixty-seven in just about the same amount of time. But that's *it*. Nobody ever got three. *Ever.* Three is just embarrassin'. I guarantee, that story was thought up by some guy in a suit who didn't know a Thunderchief from a Cessna 182."

"Probably the same guy who gave you that medal, whatever it was."

"The Air Force Cross?" Irvin said. "Oh, no. That baby was *earned*. They publicly said it was for the three MiGs, but they knew—and I knew—it was really for the other thing. No, I deserved that son-of-a-bitch. And probably the Medal of Honor. But they're both just a couple of frickin' paperweights, and who cares, anyway?"

Brad looked again at the boulder and retrieved the mattock.

"Hey, it's your turn," Irvin said.

With a violent stroke, Brad crashed the axe blade downward, shattering the rock. The old man jumped—then sat uncomfortably as Brad lobbed hunks of shale from the hole.

"So, what do you want to know about me?"

Hesitant, Irvin licked his lips. "I want to know what got into you this mornin' down at the creek."

Lifting the largest part of the rock with both hands, Brad brought it to eye level and heaved it into the yard, narrowly missing the old man.

"What's it matter?" he said, breathing hard. "I'm digging up whatever's down here. Isn't that what you want?"

"Yeah, but you'd be at your office right now if I hadn't showed you that stone."

Brad flung out several pebbles and picked up the shovel. "I told you before, it's just a rock."

"No, it's not. We both know better. And you know somethin' about what's carved on it. Those circles."

Brad stopped and wiped his sweaty, mud-smeared forehead with the sleeve of his sweatshirt. "Paul, I really don't."

"I think you do. That's *your* secret."

Brad looked squarely at the old man. "You want to know a secret?"

"You owe me one."

"Then here it is: I'm broke. I mean absolutely broke. I don't even have enough to pay for one of those hamburgers you bought for lunch."

Irvin pondered the disclosure. "You gonna keep diggin'?"

"To China, if I have to."

"Then the grub's on me."

———————

Just before dark, the old man brought more fast food and a wide-beam camping light. Brad set the light on the hole's outer slope, aiming it in the direction of the cottonwood's enigmatic taproot. As night fell, the beam lit the way, the outskirts of the hole black with shadow, but the fat, plunging root and its surrounding soil, illuminated.

"Sure you don't need some help?" Irvin asked.

"No, Paul."

"Okay, if you say so."

The night was bitterly cold—made worse by the still blustering wind. It was finally too much for the old man. He stood for some time at the hole, watching and talking of trivial things, then sat quietly on the chaise longue, trying in vain to stay warm and awake before wearily trudging home through the commons.

Brad kept at it long after. Past midnight and into the frozen hours of early morning he worked without pause. And as he went ever deeper into the earth, he felt not fatigue, but a burgeoning strength. An imperviousness to the elements and human frailties. Less and less he felt the cold and wind. Faster and harder he swung mattock and shovel. His hands, raw and bleeding through the gloves, were of no bother. Muscles and joints that should have cried for relief did not. He beat the ground with mechanized fury. And there was no thought of the world outside the hole. It did not exist. There was only power. And more power.

Chapter 43

Mornings on High

"*Keeper!*"
The voice of a woman.

In the day's first light, he came to the edge of the rise. She stood naked on the reddish stone below, her clothing at her feet. An entourage of soldiers, heavily armed, cowered in the distance.

"Holiest," she said, "I am queen of Lu-Kesh. I come to you without crown or robe. I come stripped as a beggar. I supplicate myself, and I plead for your intercession."

"I know who you are," he said, "and I have already heard your plea. It came on the wind as you traveled The Way of Stones."

"But Holiest, I beseech you, hear again. There is plague. It has taken the king and half the city. We are weakened. And wild tribes march from the north to make war upon us. Only you can save us."

"That is true."

"Then come with me to Lu-Kesh so that we may worship you and see an end to these troubles."

"I do not require your worship. And I will not leave this place."

"But we must have your help!"

"Then bring your plague here and I will heal it. Bring your war here and I will stop it. But I will not go to Lu-Kesh."

The woman fell to her knees, lowering her head. "But Keeper, if you could but see the devastation."

"I have seen. I see it now. I see your city and all others. I see the ways of Man."

"Then guide us! Walk with Man! Change His ways!"

"I would better change the grass of the prairie."

"And you could."

"Yes, I could. But the prairie would not change me. To walk the prairie is to walk alone. But to walk with Man is to assume the ways of Man. And to assume the ways of Man is to become Man."

She raised her desperate eyes, her words coming angry and impudent. "Men know how to love."

"And hate."

"And you?"

"I know neither. I am not Man."

Brad awakened, shivering in the family room, the windows still open. Day was breaking, and no more than an hour ago he had laid himself on the couch. He had not been tired, but, give or take, he had not slept for two days. And a man, he had thought, must have rest.

His shoes, jeans, and sweatshirt were covered in dark, crusty clay. In the bathroom mirror he saw his head, too, was smeared with it, his skin blackened like a coal miner, his hair matted and spiked. He looked hideous. Like a man buried and exhumed. But what sense was there in washing? Or, for that matter, in changing clothes?

In the kitchen he took three eggs from the refrigerator and, one by one, cracked them on the counter, dropping the yokes in his mouth. He tossed the shells in the sink and, bending down, took a long, thirsty drink from the faucet.

Wiping his mouth with the sleeve of his shirt, he looked out the window above the sink into the back yard, first at the cottonwood—its green and yellowing leaves, even after yesterday's blow, still largely appended—and then at the gaping cavity that all but surrounded it, only a thin neck of supporting, unbroken ground linking the tree to the side of the hole.

Around the boundary of the depression, the once vertical walls had been dug away, leaving, in their place, a shallow slope from ground level to the bottom of the pit. It was a slope that, through the night, he had attended with care, regularly suspending his effort to go deeper in order to dig toward the perimeter and further reduce the angle of incline, thereby decreasing the risk of a cave-in, and, at the same time, widening the hole.

A hole that was now several times the size it had been the afternoon before.

The sandbox, of course, was obliterated, its cast-off poles buried under mounds of excavated dirt, rocks, and roots. Here and there among the multitude of piles were light brown streaks of sand and the occasional toy truck or green army man—all that remained of a child's creation.

Will you take care of my town?

What town?

The one in my sandbox.

The boy would be devastated.

It couldn't be helped. He took another drink from the faucet, donned his gloves, and headed for the yard. Paul Irvin was coming through the gate. It was time for work.

———————

The day shaped up warmer and less windy than the last. The sun shone and, by mid-morning, the air had lost its chill. Birds chirped and the few clouds overhead hung static, the sky otherwise filled with a crisscross of jet contrails.

Standing in the deepest part of the hole, Brad could no longer see the yard, and the rim of the pit had now expanded to the point that unloading the shovel required a lengthy walk up the slope. It made for slow going.

The old man stood halfway down the incline, watching as Brad passed him, back and forth.

"You must be down a good seven or eight feet," he remarked.

Hauling a shovelful uphill, Brad said nothing.

"Sure does take a lot of time and effort for a man to move dirt like this."

"Uh-huh."

"Might be a faster way."

"Not interested."

"Suit yourself."

Brad dumped the shovel on a pile of rocky soil near the chaise longue and returned to the pit as Irvin went up and sat on the front of the chair. Sweating in the warm sun, the old man unzipped his jacket and took off his blue USAF cap, holding the bill with the thumbs and index fingers of both hands as the hat dangled between his legs. He was quiet until Brad again reached the top of the grade.

"Brad, tell me somethin'."

Poised to empty the shovel, Brad stopped short, the whites of his eyes glistening behind the mask of clay.

"What," Irvin asked, "do you think is down there?"

Brad threw the dirt onto the pile beside the chair. "I haven't really thought about it," he said, walking off.

"You're kiddin'. You've been diggin' near solid for twenty-four hours and you haven't even considered what you're after?"

"It is whatever it is," Brad said from the hole.

"And whatever it is," Irvin yelled into the crater, "it's got a power beyond anything we know. You understand that, don't you?"

On his way up, Brad looked past the old man.

"I mean," Irvin said, "if it can grow a seed into a tree twenty feet tall in six months, what else can it do? Brad, this thing has some sort of energy. Incredible energy. And probably intelligence. It's like nothin' that's ever been seen before. It could change people's lives. It could change the world."

"I don't care about the world," Brad said, putting another load on the pile.

"How can you say that?"

Breathing heavily, Brad stopped beside the old man. "I don't know. Stuff like that just sort of slips out sometimes."

Disconcerted, Irvin shook his head, staring into the hole. "Well, whatever it is, somebody smarter than us is gonna have to figure it out."

"What are you talking about?" Brad's eyes pressed down on the old man.

"Just that if and when you ever get this thing out of the ground, somebody—a scientist of some kind—is gonna have to examine it. Study it. Figure out what it does, and why it does it, and where the hell it came from."

Brad headed back down the slope. "I don't think so."

Irvin stood up with a look of disbelief. "Brad, for God's sake, what you've got here belongs to all mankind."

"It belongs to me."

"And what are you gonna do with it?"

Brad thrust the shovel into the ground, gathering the next load.

"Keep it," he said.

Chapter 44

When It Rains

When it rains, it pours.
Her father had said that. He had said it, hushed and humorless, the day he had been told he had cancer.

Three days before, he had lost his job.

"When it rains, it pours, Margie," he had said. "When it rains, it pours."

Even then, at fifteen, she had known what that meant: that when things went bad—really bad—there was a sort of cosmic piling on until it all just washed over you like an enormous wave. A hard-luck tsunami.

The weight of it had killed her father.

And now it was breaking over her. And the boy.

Only yesterday, he had been doing so well. After they had returned from the hospital, they had walked to a park, where, for over an hour, he had played nonstop on the swings and slides and climbing equipment. He had been as lively as she had ever seen him. And there had not been a single cough of any consequence. Just as there had not been such a cough the day before. Or the week before.

In the evening, he had blown the marker on the peak flow meter well into the green zone. He had been fine. Better than fine. And when she had spread out her pallet of blankets and laid down on the floor beside his bed to sleep, he had been resting peacefully.

Around midnight there had been a series of dry hacks. Nothing of note, really. But through the night she had heard that same cough over and over, and by sunrise there had been a rattle to it. Before his morning treatments, she had tested him on the peak flow. He had been tending, then, toward the yellow.

By late morning, things had worsened. He was coughing persistently. He was firmly in the yellow. However, there was no fever and the pulse oximeter had shown a blood oxygen saturation of ninety-four percent— not optimal, but only just below his baseline. In the past, he had often been at ninety-four and no one, doctors included, had thought much of it. Still, she had decided to give his midday treatments a little earlier than usual. She'd had him use the nebulizer while wearing the vest. He had not objected. After, she had done backy-whacky as well. She had thought the extra therapy might help.

It hadn't. The coughing had continued. The peak flow had remained unchanged.

The oximeter reading had dropped to ninety-three.

And he had seemed a bit restless, but that was understandable. The medications often made him that way, and there was so little to do.

"Can we go outside?" he had asked, lying on the couch.

It was certainly nice enough. A warm day, almost hot. They were both in shorts. She had hated to tell him no.

"I'm sorry, honey, but you need to rest. I think you have a touch of something."

Disgruntled, he had settled for Cartoon Network.

"I wish they had Xbox," he had said.

Eva would not allow it—and probably couldn't afford it.

"Aunt Eva does things differently than we do." Coming over from the kitchen, Sally had brought him two enzyme tablets, a glass of water, and a ham sandwich on a paper plate. "Here, honey. You need to eat."

"I'm not hungry."

She had coaxed him to eat half of it. He had wanted milk instead of water, but she knew better. When the gunk was building in his chest, milk could make things worse.

After eating, he had fallen asleep on the couch. But it had been a broken sleep, interrupted with fits of barking coughs, his groggy eyes sometimes opening slightly until the disturbance passed. Muting the television, she had sat beside him, watching and listening as the coughing continued, his breathing marked by occasional rales and whistles.

In retrospect, she knew she should have seen where things were heading. The signs were all there. But through the years she had learned (or thought she had) that a little chest congestion and a peak flow in the yellow were not cause to run to the emergency room. She had cried wolf like that a few times in the early days and they had made her feel stupid for it. She had thought that if it went on like this through the afternoon, she might call Eamon's old pulmonologist in Santa Monica for a consult. That would not be too over-the-top. But there would certainly be no need for anything beyond that.

Besides, it wasn't as if she could just dash off to a hospital. Eva had taken her car to work. She did data entry for a company over in El Segundo and wouldn't be back much before six. Anyway, Sally had told herself, this simply wasn't an emergency. And if it threatened to become one, she could always call a cab and be at an ER—either up in Inglewood or down in Gardena—long before things got critical.

Mid-afternoon, the boy was still dozing. But the wheezing had become even more pronounced, and with it had come a kind of anguished gurgling sound. Perhaps it was time, she thought, to make that call to Santa Monica. She no longer had the doctor on speed dial, but found her in Contacts—just below the number for Brad's firm.

On impulse, she paged up to the firm number, reflecting on it. She hadn't heard from Hugh since yesterday.

I went out there. He was there.

Doing what?

Digging a hole in the back yard.

A hole?

Yeah.

Why?

I don't know. He said he was landscaping, but . . .

Hugh, that's bullshit.

That's what I thought.

How did he act?

Well . . . not like himself.

So why hasn't he called me?

Honestly, Sally, I don't know.

Is he going to call me?

Sally, I'm sorry. I'm afraid he may not.

Forever, he had said. He would love her forever. That had been just last Friday. And now he never wanted to speak to her again? How could that be?

And skipping work to dig a hole?

Clearly, something had happened. Something devastating. And in some way, emotionally, mentally, he had snapped. He had literally changed overnight.

Well, almost. He had not seemed well all of last week. And been far worse Saturday and Sunday. But at the airport, he had hugged her. He had kissed her. Just like always.

Or had he? No, not quite. In his kiss, his embrace, there had been a passion vaguely different from the norm. A hint of something beyond affection. A cry for help. And the more she thought about it, the more she realized that his last words to her—the way he had said "Goodbye, Sally"—had held, ominously, an air of finality.

She had lost him. The man who had walked off that elevator—the one who had looked at her like he was ready to own her (even as she, looking at him, had wanted him to)—was gone.

She wondered what would become of her. Odds were, she would end up like Eva, broke and bitter. But that might be preferable to what lay in store for Brad. He might very well be headed for a padded cell. Yet what were they doing for him? Hugh and the rest of them? Nothing, most likely. Just covering for him to keep themselves out of trouble. Letting him dig his hole deeper and deeper.

But surely they were making some effort to investigate. To find out what tragedy had befallen their investment. Their golden boy. Yes, undoubtedly, Hugh had to know more today than he had yesterday.

She dialed the number.

"May I speak to Hugh Miller?"

"Please hold," said the receptionist.

Several notes of Muzak followed. A mind-numbing rendition of "Ring of Fire."

Hugh's secretary came on. "This is Kimberly. How may I help you?"

"I'm calling for Hugh Miller."

"I'm sorry. Mr. Miller is in conference. Would you like to leave a message?"

Something occurred to her. She knew it was crazy, but what if, by some miracle, he was there? What if, against all hope, Brad Manford had come out of his hole? If he had, then he was better. And if he was better . . .

It was worth a shot.

"By any chance . . ." She held her breath. ". . . is Brad Manford there?"

"One moment, please. I'll transfer you."

Ersatz Cash returned. She was deaf to it. She sat stunned, numbly holding the phone in place.

Good lord, he *was* there. And now he would talk to her. Because she was being *transferred*.

And suddenly, she knew everything was going to be okay. They were going to fix this thing. Work it out, whatever it was. Together. And it would all be like it had been before.

As she waited, the boy stirred. He pushed himself to a half-sitting position, awake but less than alert. She gave him a cursory glance.

"I'm going to talk to Dad," she said giddily.

"I dreamed I was with Dad," he said, a bubbling sound in his throat. "We were playing . . ." He paused for an extra breath—and then another—". . . in my sandbox."

A lounge version of "Eleanor Rigby" grating her ear, she lowered the phone and looked at him more closely. He was panting, his breaths coming thin and quick. He was actually winded.

Winded by a handful of words.

"I wish . . ." he said, ". . . I was in my sandbox . . . now."

She put the phone in her lap. She could not understand this. He had not been like this before his nap. And was it just the light in the room, or did he look different?

She reached toward the end table for the peak flow meter. "Here, honey, sit up straight and blow into this."

With a confused look, the child took the device and, after nearly blowing in the wrong end, did as instructed. The indicator scarcely moved, not leaving the red zone.

"No, honey. You didn't do it right. Blow as hard as you can."

He took several breaths, preparing to speak. "I did."

"Let's try again."

"I'm tired."

"Please, honey. Just once more."

The child held the device in both hands. He did not seem to know what to do with it.

"Honey, put it in your mouth."

His small chest heaving, he looked blankly around the room.

And then she realized what it was about him. It was his lips. Their color. And to an extent, his entire face.

He was blue.

Because he was suffocating.

Her heart became an icy block. It ceased to beat. She could not move. She watched him, wanting to reach out. To take hold of him. To scream. But her throat, like his, was locked.

You worthless excuse for a mother. Do something!

He started to lie down. Or pass out.

As if waking from a dream, she sprang from her seat.

"Eamon, no!" She caught him, awkwardly propping him on the arm of the couch. "Keep your head up. You'll breathe better. This is better, right?" she babbled. "Now stay like this. Like this."

She ran to Derrick's room and groped through the backpack of medical supplies for the rescue inhaler. A few puffs, she thought, might help until the ambulance got there.

And what ambulance would that be? *You haven't called for one.*

She hadn't called the doctor either.

God, you worthless . . .

She could not find it. It had fallen out of its zip-lock bag. Frantic, she dumped out the backpack, the inhaler spilling onto the bed among sacks of drugs.

In the chaos, almost by reflex, she returned the phone to her ear.

Brad! Answer! Talk to me!

Replacing the Beatles' lyrics, a sleepy, tedious guitar spoke of lonely people and Father McKenzie.

Oh, that idiot secretary! What was wrong with her!

She sped back to the fading child. The phone between her head and shoulder, she was helping him with the inhaler when the receptionist came on as though answering a fresh call.

"I've been holding!"

"For who, ma'am?

"Brad Manford. I need to talk to him *right now.*"

"I'm sorry, ma'am, but Mr. Manford is no longer employed here."

The phone fell to the floor. She snatched it up, ending the call and hitting 911—then, awaiting an answer, held the barely conscious child to her breast, listening to the screeching chorus that came with his every breath, and hearing, too, the voice of her sad, dead father.

Chapter 45

Parting Company

Spattering crimson on wispy clouds, the evening sun fell to earth. The day's warmth was gone. Ahead lay another frozen night.

In the hole, caked in muck, Brad worked in the gathering shadows, while, at the edge of the pit, surrounded by high piles of soil, Paul Irvin sat on the side of the chaise longue, hunched over in the vanishing light, hands deep in his coat pockets.

"Gettin' mighty cool out here," the old man said, as Brad staggered up the slope with a shovel load.

"I hadn't noticed."

Brad passed by and dumped the load on a growing pile near the fence.

"Mind if I go in your house and warm up?" Irvin asked.

"It's the same in there as it is out here."

"Yeah, but we could shut the windows and turn on the heat."

Heading back to the hole, Brad stopped beside the old man. "Why don't you go to your own place?"

Letting the question hang, Irvin moved his shoulders closer to his knees, further compressing himself.

"I wish I knew how much longer," he said. "You think it's down at the end of that root? Whatever it is?"

Brad looked at the cottonwood's taproot, still plump where it sank through ground yet unexcavated. "Or deeper."

"Deeper?" The old man made a scoffing sound. "And you think you're gonna get there with a shovel and a mattock?"

"Anything is possible," Brad said, reentering the pit.

"Brad, look, I think it's time for Plan B."

"What's that?"

"Tryin' somethin' else. Somethin' other than what you're doin'." The old man stood, speaking down into the hole. "Brad, you can't keep on like this."

Brad was coming up with another load. "I feel fine."

"You look like shit."

"I don't care." He tromped on toward the pile at the fence.

"Brad, I'm just sayin', look at this logically. Think it through. There's got to be a better way."

Brad disposed of the dirt and started back to the hole. "This is the way."

"But Brad . . ." Irvin shook his head. "Listen, you may be right. It may be deeper. A *lot* deeper. And if it is, you can't do this by yourself."

Short of the pit, Brad stopped, his hands vising the shovel with an explosive stranglehold.

"Paul, I told you, this is my hole."

The old man nodded appeasingly. "Yes, it's your hole, but if you just had someone to help . . ."

"Like you, I suppose."

"No, not me."

"Who, then?"

"A professional," Irvin said.

Brad started down the slope.

"Brad, just hear me out."

Boiling over, Brad spun to face the old man. "Fine! Talk!"

"We hire one of those Caterpillars," Irvin said hurriedly. "You know, the ones with the big front loaders? Hell, they can move more dirt in five minutes than you can in half a day. And I'll pay for it."

Brad turned and went down the slope.

"So, will you do it?" Irvin asked.

"No."

"Brad, for God's sake, be reasonable."

From the deepest part of the hole, Brad stared at the old man, his muddied form mixed with the dim shades of the darkening cavity.

"It's time for you to shut up."

———

In the east, night had fallen; to the west lay its dusky precursor. And as the last of the day died away, the plodding march in and out of the hole continued, Brad pausing only to switch on the camping light and direct its beam low in the crater.

Sitting several feet from the pit, Irvin could not quite see its bottom. Brad had been digging down—straight down—for some time. Digging a hole within the hole. It was dangerous, Irvin thought. Just inviting a cave-in. *But far be it from me to say anything. He can learn the hard way.*

The old man sat static, his tired eyes fixed on the brightening stars while a full moon rose and waves of southbound geese crossed its globe. The honking calls waned and disappeared as the sound of the mattock and the shovel and the slogging of steps up and down the slope went on, producing a rhythm nearly hypnotic. There was, in time, though, another sound. At first inconspicuous. But ever more perceptible. It came from the hole. A splashing of some kind.

Brad was coming up again. There was a squishing with his every stride. And in the glow at the crater's lip, Irvin could see it dripping from the shovel.

The old man stood and looked into the bottom of the hole. The light was shining right on it. There was no mistake.

"Brad?" he said. Then, getting no response, somewhat louder: "Brad!"

Silent, Brad emptied the shovel and returned below ground.

"Brad, you've hit water."

"You think I don't know that?"

"You can't dig through water."

"Watch me."

"But Brad, you're into the water table. And the deeper you go, the worse it's gonna get."

Brad dredged out a shovel of soggy soil and labored up the slope.

"Look, this just won't work," Irvin said. He waited as Brad slid the runny load from the shovel and started back. "We need to get one of those big Cats I was talkin' about. I'm tellin' you, we get one of those things in here tomorrow and it'll be over in thirty minutes. And I know a guy . . ."

His voice trailed off as, several steps away, Brad, all but invisible, came to a looming halt, his head and shoulders etched in black against the moon.

"I told you a while ago to shut up."

"I'm just tryin' to help."

"Don't lie to me." The voice, seeming disembodied, came low and rasping. "You're not fooling me, old man. You never have."

Irvin found himself talking faster. "Brad, I—I don't know what you mean. I really don't."

"Yes, you do. We both know why you're here." Then, in a whispered tone not altogether human: *"You want what's down there."*

In the next moment, as if awakening from some lesser state of consciousness, eyes that had been all but shut widened, their bloodied whites floating in the dark.

And slowly, they advanced.

Twice, Irvin tried to speak, but couldn't, his throat swelling against the effort. At last, he forced it through.

"I do want it. . . . But not for myself."

The eyes bore down. And in the light of the moon, Irvin saw shadowy hands gripping the shovel. He saw the blade come shoulder high.

He glanced back at the yawning pit—his only path of retreat.

Useless.

He felt himself sinking. Sinking deeper than the hole. As the ghastly eyes—eyes that would bury him—closed in. The shovel lifting higher.

The night held the quiet of death as the thing of dirt and clay stood inches from the trembling old man.

"Leave this place," it said, "and do not ever come back."

Chapter 46

Promises to Keep

It might have been midnight. Or near sunrise. He had lost all sense of minutes and hours. They no longer had meaning. They quantified nothing. Time moved solely as a product of his own effort. It advanced only on the swing of a mattock or the thrust of a shovel.

And time, it seemed, was slowing down.

He was cramping up. Losing control. In a confining pocket, its floor some seven feet below what had been, before sundown, the bottom of the pit, he stood in water above his waist, an icy bath in which his legs had become wooden pegs and his arms locked in spasm.

The old man had been wrong, though. You *could* dig through water. You could take the shovel right down through it and find its earthen base and blindly scrape out a modicum of slime. And if you did that enough, you would eventually move what amounted to a decent load. It just took a little longer.

On the other hand, hauling anything to ground level was no longer an option. He was too far down in this new excavation. The walls around him were too steep. And he did not have the physical capacity. It was all he could do to raise the gobs of ooze to the base of the crater above. And as he went deeper, that, too, became ever more difficult.

It was unwise, he knew, to have dug this secondary hole so deep without sloping it. The soil down here was sandy and loose, and the water only added to its instability. But the cottonwood's root was tapering. He could feel it below the waterline, thinner than it was above—and thinning even more as it met the soil below. Its end, he thought, was but a few feet away. Or less. And if that also marked the end of this torment—if there was any possibility of that—there could be no delay.

He would push harder.

And he did. But there was too much pushing back. There came a point where his hands simply ceased to function. He could not tell, without looking, if he was even holding the shovel. And then he could not seem to hang on to it. Again and again he nearly lost it in the murky water, lunging for it convulsively, hugging it with clumsy arms to save it from sinking. And there was no longer any way to really use it. Not effectively. Yet he continued, teetering on frostbitten legs, vainly pecking about the dirty soup as he quaked from the cold and icicles stiffened in his hair.

When the hole caved in, he collapsed along with it, the tumbling dirt slamming him below the water, pressing him to the bottom of the hollow. He flipped about in the throes of what seemed like drowning until, by sheer force of buoyancy, he found the surface, his nose and throat plugged with sludge as he gasped, reflexively, against the suffocating blockage. In another instant, gagging, retching, he felt the night's frigid air on his face.

With nothing left, he floated in the slush, unable to move. He was finished.

A string of Stratotankers passed over. They came and went like sheep jumping a fence. And in his drowsy confusion, he heard the last one ringing. Ringing as it ran to fields far away.

And the ringing became a voice.

Her voice.

"Hi, you've reached the Manfords. At the tone, please leave a message."

A beep. A pause. Then, smooth and sarcastic, a second speaker.

"Hey, partner. Guess who?"

Strange. He had totally forgotten about this little mess.

"It's your old buddy, Skip. Say, I just wanted to remind you about that little package you promised to send. I sure hope it's in the mail by tomorrow, because if I don't see the postman this weekend, well . . ." Laughter, measured and diabolic. "Anyway, you take care."

What did it matter? Soon, nothing would. Already, the pain was gone. No more shivering. No more throbbing of joints and relentless fatigue. No feeling at all.

Another string of planes. And in the vanishing rumble of the last passing sheep, he felt himself moving away. Losing contact with all that surrounded him.

Then, like a curtain falling, came utter blackness. Without shape or size, he drifted in a place that seemed as vast as a universe and as small as a hole in the ground. Somehow, he felt he had been here before—that, in a way, he had always been here. A place of endless dark and solitude. Of nothingness.

Yet the void was not absolute. For within it lay a sound. One he knew well. An unmistakable humming. But it was different here. Louder. Constant. Nearly unbearable. It shook him like a tuning fork and brought with it echoes from another world: the sound of a child wheezing and coughing, a woman wailing and moaning.

And it gave voice to memories.

Is there something that can make me well?

You mean like medicine?

Uh-huh.

I don't know.

If there is, will you get it for me?

He had promised. He had promised the boy in the calm of an autumn evening.

He had promised her, too—that he would love her. Forever. And a man was supposed to—*had* to—make good on such things.

He felt the return of something and realized it was, in fact, feeling itself. A sensation of bobbing in water. And in the next moment, through eyes straining to open, blotted with mud and unable to focus, darkness was replaced by a glowing cloud. An orb of light.

It rose from the great root. It breached the water without a wave.

It hung before him.

It spoke to him.

And its voice was his own.

PART SIX

WINTER

Chapter 47

Vacancy

*L*ong after the final days of Lu-Kesh; after its supplanters had become dust and The Way of Stones broken and buried; after the Clovis People had swept the plains and hunted the great beasts—mammoth, sloth, mastodon—to extinction; after others had taken their place and the villages of the Wichita dotted the prairie; after armored men had come on horseback seeking gold, and men in buckskin and blue uniforms had come from the east speaking of a Great White Father; after all that, and more, the one who had been called Keeper dwelled on within the hill.

He dwelt, as he always had, in isolation. But he heard the racket of the world around him. And of all that racket, the noise of Man—as it had been since Man had been Man—rose most prominent. He heard Man's shouts and laughter. His fine verse and bawdy tales. His sweet songs and grieving cries.

And he saw, as well. He saw Man's wars and suffering. His pleasures and jubilation.

He wondered about Man. He always had. For while he knew the ways of Man, he did not understand Him. Because Man did not merely create. Man did not merely observe. Man did not merely destroy.

Man felt.

And he did not.

He tried to imagine what it would be like to feel. To feel love. To feel hate. To feel something. Something beyond the eons of emptiness.

But he could not. It was not in him.

Because he was not Man.

But were not all things possible? And had he not denied himself long enough? It was time, he thought, to walk with Man.

And he came down from the hill.

For a week, the old man did not walk the commons. And when he again crossed the creek, he did not dawdle at the fence. The gate bore a new padlock, and as he moved east of the property line, he could see a patrol car in the drive out front. In the house, a single police officer sat at the island in the kitchen, reading a newspaper and drinking coffee. Upstairs, the broken window had been boarded over.

The next day brought more police, scouring the house. And that evening, they had come to his door. A detective had asked about the hole.

"Tell me, sir, what was going on there? Was he burying something?"

"No, he was tryin' to dig somethin' up."

"What?"

"I don't know."

"But weren't you helping him?"

"Not really."

"A man he worked with, a Mr. Miller, says you were there."

"Well, yeah, I was, but just off and on. I was just watchin'. I was curious, you know. It was a little unusual, a man diggin' a hole that size."

"You didn't assist him in any way?"

"Not with the diggin'."

"What did you assist him with?"

"Just brought him stuff. Food and water."

"Anything else?"

"Well, a shovel, 'cause I knew he was fixin' to dig and I didn't know if he had one. Gave him a mattock, too."

"A mattock?"

"Yeah, you know, with a chisel and an axe head? It's good for loosenin' ground and choppin' roots and such."

The detective had shown him a picture. "Is this what you're talking about?"

"Yeah, that's a mattock."

"Is it *your* mattock?"

"Could be."

"Colonel, I need to ask, have you ever heard of a man named Ronald Delvechio?"

None too soon, they had left. But the following day, they had returned across the way with shovels of their own. They had sifted through the piles of dirt and sand and clay. And they had gone into the hole, cracking the ice at its bottom and trying to dig further down.

But Irvin could have told them it was folly, trying to dig through water.

And he could have also told them there was nothing to find. The leaves of the cottonwood had stiffened and fallen. The tree's barren carcass listed toward the hole. And the great root that had once sustained it lay as withered as a molted snakeskin.

At first, with photos of the missing family on national display, the reports of sightings had come in waves. The child, alone, was purportedly seen in seven states, but every such claim was proven a case of misidentification. It was much the same for the boy's mother, who also had her share of near lookalikes—although the police noted that none had quite the shade of eyes as the woman for whom they were searching.

As for the one called "the suspect," he was likewise allegedly spotted in varying locales. But the authorities had, understandably, expressed their greatest interest in accounts gathered from Southern California, where, during ten-days' time, a man of matching description—often characterized as dazed and wandering aimlessly—had been seen fleetingly in Pomona, Riverside, Yucca Valley, and progressively at other points east until, at last, seen by a hiker entering the wilderness of the Turtle Mountains, he was seen no more. Soon after, with no further information to stoke the news cycle, interest in the story began to wane. And within a month of their disappearance, the Manfords were all but forgotten.

The occupant of cell five had been brought in that morning. He had been found not along a road, but in a snow-covered pasture, a mile or more from the nearest thoroughfare. The owner of the property had reported him. He was confused. He spoke largely in groans and grunts. He had no identification.

He did not even know his name.

It was thought he must live nearby. Dressed only in jeans, a sweat-shirt, sopping tennis shoes, and work gloves—the whole of his garments badly worn and tattered—he certainly could not have survived the freezing wind chill for long. And though the county was thinly populated and neither the landowner nor either of the deputies on the scene recognized him, that stood for little, because who could say what this individual really looked like? Covered with a layer of filth, his face torn and pocked with scabs, he had appeared as a wounded animal risen from a grimy lair. And there had been an odor to match. The two lawmen had pounded hands to decide the car in which he would ride to town.

At the jail, he had been taken straightaway to a shower. He had cooperated, washing and drying himself—albeit slowly, as if he was just learning how. He was then given a shave and clean clothes—underwear, a t-shirt, socks, a pair of second-hand loafers, an orange jumper—and placed in his cell. One of the deputies had brought him a chicken salad sandwich. He had eaten none of it. For several hours, personnel from both the sheriff's office and the courthouse next door came by to look at him through the bars, trying to identify him. No one could.

Late in the afternoon, the one called John Doe was taken to a cramped room with a small folding table, four chairs, a sink, a refrigerator, and a microwave, which, when not in use for interrogation, served as a break area. He sat at the table, with the county's wrinkled and morbidly obese sheriff directly across. Two deputies sat lazily on either side of their superior. One of their nameplates said HOWARD, the other MORRELL.

"I'm Ned Gasper," said the sheriff. "You know why we picked you up?"

Dead-faced, John Doe awaited the answer.

"You were trespassing on private property," Gasper said. "Now, you're not charged with anything. Not yet. But I'm keeping you here because I'm not about to turn loose of you until I know who you are. Understand?"

In response, a sluggish nod.

"Can you talk?" the sheriff asked with a snotty air.

The reply was not immediate. "Yes."

"Then you need to tell me about yourself. Who are you?"

A shrug. "I don't know."

"Really? You're sure about that?"

"Yes."

"Have you thought hard about it?"

"No."

"Then do that," Gasper said. "Think hard."

For a time, eyes down, the subject seemed in compliance. The sheriff waited. A clock on the wall ticked audibly.

"Have you figured it out?"

"No."

"Well . . ." Eyes bulging, the fat inquisitor studied his witness. "Do you know where you live?"

"No."

"Do you live around here?"

"Where is *here?*"

"This is New Mexico, buddy. Does that ring a bell?"

"No."

"So you don't live here?"

"I don't think so."

"How did you get here?"

"I think I walked."

"From where?"

"I don't know."

Frowning, the sheriff slouched in his chair, lightly drumming his belly with the fingers of both hands, then exhaling a frustrated breath as he pulled a pack of Wrigley's Spearmint from the breast pocket of his uniform. He wadded a piece of gum into his mouth and flipped the wrapper onto the table.

"Sir," he said, "do you know where you were going this morning?"

"Yes."

"You do? Where?"

"Home."

"Home?" The sheriff leaned forward. "You said before you didn't know where you lived. So now you do? And where is that? Where is your home?"

"It is where it is."

"Don't get smart with me, buddy. Now, answer me. Where is your home?"

John Doe silently aimed a finger toward the refrigerator.

"Excuse me?"

"He's pointing east, boss," Howard said.

"East?" The sheriff seemed unsure of his deputy's interpretation. "Is that what you're telling me? You were going east?"

"I still am."

Ned Gasper chewed his gum and huffed a small laugh. "Not till I get some answers, you aren't." He leaned back and looked at Howard. "You got the file?"

"Not much to it." Howard passed over a folder containing several loose sheets of paper.

"What's this?" Gasper asked the deputy, running a finger over one of the pages.

"That's what Grady told us."

The sheriff looked at the paper as he spoke. "Sir, when you were taken into custody, you were on land owned by a man named Grady Harlock. And Mr. Harlock told my deputies that when he first saw you, it looked like you were carrying something. What was it?"

"I don't know."

Gasper made a face. "But you were carrying something?"

"Yes."

"What happened to it?"

"Nothing. I have it."

"Where?"

"With me."

"In your pocket?"

"No." The anonymous hands rose from the table, their palms less than a foot apart, as if holding something. "Right here."

The sheriff looked at the hands—scarred, empty mitts of torn flesh—then at his deputies.

"He's clean," Morrell said. "I swear."

Howard nodded in agreement.

"Mr. Doe," Gasper said, "I think we better take you somewhere and have some nice folks look after you."

Someone was coming fast down the hall. A tall, black-haired deputy with LOPEZ on his nameplate opened the door and looked in. He spoke with an urgency.

"Boss," he said, "you better take a look at this."

Gasper strained himself out of his chair and waddled into the hall. There was the sound of rustling of paper, and seconds later, the sheriff's disbelief.

"Ho-lee shit."

Chapter 48

Ghost in the Machine

An hour later he sat in handcuffs and leg irons, the two deputies who had before reclined with disinterest now standing at his flanks.

The tall man, Lopez, stood to his rear, a Taser at the ready.

"Your situation has changed," Ned Gasper said, reseating himself at the table. Chewing his gum, the sheriff seemed about to grin. He looked at his deputies. "Has anyone Mirandized him?"

"I did," Morrell said, "this morning when we took him in."

In thought, the sheriff nodded slowly. "Well, what's good once is always better twice." He pulled a card from the same pocket that held his gum and read from it. "Do you understand each of the rights I have explained to you?" he asked after.

John Doe nodded.

"Is that a yes?"

"Yes."

Gasper stole a look at the surveillance camera mounted above the refrigerator. "And with those rights in mind, will you talk to me?"

"I already have. What else can I tell you?"

"First thing, you can tell me who you are. And we're not going to play any more games, understand? Now, what's your name?"

"I told you, I don't know."

From the file, now thicker than before, the sheriff produced a sheet of paper and placed it in front of his prisoner. It carried a drawing of a face, words in Spanish, and a number with a dollar sign.

"Does that refresh your memory?"

"No."

"You don't think that's your face?"

"I don't know whose face it is."

"Do you know what this person did?"

"No. It says he's a monster."

"So, you read Spanish?"

"I guess I do."

"Do you also read English?"

"I don't know."

"Let's find out."

The sheriff placed another paper on the table. It showed three prominent capital letters: an F, a B, and an I. There was other writing and a color
photograph.

"See that picture?" Gasper said. "That's you, right? And you see that
name?"

"Bradley Manford?"

"Yeah."

"I'm Bradley Manford?"

"No, not really, because, you see, it goes on to say that Bradley Manford,
a/k/a Brad Manford, is just the name you've used for the last ten years or
so. It's not your real name. It's an alias. It's made up. And that's true, isn't it?"

"Maybe. I don't know."

"And it says also that you passed yourself off as a lawyer out in California, and then in Wichita, Kansas. But you aren't really a lawyer, are you, sir?"

"I don't know."

"Okay, let's see if you know some other things. For instance, do you
know that you beat up a police officer last month in Wichita?"

"No."

"Well, you did. I just got off the phone with the police there, and they
told me the officer was wearing a body cam. Got you dead to rights. Got
your license plate, too. And that's how they started putting all this together.
So, whatever your name is, they know it was you. And now, so do I."

The one in chains looked unaffected.

Ned Gasper chomped his gum. "Why did you beat up that police
officer?"

"I don't know. I don't remember doing it."

"Do you remember what you did after you beat him up?"

"No."

The sheriff gazed into the dark eyes across the table.

"You went home and dug a hole in your back yard," he said. "The officer I talked to in Wichita said it was the God-Almightiest hole anyone's ever seen. And you're telling me you don't remember that?"

A hole. Something about that seemed to register. A hole and the need to dig it. But that was all. The rest of it—whatever there had been—had not persisted.

The small room was stuffy. Rings of sweat grew under the fat sheriff's arms.

He looked through his notes. "There was a man that was with you when you dug that hole. A neighbor of yours. You borrowed some tools from him. Remember that?"

"No."

"A shovel and a mattock?"

The prisoner stared at the sheriff, unblinking.

The sheriff looked back at his notes. "Do you . . ." He paused to correct himself. "*Did* you know a man by the name of Ronald Delvechio?"

"I don't think so. Who is he?"

"He's nobody. He's dead. He was found that way last month in his apartment in Los Angeles. Do you know how he died?"

"No."

"Yes, you do."

The other said nothing.

"He died," Gasper said, "because that mattock you borrowed from your neighbor found its way from Wichita, Kansas, to Los Angeles, California. And it further found its way into Mr. Delvechio's apartment. And from there it found its way into Mr. Delvechio." The sheriff leaned forward and tapped the Mexican wanted poster. "This was also found in Delvechio's apartment. But I think you know that. And I think you know what it means."

Working his gum, Gasper looked again at the surveillance camera, giving the accused a moment to mull things over.

"Mr. Manford—or whoever you are—it's time to stop pretending you can't remember things. It's time to come clean. It'll be better for you. It'll be better for everyone. And obviously, we can't help Delvechio, and we can't help those poor people in Mexicali. But maybe, if you'll let us, we can still help your wife and son."

"My wife and son?"

"You're not going to tell me you don't know about them. Don't tell me that, buddy."

"I don't know what else I *can* tell you."

"Good God," the sheriff grumbled, pushing back from the table. "I told you, boy, I've had enough of this."

"But what are their names?"

"You know their names. Now tell me where they are."

"How would I know that?"

"Because you're the one that took them from the hospital. Isn't that right?"

"What hospital?"

Running with sweat, the sheriff's bloated face turned a livid shade of red.

"The hospital in California! Where your son was! Your son who was damn near about to die!"

"And I took them?"

Gasper jutted his jaw. "Didn't you? How else would they just disappear? And we know you were out there then, because that's when Delvechio was killed."

"But I don't . . . I can't . . ."

"Look . . ." The sheriff took a deep, angry breath. "If you want to do this all night, then that's what we'll do. But if you'll just be straight with me and help us find these people, then we'll take you back to your cell and get you some food and some rest and everything'll be a whole lot better. So please, just tell me what you did with your wife and your boy."

Ned Gasper and his deputies waited.

The clock on the wall ticked away, the sheriff's heavy breathing, the grinding of his gum, the only other discernible sounds.

Gradually, the suspect lowered his eyes. He seemed, at first, to be looking at his hands. He wasn't. He was staring at the space between. And with his wrists held by the cuffs only inches apart, he splayed his palms outward, creating a wider distance from one set of fingertips to the other as he appeared to again take hold of something. Something not seen.

The sheriff began to speak—but did not. A bead of sweat, having streaked a liver spot on his temple and run to his jowl, was ready to fall.

But did not.

And there was no more of the chewing sound. No more labored breathing. The ticking of the clock was not heard.

Something else was.

A humming. A deafening drone.

And a thousand years passed. Ten thousand. More. Enough time to understand. Enough to look into that which he held, which he kept, and know, finally, that he was holding, keeping, himself.

Enough time, too, to find within that self the unbearable memory of total darkness. The darkness of an eternal abyss. A place dead and frozen where he alone—he, a thing made perfect in symmetry, perfect in function, more constant than the stars—had seen the last point of light flicker and fade and become useless matter; and had felt himself float endlessly among the burned-out cinders that had once given warmth and life; and had heard, in the depth of the oblivion—heard from within the smallest corner of himself—a message from his programmers, themselves gone long before the last of the galaxies, but their directive—their plea to replace that which was lost—surviving.

Speak, it said. Speak and that which is spoken shall be.

He had spoken. He had *commanded*. And within a virtual cosmos born of his own will—a new world within the old—a world within a world—there had been light. A vast explosion. An expansion.

He felt himself gliding among a radiance of new suns more countless than countless. Then settling. A sinking amid fire and steam. And after, days in the billions. The birth of creatures from watery bogs. Mere specks of life morphing to animal titans. Swimming, crawling, flying. Snarling and screeching and taking hunks of one another.

A flash of light and thunder. A great dying among the giants. Then, other beasts, some scurrying to the trees, some in chase. And a furry thing that grew and straightened itself and became master of itself and then (so it thought) master of its world.

He felt himself atop a rise—a lone hill on a grassy plain. And coming down from it. He saw, then, other things. The computations that were his thoughts skipped through them. Disregarding one after the next.

Until alighting upon a vision of a morning sun, its rays warming the captive space of a glass atrium. And with that sight, the sound of hard heels on a harder floor. The ding of an elevator.

And a sense of ascending. Of losing himself. Of leaving behind all thought of who and what he was and becoming more and more something once only imagined.

Then, doors parting.

And yes, yes, the eyes.

That look.

A woman.

His.

And a tiny voice. A child: *Will you get it for me?*

And he saw, then, the form of a man, writhing in the depths of a great hole. In the dirty, watery bosom of this place men called Earth. There, he had suffered. Suffered as men suffer. But a light had risen from the mire and told him—*reminded* him—of things he could do beyond all conception of Man. And in a moment—the very next moment—he had. With perfect speed he had traveled. And all he had willed be done, was done.

Yet, gaining much, he had lost more, the dream of Man within him sensing its fabrication even as the cold mechanism of his true self struggled to deny its existence. And in that disordered state of doubt and incredulity, he had become nothing. Neither man nor machine. An all but lifeless shell, devoid of identity, without function, mindlessly wandering cities, mountains, wastelands. Only to come here. To gaze into himself and find himself. And to find himself desperately wanting, much as his creators had wanted, to recapture a thing of infinite value. No, not a universe. But for him, a thing more precious: The belief—the *absolute* belief—that he was something he was not. For without that, he could not have the things of Man. Not in the way Man had them, with His mortal thoughts and feelings. Knowing, without question, that He was Man.

It had fled him, all of it—those thoughts, those feelings, those *things*— as if fallen into some black hole. Gone.

Could he ever regain it?

It was time, he thought, to try. To find a way—some way—again, to *believe.*

There resumed a ticking from the clock. The bead of sweat fell from the sheriff's jowl. He chewed his gum, as before, breathing in noisy, nasal rhythm.

"Okay, buddy," he said, "I'm done waiting."

"So am I."

From beneath the table came the sound of metal snapping. He stood, and, with the slightest jerk of his arms, popped the chain of his handcuffs.

"What the . . ."

"Son of a bitch!"

"Hold him!"

"I can't!"

"My God!"

"Victor! The Taser! The Taser!"

"I am! I am!"

Chapter 49

Sortie

Paul Irvin had continued his trips to the fence. But the effort had been born more of habit than hope. Day after day, the scene lay unchanged: The desolate lot with its absurd hole. Piles of soil ringing the pit like some amorphous army. The dead cottonwood collapsed and fallen as if into its own grave.

And the house dark, dormant. The window on the second floor still boarded over.

They wouldn't be back, he thought. The woman and the boy had been missing too long, and what might someday be found of them would probably require dental records. That was how it usually turned out. And Brad Manford—or whoever he was—would surely not risk a return. His litany of crimes was far too staggering. He had fooled everyone. Though not in the way of some ordinary scammer. He had been a fake, all right. But apparently a very lethal one. That cop, they said, had brain damage. And all that grisly stuff in Mexico . . .

But the police were wrong about the kidnapping. There was no way he could have taken his wife and son from that hospital. The P.I.'s murder, too. He couldn't have done it. Irvin had tried to tell them that day at his house. It had been the Tuesday before Thanksgiving, he had said. That night. That had been the last time he had seen Brad.

No, I'm sorry, Colonel, but you're mistaken. You have to be. The woman and the kid, they disappeared early that Wednesday. Like one, two in the morning, our time. The coroner in L.A. says that's also about when Delvechio was killed. And there's no way he gets from here to there that fast. Not unless he has some kind of magical powers.

I know, but I'm tellin' you, it was Tuesday.

It was Monday, sir. A day earlier. That's the last time you saw him. Had to be. And he left for California either that night or first thing the next day.

But no one answering Brad's description had boarded a plane during that period. And he couldn't possibly have gotten there so quickly by train or car. No, even under the theory the police were proposing, it didn't make sense. And if they were wrong about that, couldn't they be wrong, too, about that wanted poster they had supposedly found in the dead man's apartment? Could be, Irvin thought, that poster had no connection to Brad whatsoever. Could be that face belonged to someone else.

But the way he had looked at him, holding that shovel. And that voice, so full of something strange and malevolent.

Do not ever come back.

Since that night, the old man had thought of those words every time he stood at the fence. And he thought of them now, his hands on the locked gate, the day's last light dropping red in the west, as it had that evening.

He jiggled the gate just enough to hear the latch clank against the iron post.

No, Irvin thought, he wouldn't be back. Not ever. Besides, he had found what he wanted.

But then again, was it possible that when he left the house that last time—and who could say for what reason—he had planned to come back? That he had left something, intending to return?

The old man jiggled the gate again.

He stared at the house.

The police had done their investigation, but he—he who had invested so much—had been given no access. And no, he hadn't asked. But if he had, they would have undoubtedly shooed him away. They didn't understand. They didn't understand any of it. Of course, he didn't understand much either. But he was way ahead of everyone else.

Everyone, that is, except the one who had dug that monstrosity of a hole. A hole whose secrets had vanished. There was nothing to be found there.

But in the house, who could say? The police could not possibly have known what to look for.

Or listen for.

And even if it—whatever *it* was—wasn't there (and it probably wasn't), there might yet be some clue. Some answer, however insufficient.

He glanced at the boarded-up window on the second floor, then at the padlock on the gate. And an idea that had festered for days and weeks at once became too tempting.

A full moon rose with the sunset and, by midnight, hung high and bright. Too much light, he thought. But within an hour, a bank of clouds crept in from the west, covering Perseus and the Pleiades and moving steadily eastward to eclipse the entirety of the celestial sky. The night suitably darkened, the old man donned a heavy coat and new work gloves, and quietly stepped out of his sliding back door with a hand towel, a flashlight, and a pair of 36-inch bolt cutters.

Against the city's faint backlight he could see the outline of trees ahead. As he entered the commons, things grew darker; the silhouettes disappeared. Yet he had no need for the flashlight. He knew the way, stepping to his right to avoid an unseen Osage orange, left to dodge another. In such fashion he reached the pointed stone and crossed the creek.

In the near pitch black he took care on the steep path, going slowly to avoid a slip among the dry leaves and rotting hedge apples. Halfway up, the instep of his left foot nevertheless found a clump of the useless fruit and he nearly took a tumble, but, grasping a tree trunk, righted himself and moved on.

It was darkest in the cedars. He emerged to find the house profiled against the city's pale glow. Reaching out, he located the fence, and reaching a second time, the gate.

The bolt cutters made short order of the padlock. Slow and cautious, he swung the gate without a squeak.

The hardest part was getting across the yard. He steered well clear of where he knew the hole to be, but en route to the deck stairs, stumbled blindly among the dirt piles. More than once he considered using the flashlight, but thought better of it.

On the deck, he glanced warily about, but assured himself that, so late, in the dark, and with no other houses in view, there was almost zero chance of being caught. In fact, he thought, as secluded as it was back here, he would have been almost as safe doing this in broad daylight.

Still, he hesitated.

Somewhere you shouldn't be, doin' somethin' you shouldn't be doin'.

And tomorrow was Christmas. Be a bitch to spend it in jail.

But at least he wouldn't be alone.

He wondered what old William B. Travis would have to say. Probably draw a line in the sand and dare him to cross it. Yeah, he thought, that's what he'd do.

He couldn't let old William B. down.

Remember the Alamo.

He looked through the small windows of the back door. Unable to see inside, he tried the knob. It wouldn't turn. Just above, he felt the keyhole to the deadbolt.

He folded the hand towel to roughly the size of one of the door's glass panes and placed it over one that, he judged, would allow him access to both the thumb-turn of the deadbolt and the lock on the knob. He took another quick look around, then, centering the butt of the flashlight over the towel, punched through the glass.

He stood listening to the dogs. The glass had broken with relatively little discord, but the falling shards had caught the attention of at least one local canine. Now, the barking came from all directions. He wasn't concerned, though. He was sure he hadn't been seen. And he was in the house.

This, of course, was the kitchen. He could remember where the table was. The counters, the island, the stove. The problem would be the rest of the place, none of which he was familiar with. No doubt, at some point he would need the flashlight to get his bearings, but hopefully not in rooms that faced the cul-de-sac. Folks down the block would crap their pants to see a light roaming this house.

Where to go first? He wondered about that room upstairs. The one with the broken window. He knew that had happened the night before the digging started. He had seen it that morning, Brad sitting at the top of the deck, waiting for him. Nothing had been said about it. But there had been that gas smell. Something had not seemed right.

He felt his way along the kitchen island, his hands running into a pile of papers, knocking some to the floor. He tromped over them. Newspapers, he thought. Probably one for every day the cops had been here. And there was something else on the counter. An empty box with a cellophane panel across its top.

Doughnuts.

He almost laughed out loud, forgetting, for just an instant, that he was in the process of committing a felony.

He moved toward the dining room. Through the sheer curtains, a porch light down the block shone bright enough to guide his way, and in its gleam he saw the fog of his own breath. He figured the cops had probably turned on the heat for themselves. But since then, either someone had turned it off or, more likely, the power company had pulled the plug. It didn't really matter, he thought at first. But then again, it might. He had never seen anything resembling a security system in the house and had assumed there was none. Yet if there was, and they had cut the electricity, the problem had been conveniently eliminated.

Unless the system was battery operated. With a silent alarm. In which case, the doughnut-eaters were already on the way.

Oh, you old man! You never used to think like that. You never used to worry about anything. Now quit being such a yellow belly and get your ass in gear.

From the dining room he found the staircase, and, upon ascending, total darkness. A closed space. A good place to use the flashlight.

He flicked it on and found himself in a hallway, his breath steaming the corridor. On the right were two doors, one closed.

That one, he thought. The closed one. That was it.

The dogs had gone quiet, and as he turned off the flashlight, he listened. Listened for the sound—the gentle hum—he had come to know. But there was only stillness. A silence so acute it seemed to make its own noise.

Then, startling him, a clunk. A muffled bump. Like a car door slamming down the block.

Or closer.

He stood frozen.

And there it was again. Only not outside. More like in the house. Down the hall. There had been another door closed at the end. The master bedroom, he guessed. It had come from there.

He put the flashlight in his coat pocket and, with both hands, raised the bolt cutters.

This bastard'll do some damage.

He waited. For the door to crack. Or a footfall.

And waited.

Nothing.

Dumbass. Houses expand. They contract. They settle. Yours does. They all do.

He gave it another minute, poised with the bolt cutters.

He told himself he was wasting time. He moved down the hall toward the closed door on his right, turning on the flashlight just long enough to find the knob. He pushed the door, feeling it drag along the carpet as he stepped inside.

The room was nearly as dark as the hall. A Venetian blind covered the single window opening, only the weakest of light diffusing through its louvers from the window's undamaged upper pane, nothing through the tightly boarded lower space. It was a small room. He could sense that. But what was its function?

He turned on the flashlight to find a roll-top desk and a chair, and on the wall to his right, pictures of Sally Manford and her little boy. Beautiful woman, that Sally. But the child had never seemed healthy. He looked worse here, though.

And again it came. That sound. Like the thump of something heavy falling against a wall.

Enough light. He turned it off, waiting, his thoughts wandering. Thinking of the woman and the boy. How innocent they had been. Like so many he had seen shoved into holes distinctly resembling that in the back yard. Their resting place forgotten. A stand of weeds their only marker.

He popped the light on, directing the beam to the wall adjacent to the door. One of Dali's horrid works. That sort of crap had never done much for him.

That sound *again.*

Off the light.

Waiting. Waiting.

God, what was he so scared of? It was only the damn house.

Get on with it.

He had seen a closet near the room's entrance. He turned on the flashlight and opened the folding doors.

Empty space.

There was still the desk. Dropping the bolt cutters, he moved in behind the roll-top, searching. Pulling the drawers out. Finding a printer in one. In others, pens, pencils, paper. Meaningless items.

An icy breeze blew through the slimmest of cracks between the board and window opening. Something about it pissed him off. The whole house did. It was like the cottonwood. Dead. Broken. Ineffectual.

In a rage, he swept the light about the room, demanding a sign. A clue. Some small piece of validation. But there was nothing. It had been a waste, this quest. His long effort. His anticipation. His tremendous hopes.

All taken away.

He swung the light without thought, shadows spraying the walls, the corners. Then . . . stop.

It hung on the wall, several feet from the closet. He came closer, the flashlight falling on crudely written words that, in the shifting incandescence, he could scarcely read. But he knew some Spanish.

MIS MUNDOS.

My worlds.

And below. He trained the light squarely on it. Some kind of symbol.

There was a bewildering moment before he fully realized. And when he did, another moment of just standing, refusing to believe.

Then, awkward steps backward, hitting the far wall, knocking a picture to the floor, losing the flashlight.

He did it after, he told himself. *After he saw the rock.* There was no other way.

And yet he knew that was not possible. No more possible than a man flying to California without a plane.

He felt unwell. The room moved to his right. And around. And to his right again. He heard himself breathing. Gasping. And as he panted, in the dead air between each respiration, a sound.

A humming.

In the hall, a light sped past the door. Car lights, he thought, swinging in the cul-de-sac. The police.

But no, no. Not lights from a vehicle. From this room you could not see such a thing.

Suddenly, he felt too feeble to stand. He fell to his knees.

The light again, in the hall. A ball of it dashing. Back and forth.

Get out, he thought. *Get out!*

He threw himself forward. Old joints pushing hard. Forcing himself to the door, into the hall.

Shadows and whirling light filled the corridor. And at its end, at the stairs, a figure. A thing enormous, undefined.

He fell prostrate, hiding his face, whimpering.

Something came from behind. Then from everywhere.

And he was falling. Falling into a place darker than the house. A hole. An oblivion. The humming there split his ears. But amid the din, there were yet other sounds. Voices. Of a child. And a woman.

Chapter 50

Out of the Rabbit Hole

It was a familiar sound. The passing of jet engines.

KC-135, she heard the old man say. *Stratotanker.*

But in the plane's fading rumble, she opened her eyes to find herself alone. She could not see much. The room held the faint light of late evening or early morning. She had no idea which.

And why was that? Well, it was obvious. She had gotten drunk. So drunk she had passed out.

But how, she wondered, could she have done such a thing at Eva's? Where liquor was anathema?

Yet, as her eyes adjusted to the light, she recognized furnishings unlike her sister's. And she did not lie on a floor, as she had in Derrick's room, but on a bed. A bed to which she was well accustomed.

Her own bed. In her own room.

This was Kansas.

She sat up, expecting the room to spin, but it didn't. There was no headache, either. No dry mouth. No queasy stomach. In fact, she felt quite well.

What kind of gin does this?

Could it be she hadn't gotten drunk? If she had, she certainly didn't remember it. Not even the first sip. No, she thought, there had been no drinking. None. She hadn't had a drop since . . . when? That night in her mother's trailer?

But if that was true, then why was she sleeping in tennis shoes? And a pair of Liz Claiborne shorts?

Something was awry.

She laid back the covers to get out of bed and felt a shuddering chill. The room was like an icebox. Goosebumps on her legs, she strode quickly to the bedroom door, stepped into the hall, and flicked the light switch beside the upstairs thermostat.

Nothing.

She played with the thermostat controls.

More of the same.

God, what was it in here, twenty degrees?

She rubbed her arms below the sleeves of her t-shirt and stared about the hall with the vague feeling she belonged somewhere else.

In a hospital, perhaps.

But she could not think straight in this cold. She scampered to her closet and, in the dark, threw on the heaviest thing she could find: an old ski jacket she had not worn since a trip with Brad to Bear Mountain. They had been just a couple then. The days before Eamon.

Eamon.

Reaching for a pair of jeans, she drew her hand back, cursing herself. The child was probably freezing to death. She left the pants and rushed from the closet, through the bedroom.

But as she entered the hall, a vision. A picture of the boy lying so very still. Eyes closed. Face ashen. And she could hear, in her thoughts, a sound. A pumping rhythm. The motorized indifference of a ventilator.

And a doctor's voice: *We won't know for some time.*

Feet smacking the carpet, she came to a rigid stop. Her mind, in that instant, seized by a possibility unspeakable.

She braced against the wall, heart pounding.

His door was open.

"Eamon?"

She moved slowly down the hall, past the closed door of Brad's office, then, nearing the boy's room, slower.

She looked in. His bed was made. Everything in its place.

An empty room.

Another plane was coming, and with the building thunder came a bursting panic. She shot to the stairs, calling down.

"EAMON!"

The roar of the plane peaked and ebbed, and in its passing left the house in abject quiet.

"Eamon? . . . Honey?"

Her words echoed in the stairwell, mixing with the cold dead air. Fading like the plane.

She stood motionless, gripping the newel post. Her head feeling light and starting to spin.

Then, in a second frenzied spurt, she took the stairs with abandon. Two at a time. She slipped near the bottom. Fell against the banister. Bounced off and banged the wall. Caught herself. Leaped forward. Hit the landing.

At full gallop, she turned toward the family room, shouting the boy's name. Shouting it over and over. Running without thought for direction.

But nearing the picture window, she slowed and fell silent. Then stopped.

She sucked in a breath and held it. Trying to comprehend.

A bomb had gone off in the back yard.

Hugh Miller had said something about a hole.

A *hole?*

The man was an idiot.

This was a reservoir in need of water. Lake Manford waiting to be filled.

And a yard littered with enough excavated soil to dam a river.

So, it was true. Brad had lost it. Cracked up. Even worse, it seemed, than she had feared.

Nauseous, she turned away from the window and noticed the couch smeared with hardened clay, a trail of which led to the kitchen. The worst of the mess lay near the French door that opened onto the deck, where splinters of what appeared to be glass sparkled on the soiled wood floor.

She came closer. Indeed, it was glass. A broken pane from the door. Cold air wafting through the breach.

Screw it, she thought. Someone had broken in, but screw it. And screw the filth and the ridiculous cavern in the back yard and the man who had dug it. Screw it all. For the time being, they were but distractions.

Where was Eamon?

Surely she knew. She had to. *You're his mother, for God's sake.*

Okay, she thought, start with what you remember. The hospital. The one in Inglewood. Centinela Hospital. Pediatric ICU. She had sat next to his bed. She remembered the ventilator, the doctor. Then what?

Think.

Then what? WHAT?

Then . . . waking up. Here.

And in between, nothing. Literally nothing.

Gradually, a realization swept over her, and with it, a fresh horror—a fear not for the child, but for herself. She put her hands to her face, covering her mouth, gasping frigid air through her fingers. Shaking, but not from the cold.

She was missing something.

Time itself.

Frantic, she felt the pockets of her shorts for her cell phone. It wasn't there. It wasn't in the kitchen, either. Nor the family room. And, of course, the house phone was dead.

There was nothing left here. This place was no longer meant to be lived in.

Yet someone—the back-door intruder, or Brad, or God-knew-who—had, at some point, been making himself at home. On the kitchen island sat an empty doughnut box and a collection of equally empty McDonald's coffee cups, their plastic lids still in place. Nearby lay a rumpled stack of newspapers, several sections having fallen to the floor, one with a dusty boot print stamped across it.

She picked up the dirty one—a front-page section—her eyes wandering to its upper left corner. The date of publication.

She sucked in a breath, feeling herself grow colder than the air around.

She cursed in an incredulous, trembling whisper.

A week. She had lost a week.

In something like a dream, she shuffled to the dining room and looked blankly out the window. A light snow was coming down, and through the flakes she could see a Christmas display in a yard down the street. Blow-ups of Santa and a reindeer floating on tethers. And in her drive lay more newspapers. A pile of them in plastic sacks. Perhaps a dozen. No, two.

One, she thought, for every day.

A month? Was it possible?

She looked again at the newspaper. The footprint obscuring its top half, she scanned the bottom.

She had almost expected the headline: MOTHER AND SON STILL MISSING.

But the kicker, just above, she had not foreseen.

In a progressing stupor, she followed the lines of the story below. Reading until her mind felt as thick and numb as a stone and she could not go on. Could not even hold the paper.

And as it fell, even as she told herself *no-no-no*, the words of the kicker rang in her head:

Husband, Father Sought in Killings, Fraud, Assault.

Eyes glazed, she felt herself unable to move. To breathe. To *think*.

Then, a noise. A thud from within the house, shocking her to a more conscious state.

"Eamon?" she quivered.

Silence.

On instinct, she called for another. "Brad?"

A second thud. The floor upstairs creaking under a massive weight.

The sound of a knob turning. A door opening.

Measured footfalls on the staircase.

"What is it?" he said.

Chapter 51

The Stranger

He descended, watching her. His eyes never leaving her. He wore a suit and tie. Dress shoes. A soft cologne that filled the house.

On the landing, he stopped, awaiting an answer.

"Brad . . ." It was all she could manage.

"Are you okay?" he asked.

"Yes, just . . ." She could not get enough air. ". . . very surprised."

"At what?"

"You're here."

"Of course I'm here. Where else would I be?"

The question was not meant as rhetoric.

"Well, I don't know. It's just that I was yelling and no one answered."

"I heard you."

"Where were you?"

"Upstairs. In my office."

"Doing what?"

"Oh, you know."

His lips traced a smile in a way she had never seen. And his eyes. She did not like them. Something different there as well.

She put the question with a delicate innocence: "Brad, where is Eamon?"

The smile widened. "He's fine."

"No, *where* is he?"

"Somewhere safe."

"Here? In the house?"

"You might say that," he said. "Or you might not."

She felt herself losing control, her ruse of nonchalance about to fail. She fought against it.

"Brad, I want to see him."

"You will. Soon."

"No, now, please."

He shook his head. "I want us to be alone. Just for a while."

He started toward her. Slow and deliberate. Heels sounding on the hardwood.

That suit and tie. She remembered it from somewhere.

But those eyes. Glassy. As cold as the room. Not the ones she knew.

Facing him, she felt behind her for the dining room table and took a step back. Then another.

"Brad . . . sweetheart . . . please tell me what's going on."

"Going on?" he said. "What do you mean?"

Stride for stride, her retreat matched his advance.

"Well, it's just that, I don't know how I got here."

"I brought you here."

"From where?"

"It doesn't matter."

"But Brad, where have I been for the last . . . however long?"

"You've been with me."

"But *where?*"

"I told you, it doesn't matter."

Rounding the dining table, she felt for the kitchen threshold. "Brad, honey, look, I know you've had some . . . difficulties."

"Not really."

"You lost your job."

"That's nothing," he said. "I'll get it back. Or I'll get another. I can have any job I want. I can do any-*thing* I want. *Any-thing.* I know that now."

She was well into the kitchen. He, just entering. Strolling with serene confidence.

And she knew then where she had seen that suit and tie: He had been coming off an elevator.

"I'm sure it'll all work out," she said, hearing, in her own voice, the lack of sincerity. "But I'm just thinking about Eamon. He needs things. Expensive things. Doctors, medicine . . ."

"No, he doesn't."

"Brad, what are you saying? He *does*."

"No, he doesn't. Not anymore." He offered another smile—or rather, an imitation of one. "Sally, don't you know? All things are possible."

A forbidden thought crossed her mind—just as the kitchen island hit her squarely in the back, pinning her.

Still sauntering, he closed in.

"Brad, is he okay? Eamon?"

"I already told you, he's fine."

"Brad, you wouldn't . . ." She took a breath and held it.

"Wouldn't what?"

"You wouldn't hurt him, would you?"

There was a look of annoyance. "Hurt him? What kind of father do you think I am? What kind of *man*?"

"A wonderful father," she said at once, hoping to placate. "A wonderful man."

"I would never hurt him! And I would never hurt you. I love you. Forever."

But his words came like dirt from a hole. Lifeless. Meaningless.

A foot away, he stopped, staring at her. Head down, she dodged his gaze.

"Look at me," he said.

She looked up for a second, then away.

"*Look* at me."

She tried. She couldn't. It was horrible. And not the eyes as much as something that seemed to lie behind them.

He leaned closer, the fog of his breath merging with hers. Their vapors clearing and mingling and clearing again.

He would not quit staring.

She did her best to hold it back. But she couldn't. Not all of it. Crossing her arms tightly, she pursed her lips as her chest and shoulders shook, tears quietly running her face. He stood watching, a mere observer, seeming not to understand as she wiped her eyes. Mascara smearing her cheeks and nose.

She took a deep, steamy, shivering breath. "It's cold in here."

He glanced around the room as though looking for something.

"They've turned off the power," she said. "There's no heat. No lights. Nothing."

"Oh, but there is."

He reached for her. She moved away, arching backwards over the island. But along her jaw, in a slow, sweeping stroke, his touch found her. And with it came the sense of an electric shock. A painful spasm.

Yet in the next instant, a showering, comforting warmth. A warmth that held her and cloaked her and coursed through her like hot blood. A warmth that became a fire that shone with a light made just for her. A light that promised to satisfy all needs. All hungers. And in it, the world around her threatened to seep away like the memories of a dream lost upon awakening.

Already, it seemed, the room in which she stood had vanished, the man before her dissolving. His features—his very self—a mere façade, all falling away to reveal a glimpse of a nameless other beneath.

The thing behind the eyes.

She let loose a short, muffled screech, and, with a violent jerk of her head, cast off his hand.

"Something's wrong with me!"

"No," he said.

"I've lost my mind." With a quick side and backstep, she put the corner of the island between them. "And so have you."

She took a fleeting look behind her, toward the back door. Through the French windows she could see the snow still falling. But the deck wasn't yet covered. No slipping or sliding, she thought. And there would be little delay with the door; courtesy of whoever had broken that pane of glass, it was unlocked.

She thought she could beat him to it.

"Sally, don't," he said, warning her in a voice hard and desperate, while outside, the rumbling of an approaching KC-135 was squelched by the rising of a furious wind, the house bending and creaking.

She turned to make a dash.

He snatched her wrist, the house seeming ready to break in the gale.

"Let me go!"

"You can't leave!"

His grip tightened.

"You're hurting me!"

At once, he released his hold, clenching his fists and teeth in a visible struggle to calm himself.

The wind settled.

"I'm sorry," he said.

She stepped back, doubling the space between them as she rubbed her throbbing wrist. "I thought you weren't going to do that."

"I won't. Not ever again."

"Why should I believe you?"

He seemed about to answer, but didn't.

She moved further away.

"I want to ask you a question," she said, hesitating, as if to await permission, "and I don't want you to hurt me for it."

"I won't. I promise."

On the back of her bare legs she felt a blast of cold air and snow from the broken pane. A sign the doorknob was somewhere just behind her, within reach.

"Have you hurt other people? I mean, hurt them, you know . . . bad?"

He shook his head. "No. Never."

"I read something in the paper . . ."

"It's not true. Someone else did that."

"Who?"

"Someone you don't know. Someone troubled."

With a doubting nod, she looked away. "And do you know this troubled person?"

"I do."

"He sounds like some kind of psycho."

He shook his head in vigorous denial as the wind, in a burst, again rattled the house.

"No, it's not like that! If you could just understand. He's different. Not like you. Not like anyone. But he wanted to be. He *tried* to be. He just wanted to feel what people feel."

"By doing terrible things?"

"Not at first." He paused at length, as if not wanting to go on. "He tried so hard to feel happiness. To feel love. He tried, but he couldn't. So he tried to feel the very opposite. To feel disgust. Revulsion. Hatred of things. Even himself."

"And did he?"

She took a glance out the French door. The snow, though still rather light, was starting to pile up. A white film covering the deck and yard.

When she looked back, his eyes were turned to the ceiling.

"Not really," he said, his voice weakening. "He felt no sorrow, no regret, for any of it—other than for his own inability to have such feelings." He dropped his head, his face drawn and seeming suddenly much older. "But he tired of it, the violence. Nothing ever coming of it. And then, one night, in an alley, a drunken man begged for his life. And not merely for his own sake. But for others. A wife. Children. The things that men have." He drew a long breath. "He wanted those things, but he knew he could only pretend to feel about them in the way that men did. And so, he resigned himself to that. To simply pretending. Pretending to be a man. And then, by some miracle . . ." He hung on the verge of a smile. ". . . he *became* one."

She was cold. She had never been so cold.

"I don't know what you're talking about," she said, haggard and indifferent.

"Just as well."

She put her face in her hands, her fingers grinding her eyes as if to rub something away.

"I thought I knew you," she said. "I thought I knew everything about you. But I don't know anything. I never did. I don't even know who you are."

"Of course you do. I'm Brad Manford."

"No, you're not," she said. "I saw that in the paper, too."

His eyes shifted about. "They're wrong."

"I don't think so."

"I am *Brad Manford!*"

The wind hit the house like a fist.

"I know better."

"Then I'll make you forget what you know. I'll make the whole world forget."

"And can you make *yourself* forget?"

As though in prayer, he pressed his hands together, moving toward her.

"Yes," he said, "if you help me."

She glanced back to see the snow, as if on a switch, turn from misty downfall to a far thicker veil of white, the flakes suddenly drifting and mounding against the door in a way not altogether natural.

"And if I don't?" she said.

The answer came with a vicious twist of his mouth, eyes hot aglare. A show of untempered rage like that of a child about to scatter the pieces of a board game.

She spun round, her hand just reaching the knob as he pounced, slamming her against the door, her arms flailing in vain as she shrieked and sobbed and the wind, rising further, bellowed and beat the house.

"You're not leaving! You can't!"

He was crushing her.

"God . . . don't . . . please . . ."

"Sally, I'm begging you! I need you!"

Whimpering, she dropped her head. With a hand, he forced it upward, clamping her face—then her throat—in the vise of steely fingers.

She heard the wind roar. Felt it move the house with a mass of ice at its fore.

"Look at me," he ordered.

Through her tears, he was a blur.

"Gimme that look!"

She couldn't think.

"C'mon, you know that look!"

"I don't know what you want from me!"

Slowly, but not completely, he loosened his hold, searching her face, her eyes. Looking for something he could not find.

"I should never have come here," he said. "Never brought you here. But I thought I had to be in this place. I didn't know why. I do now. But I also know I don't have to stay. *We* don't have to stay. Because that which I keep is with me now always. And I am with it. I *am* it. And it is me."

She was past caring. Her eyes fell shut.

"We can go anywhere," he said. "Far away. So far it will be like this place never existed. It won't even be a memory. And we'll start over. A new you. A new me. It's possible, Sally. All things are."

The eyes reopened. "Some things are not."

"But Sally, if I can't have you . . . If I can't *believe* . . . then I am nothing."

His hand still framing her jawline, she looked directly at him, her strength—and fear—exhausted. "Let go of me."

"You won't leave?"

Behind her, the storm had grown to a maelstrom of ice and wind. A swirling wall beyond which nothing was visible.

She turned her head just enough to look through the panes of the door.

"You can't go out there," he said. "I've heard of storms like this. People go out and never find their way back."

The hand on her throat tightened its grip.

"I wouldn't even try," she said.

"Sally, you can't mean that. I can't live in this world without you."

"Then live somewhere else."

There was a final effort. A futile bid to glimpse a light gone dark. Once green fires no longer burning.

He looked off and became as absent of color as the world outside. Drained of hope. Of life. She saw then the last vestige of the man she had known fade and die, the whole of him replaced entirely by something else. A thing unhuman. Callous and mechanical.

Moving stiff, robotic, he released her.

And in that moment, on the winds of the roiling tempest, she heard the cry of a child. A child lost, calling its mother.

With a disbelief surpassing all comprehension, she opened her mouth wide—and ever wider—trying to speak. The words at last coming hushed and wavering.

"He's out there?"

The one who had been Brad Manford said nothing, watching with dull eyes as, in a flurry, the woman flung open the door and disappeared into the snow.

Chapter 52

Memento Mori

Paul Irvin heard the voices as he stood at his bedroom window. Cries that seemed to come from a place hidden by the driving snow, somewhere to the south. He knew little of what lay in that direction. Some trees, he recalled. Nothing else. It was nowhere he had ever been interested in going.

But voices? Really? He reconsidered. Wind like this made for noises strange and cacophonous. Sounds that mocked howls and moans and shrieks of pain. And my God, who would venture out in such a storm? No. Hell no. He was hearing things. There was nobody out there.

Incredible, he thought, the force of this wind. What was it blowing? Sixty, seventy miles an hour? And he'd never seen snow this heavy. None of it had been in the forecast. Clear days ahead, they had said. And now, this. A full-on blizzard. No less, he figured, than the one the old-timers in Pampa used to talk about.

But that one had gone on for days, and he didn't have much food in the house. Well, no great loss, he thought. If he didn't have it, he wouldn't have to cook it. Or sit alone and eat it.

Through the squall he heard a plane overhead. At first he thought maybe that, too, was the wind. But no, if he knew anything, he knew that sound. KC-135. What in God's name were they doing up there in this weather? Must have gotten caught unawares. Stinkin', lug-headed weathermen. Well, they sure as hell couldn't land in this soup. Better try somewhere else, he thought. Tinker AFB in Oklahoma City or Vance in Enid. Or if they were socked in, the base down in Altus.

At intervals, it had continued—that anomalous noise from the south. Something, it seemed, like the wailing of a child. And something else remindful of a woman calling a name, over and over. Could the wind sound so desperate?

He listened closer. It kept on. The wailing. The frantic shouts. Cries no less real than the passing aircraft.

No, there was no denying it. People *were* out there. And in this wind chill they didn't have long. A short time to frostbite, and soon after, hypothermia. Then death.

Call someone, he thought. *911.*

And what were they going to do? Not a damn thing. They couldn't. Not until the storm broke. And when would that be?

Too late.

He began making a list in his head: hiking boots, long underwear, coveralls, his heaviest coat and gloves, a length of rope . . .

He was heading for the closet as he stopped himself.

Are you out of your mind? Seventy-five years old and you think you're gonna go out there and be some kind of hero? Chances are, you won't make it. And neither will they.

But somebody had to try. Just like somebody had to do that nasty little job back in '68.

And hell, seventy-five was old enough.

He had left the house in such a hurry, he was somewhere near the end of his small patio before he realized he had not gotten a heading. Without that, he knew, this trip could well be one way only.

He hunched against the biting wind and pulled up the trank of his glove to check his wrist compass. The thing had been gathering dust since 'Nam, but it still knew the way. One side of the needle was pointing right at him—and at the sliding glass door to his rear, barely visible through the snow. Due north. Humped over and tottering, he went the opposite direction. Within twenty paces, he looked back; the house was gone.

He moved on into what seemed a blank screen. A white nothingness. He was in fine shape for his age, but he quickly found himself panting, his chest heaving. The drifts, in places, were up to his knees, and the driving snow came in whirling waves, like buckshot, pelting him from every side.

The hard flakes stung his face through his ski mask and rattled off his coat and sunglasses. He felt them, too, on the skin of his neck, somehow finding their way past his tightly drawn hood. With his arthritic hands, he fought to hold the collar of his coat higher and, as he did, the wind caught him from behind, off balance, throwing him down just as he reached the shallow slope at the end of his yard. He rolled a ways before righting himself on all fours, his stubborn joints aching, his sense of direction lost in the whiteout.

He rechecked the compass. He doubted, in the short distance he had come, that he had veered much off line. And true to his instinct, the needle still pointed opposite the continued slope of the ground—what he could see of it.

He forged on. The wind, if anything, was picking up. He could stand and walk only in something like a half squat. Under the strain, his legs and back burned with a misery beyond anything he had felt since the Academy. That had been tough.

This was tougher.

A blast of wind, icy hot, shot into his face and down his throat, injecting itself into his lungs. He felt himself gagging, suffocating. Drowning in cold. He staggered, tossed about by the wind, ready to quit.

But there was something ahead, dark and vertical. He reached for it and fell against it, dropping to his knees.

A tree. He embraced it, pressing his face to its bark, away from the wind. Warming his throat and lungs with air less toxic.

You could turn back, he thought. You could turn back and still make it.

Maybe.

But an agony-laden cry came from the south. An awful sound. Someone else near giving up.

He gathered himself and, staying fast against the tree, worked his way as far upright as he dared, then pushed on into the colorless hell to find, almost immediately, another tree. The ground, it seemed, had flattened.

He looked again at the compass. He was still on line. Still southbound.

But then, a loss of traction. A sliding of his left boot and a corresponding spill to the opposite side, where his right hip met a brutal, unyielding slab, and the weight of his legs pulled him off a slippery shelf and downward to strike another hard plane—but which, in an instant, gave way with a cracking noise, dumping him into a shocking cold.

He thrashed about in utter confusion until, as the chaos of the moment abated, he realized: Ice. A creek. He had fallen in.

His feet met a shallow bottom, but as he attempted to stand, his right leg crumpled, and a pain like the stabbing of a fire-hot blade ripped through him from his hip to his toes.

He reached out and found the edge of that from which he had tumbled: A rock. A hell of a big rock. Reddish under the snow. He put his wet-gloved hands atop it and, with all he had, thrust his head and torso to its platform. Stiffly, he raised his left leg from the water, then the other—the tortured, useless other—rolling himself over, face up.

The hip was broken. He knew it.

He was done for.

Goddamn you. Why did you get so old?

He was soaked, freezing fast. The cold numbed his pain, but would soon leave his every extremity unworkable. He was low to the ground, though, and the trees were blocking some of the wind. It wasn't so bad here. A good place to rest. A good place to die.

Another tanker passed over. Flying low. Another followed close behind. And another and another. All just hanging around, circling, each waiting the chance to bring its many thousand pounds of fuel and machine back to earth. But with all that juice on board, they were in no hurry. Hours from now, if need be, they could still be up there cruising. But Paul Irvin knew he wouldn't be hearing them. By then, for him, there would be only silence.

The snow was drifting over him and he was closing his eyes as the woman's call came again. It was growing fainter. But so close. Perhaps no further than the top of the hill that lay just ahead—a short but sharp rise hazed in the mixing white.

Surely, he thought, he could make it that far. Hell, he could *crawl* that far.

And what kind of lousy excuse was a broken hip, anyway?

He pushed up from the rock, trying to stand, but, with a single frostbitten leg for support, could manage only a pathetic hop. The wind rocked him and played with him and he tipped over, falling prone, only half catching himself and banging his face flush on the stone. Blood dripped from his nose, saturating his ski mask as, for a time, he lay dazed from the blow.

All right, he thought. He *would* crawl.

On his hands and left knee, dragging the other leg, he lugged himself to the end of the rock, honed, as it was, like an arrowhead, pointing the way. Perfect south.

Up the hill.

He had a feeling, a strange sense, that he shouldn't go there. He wasn't supposed to. But why?

To hell with it.

He shouted up the slope. Words of encouragement. Hang on. He was coming.

The voice, in distress, sounding ever closer, ever weaker, answered. Still calling what had before seemed like a name, but now more the last word of a prayer.

———————

The boy's cries had seemed to come from one point, then another. And she had chased those cries through the raging wind and ice. Stumbling and falling and pushing on through an expanse that, once familiar, had lost all semblance of its former dimensions. Wandering sightless through a boundless, frozen maze. And screaming. Screaming for him. For anyone. Screaming and screaming.

She was screaming even now, through lips slack and clumsy. Screaming a scream only she could hear. A scream that went on in her mind as she lay hushed and buried in the swirling snow.

The pain of the cold, though, was gone, her legs and arms seeming no more a part of her. The horrible shivering had stopped, too. And in time, so did the noise in her head.

A while ago there had been another voice. It had said something about being on the way. It had seemed important. She couldn't remember why. Anyway, she was all right. It was warm here, and so comfortable. Like floating on a wide, wonderful bed of cotton. She felt herself dozing off.

Or was she waking up?

The sun was high in a cloudless sky, and she walked in tall grass amid countless blades waving in a placid breeze. She had come far. Stones had led the way. The journey's end was near.

Ahead, on a short, steep rise, stood a waiting figure. That of a man.

But not a man.

She came to the final stone, marked, as all had been, with two circles, one within the other. And there, she looked to the crest of the hill. The

wind died and the air, in its static silence, betrayed the sound of the hill
itself. Of the thing that reposed within. A gentle hum, audible to only
those most vigilant, calling in a language of ones and zeros. She felt its soft
rhythm as the sun slowly withered. And as darkness overcame the light,
she ascended the rise, as did others in their millions. Bits of data drawn to
their source. All for reuse.

His hands without feeling, his right leg numb and limp, and his left nearly
as worthless as the other, he kept on until his arms gave out and he sank
to the ground. Yet, even then, through the wind and drifts and broken
branches, he continued, crawling flat against the slope, pulling himself from
the base of one tree to the next. Forcing his feeble, wilting self forward.
Upward.

Mere yards from the top of the hill, he felt his last measure of strength
sapping away. But as the ground leveled out, there gathered within him
a newfound power. An energy surging through those parts of him that
weren't ready to die. Challenged by what seemed an impenetrable clump
of cedars, he moved on, by instinct—by some odd and undefined sense of
familiarity—winding through the evergreens as their branches thrashed
above him, the thick boughs giving some respite from the battering wind.

But as he emerged from the trees, he was met with an explosion of
snow and air that struck him like an immense, crashing ocean breaker. He
buried his face, covering his head. Then, timidly, glanced up.

Ahead, a churning curtain of sheer white. He shouted into it, an-
nouncing himself. It had been some time, though, since he had heard the
voices. The wails of the child had long ago fallen silent. And he had not
heard the woman's cry since he had left the rock. Her call had seemed to
come just east of here. He checked his compass for a heading.

But something was amiss. The damn thing had gone haywire. The needle, unsettled, spun slowly, as if true north were in orbit around him.

Or had ceased to be.

The tankers were still there. Themselves in rotation. But the one that
had just passed over had seemed so incomprehensibly low. And as it trailed
into the north, its rumble vanished with an alarming suddenness. All at
once. As though a door, long open, had shut behind it.

He yelled once more into the din, but in the screeching and whistling of the wind could not contrive a human reply.

He put his head back down, wishing he did not have to wait for it. Wanting it to come now. That last moment of seventy-five years. But he knew it would take some time. Death like this was a process.

He felt himself shaking and thought that was good. It was starting. And yet it seemed almost as if it was not he that was producing the sensation, but, rather, the ground. The earth rocking in the throes of a mild seismic tremor. He knew, though, that under the circumstances, such perceptions were to be doubted. Among the dying, hallucinations were common.

He lifted himself to take a final look.

Something was approaching. A light, darting and hovering in the wintery onslaught.

Another illusion, he thought. A mirage.

But then, the figure of a man. Moving through the savage gale unhurried. Unaffected. Ambling as one might through a park on a sunny day.

"Over here!" the old man said.

The other stopped, a snow-blown shadow.

"I can't walk. It's my hip. And I'm frostbit." The old man struggled to push himself as high as he could. "My name's Irvin. I live just north of here."

The silhouette did not raise his voice, his words nonetheless piercing the wind: "You used to."

Another plane came in low. Insanely low. Skimming the trees. Splitting the sky.

"There are two others out here," Irvin said, shouting in the violence of the tanker's passing. "A child. And a woman."

"There is no one here but us."

"No, I heard them. They need help."

He had not imagined it. The ground was indeed quaking. Vibrating with a rising intensity. And the once random wind now pulsed to the same beat, the snow itself falling, dancing, in time.

"What's happening?" Irvin asked.

"I am done with this place. I am going elsewhere."

"I don't understand."

"You are not meant to."

The profile came closer. The old man could see him well now. In one hand, he carried an object. A thing round and black. As black as a hole in space. A lightless chasm that seemed to the old man like a place he had been in a dream.

"Who are you?"

"No one."

The old man narrowed his eyes. "I think I know you."

"You do not."

"No, I remember you! I do!"

The other looked aloft.

"Then forget."

The speaker jutted the object overhead, and from it came a glowing orb of matching size, flying into the storm and circling about in ever tightening revolutions, each faster than the last. Its speed increasing, until, to the eye, there shone but a single, luminous, contracting ring. And as it contracted, so did space itself. The earth and sky and all directions and everything within being drawn to a midpoint.

There was a humming sound louder than the wind. And surmounting it, the whine of jet engines rose in pitch to become a shattering roar—the light, in its final, tapering orbits, fusing with its dark twin and the man-form, all, in a fiery brilliance, becoming one—as winged metal, black and gray, pierced the snow. A missile falling to the blazing vortex.

The old man started to cry out.

There was a flash. The birth of a new sun.

AFTER

Another Season

Late in the spring, on clear days, the old man went for long walks. Not far from his house was a flowing creek, and he would stroll its bank, along which a rough trail had been worn by himself and others. The path wound through deep woods to the Billups Mill, where the creek joined with a larger stream and their mingled waters filled the millpond, then ran hard down a flume and drove the wheel. Beyond that, only a short ways, lay a meadow, then the village.

On the road in, he would pass a rock fence that was so old, folks didn't know who built it. And going on, he would walk the village green and past the courthouse. He would stop by the tavern at the inn for a hard cider, and sometimes by the sundries store for tobacco and, if the mood struck him, a stick of licorice.

He might turn back then. But if he didn't, he would move on to where the road dwindled to dusty tracks and terminated at the white picket fence of a yellow, two-story house with blue shutters. That was Doc Manford's place.

Nice fellow, the doc. Folks thought a lot of him. His wife, too. Best-looking woman in the county. And they had themselves a cracker-jack of a little boy. He had his father's build. Big and strong for his age. But he had his mother's eyes.

Some days, when he felt a younger spring in his step, the old man walked on past the end of the road, trekking through scattered trees and light brush a good half mile to a thin brook that would lead him round the village to intersect with the creek from which he had started. And reaching the brook, he would see, in the distance, a hill—not quite a mountain—its summit crowned with lush grass and a single tree. A massive cottonwood, its branches spreading like the tentacles of a thing deciding its own many directions.

About the hill, at night, there was sometimes a strange light, and the height of the rise was known—had been known forever—as a place of big magic. It was a place where no one went and everyone knew, somehow, they were not supposed to go. And in the spring breeze, wafting from its prominence, the seed of the great tree dusted the land and swirled in currents of fluffy white, calling to mind the snows of a storm never seen. Or forgotten.

Belle Lutte Press would like to thank the following people, in connection with The Things of Man:

Vince Wheeler
Joanne Gledhill
James Percy
Thomas Fincke
Roy Scott
Vanessa Maynard
Maja Wronska
Christopher Derrick
And, the CysticFibrosis.com community. To learn more about cystic fibrosis or to support the search for a cure, go to cff.org

Vince Wheeler

Vince Wheeler's interest in speculative fiction was fostered at an early age by such television classics as *The Twilight Zone, The Outer Limits,* and *Night Gallery. Later,* he came to admire the works of Arthur C. Clarke, Isaac Asimov, Philip K. Dick, and Stephen King. He holds degrees in both journalism and law, and has worked as an attorney for 30 years. However, his debut as a writer was delayed not nearly so much by the demands of his law practice, as it was by the job of helping his wife raise their two sons—both of which, Vince is happy to say, have turned out quite well. Vince has lived his entire life in the Midwest.